DEATH AND
THE BLACK PYRAMID

DEATH AND THE BLACK PYRAMID

Deryn Lake

This first world edition published 2009
in Great Britain and in the USA by
SEVERN HOUSE PUBLISHERS LTD of
9–15 High Street, Sutton, Surrey, England, SM1 1DF.
Trade paperback edition published
in Great Britain and the USA 2009 by
SEVERN HOUSE PUBLISHERS LTD

British Library Cataloguing in Publication Data

Lake, Deryn
  Death and the black pyramid. - (A John Rawlings mystery)
  1. Rawlings, John (Fictitious character) - Fiction
  2. Pharmacists - England - Fiction 3. Great Britain -
  History - 18th century - Fiction 4. Devon (England) -
  Fiction 5. Detective and mystery stories
  I. Title
  823.9'14[F]

ISBN-13: 978-0-7278-6770-4   (cased)
ISBN-13: 978-1-84751-143-0   (trade paper)

All Severn House titles are printed on acid-free paper.

Typeset by Palimpsest Book Production Ltd.,
Grangemouth, Stirlingshire, Scotland.
Printed and bound in Great Britain by
MPG Books Ltd., Bodmin, Cornwall.

One

The horses were being backed into the traces, the guard – heavily loaded with blunderbuss and pistols – was clambering up to take his seat beside the coachman, the passengers were all aboard. The stagecoach bound for the West Country stood almost ready to leave, the relatives waving a farewell, two or three of them gathered on the covered balcony of the Gloucester Hotel and Coffee House for a better view and also to keep out of the rain. For, even though it was September, the weather was inclement, the shower being of the fine sort that drove into one's face and rapidly made one's clothes damp and unpleasant.

A figure came running through the gloom; a figure holding its hat firmly upon its head as it sped along shouting, 'Have you any room left?'

The coachman called an answer. 'Only in the basket, Sir.'

There was an audible groan. 'Oh dear. I feel I'm getting a little old for that.'

But at that moment the door of the stagecoach swung open and a young man, looking very pale and covered in a clammy cold sweat, got out, reeling slightly. A girl popped her head out of the window.

'Are you not well, Sir?'

'No,' he gasped. 'I'm afraid I feel very poorly. You must proceed without me.'

'But . . .'

The young man made a gesture towards the heavens, said, 'Excuse me,' and bolted off into the dismal night.

'It's an ill wind,' called John Rawlings, and cramming his hat on his head, sprinted the last few yards and leapt into the coach before anyone on the roof had had time to descend and take the seat.

The hands of the coachman's watch were pointing at eight o'clock and it was time to depart. With a loud crack of the whip the stagecoach rumbled out of the yard, past Boone's the hat maker and Joseph Miller the fish salesman, who also had premises at Billingsgate according to the sign on his shopfront.

'First stop Brentford, ladies and gents,' called the guard, and with that they were off on the start of their long journey.

John Rawlings, still gasping from his exertion, settled in his seat, removed his hat, and looked around him at his fellow passengers. Immediately opposite him was sitting a very pretty dark young woman, who inclined her head graciously as John bowed to her. Next to her was a seedy looking individual, somewhat sad of appearance and giving the impression that he had fallen on hard times. But it was to the man in the corner of the coach that the Apothecary's eyes were drawn and on him that they lingered. For he was one of the finest specimens that John had ever seen.

Jet black and extremely handsome, with elegant, regular features and melting black eyes fringed by voluptuous lashes that would have well become a woman, the man had a finely toned physique. John reckoned that the Negro must have stood well over six feet and boasted a powerful pair of shoulders, at present concealed in a damson velvet coat and a travelling cloak, slate grey in colour.

John glanced to his right and saw a large woman sitting in a huddled posture. She had a fishy, colourless eye which immediately caught the Apothecary's, causing her to glare at him suspiciously. Beside her and immediately next to John sat a neat little man, all tidy feet and hands, with a white wig placed at a correct angle on his natty head. John at once decided that the man was a dancing master, mainly because of the precision of even his smallest movements.

The woman with the fishy eye suddenly let out a great sigh and speaking in a pronounced German accent said, 'Ach, I am so worried about mein luggage. Will it get safely to Exeter, I ask? I doubt it. I truly do.'

'Why, Ma'am?' enquired the dark young woman opposite.

'My dear young lady you obviously have not travelled much or you vould know that the vays are littered with rogues and vagabonds. Think of the coaching inns, the posthouses, the horse keepers, the hostlers – to say nuzzink of highvaymen and other robbers. I tell you vun's baggage is not safe anyvere except under vun's nose.'

'But there are no facilities for that in a stagecoach,' said the dancing master mildly.

The fishy-eyed woman rounded on him. 'Zat is obvious, Sir. Othervise I vould be guarding mine with mein life.'

John produced a book from inside his cloak and tucked his nose in it, determined not to get drawn into such a pointless and silly discussion. The ploy worked and the conversation flowed round him, the German woman growing tetchier by the second, the young lady playing the innocent and taking the rise out of her, but oh so gently. The dancing master, very sensibly, relapsing into silence.

They had been travelling an hour and quiet had been restored when suddenly the black man spoke into the hush.

'Does anybody know what time we reach Brentford?'

John looked up, surprised indeed by the man's voice, which was educated and pleasant to listen to. He glanced at his watch.

'In another twenty minutes or so.'

'Excellent, my friend. Allow me to introduce myself. My name is Jack Beef.'

'And mine is John Rawlings. Are you travelling all the way to Exeter?'

'I am indeed. May I present my manager?' He gestured towards the seedy-looking man. 'This is Nathaniel Broome.'

John bowed as best he could. 'Delighted to make your acquaintance, Sir.'

'Delighted to make yours,' replied the other, in a high, tight voice.

'You may be wondering why I travel with a manager,' Jack continued, laughing gently. 'The answer is that I am a bare-knuckle fighter and I am going to Exeter to take part in a bout.'

'How interesting,' said John, meaning it.

Jack Beef looked melancholy. 'In fact it is a hard life. I admit that I get to see some interesting places but that is the sum total of it.'

Nathaniel spoke up in his congested tones. 'Oh come now. What about your fat purses? And the lords of the land whose hands you have shaken?'

The black man gave a broad grin and explained to his fellow travellers.

'My professional name is the Black Pyramid, apparently because my torso resembles one – inverted I might add,' he informed the others with a rich laugh that made several people in the compartment smile, other than, it need hardly be said, the German lady who continued to cast her eyes towards the roof and mutter, 'Ach'.

Then, as quickly as it had started, the conversation died away and they continued to journey in silence until at twenty minutes past nine the coach pulled up in the stableyard of The Three Pigeons in Brentford. John, recalling the terrible Christmas he had spent on the run heading for Exeter, when he had been accused of the murder of his wife, gave an involuntary shiver as he stepped down onto the cobbles.

The dancing master noticed and said, 'Are you all right, Sir?'

John smiled down at him. 'Yes, perfectly. It is just the inclement night, don't you know.'

The little man bowed. 'Allow me to present myself. My name is Cuthbert Simms. And who might I have the honour of addressing?'

'John Rawlings. I am an apothecary by trade. And you, Sir?'

'I teach the art of dance to folk young and old. For many years I was attached to a great household but . . .' He sighed. 'Things change, alas.'

John silently gave himself a good mark for guessing correctly.

'Indeed they do. Allow me to buy you a drink, Sir. I think we have thirty minutes before we plunge on again.'

The little man looked gloomy. 'The coach travels through the night I believe.'

'Yes. They're changing the horses now.'

And it was true. The original team was being led out of the traces and the horsemaster was backing in four fresh beasts.

'Well, we'd better drink up in preparation,' said Cuthbert and followed John into the inn.

Half an hour later and all the passengers were getting on board. The German lady had spent the time half threatening, half pleading with the guard to check her luggage.

'Please to make sure that everyzing is in its place.'

'I assure you, Madam,' the man repeated, with just the slightest edge in his voice, 'that there are three bags and one hat box in the basket.'

'But are zey mine?'

'Yes, Madam. I put them in there myself.'

Slightly mollified the woman got in and plonked herself in the corner where she petended to fall asleep immediately. John, studying her, noticed that one of her eyes remained slightly open and drew his own conclusions.

It was now almost three years since the life of his wife, his beloved Emilia, had been cut so brutally short in the gardens of Gunnersbury House. Three years in which he had run the gamut of emotion, from grieving widower to a man in love once more. For in that time he had again met the capricious Elizabeth di Lorenzi, older than he was and as different from him as a nun to a courtesan. Where he wanted marriage, she would have none of it; where he wanted to settle, she wanted to rove wild and free. Indeed he had almost given up all hope of her when a mysterious letter had arrived, virtually commanding him to go and see her at her magnificent home just outside Exeter. And it was for this reason that he had caught the all-night stagecoach driving to that city, leaving his daughter, Rose, in the charge of her grandfather, the formidable and fascinating Sir Gabriel Kent.

What, he wondered, could Elizabeth possibly want with him now? He had thought when he had last seen her that there was no chance for them. That there was hardly a word left to say. And now this extraordinary summons. With a sigh, John snuggled down into his cloak and attempted to go to sleep.

Beside him Cuthbert Simms, neat as a dormouse, slept quietly, his head falling gently onto the Apothecary's shoulder. Opposite, the dark young lady, bonnet removed and held in her lap, slumbered, leaning her head against the wall of the coach. But it was the Black Pyramid and Nathaniel Broome who amused John on the odd occasions when he opened his eyes. They inclined inwards, resting one upon the other like a pair of elderly ladies, snoring gently, Broome softly, the Black Pyramid with a deep sonorous note that befitted his size. John's thoughts stole upwards to the two unfortunate women who sat on the roof, and his conscience pricked him that he had taken a seat inside at the very last moment. So much so that he considered giving it up at the next stop.

He slept as best he could and when next he raised his lids he saw that dawn was just starting to streak the sky and the coach was slowing down as they drove into the village of Thatcham. At The Swan with Two Necks they changed horses again and the passengers were given a forty minute stop for breakfast. Stretching and yawning outside while the others made their way within, John gallantly assisted the two females sitting above to descend. One of them had a very familiar face and the Apothecary became convinced that he had seen her before somewhere. The other was an altogether sensible type of woman with a friendly visage and clear blue eyes. This, despite the fact that she had spent the night sitting bolt upright in the chilly and damp conditions.

John made a bow. 'May I offer you my seat for the next stage of the journey, Madam?'

She shot him a look of pure gratitude. 'I would be delighted to accept, Sir. And at the next stop I shall surrender it to Mrs Gower with whom I have just shared a terrible night in the elements.'

The Apothecary nodded. 'I can imagine. I shall see if any other gentleman would be willing to change with her.'

The woman curtseyed. 'Thank you. Allow me to introduce myself. My name is Lucinda Silverwood.'

'And I am John Rawlings.' He bowed and she responded with a brief bob.

'I am going to Devon to join my daughter who is expecting her first child shortly,' Mrs Silverwood continued.

And John, remembering the fuss that Emilia's mother had made at the time of Rose's arrival, felt a momentary touch of bittersweet sadness as he recalled the time when he had first laid eyes on his daughter.

'I am sure you will be a great comfort to her,' he said. 'And now, Madam, allow me to accompany you in to breakfast.'

As they went inside the last two remaining passengers climbed down from the roof and John glanced at them. One was a plumpish fellow, clearly bald beneath his somewhat ornate wig of curling brown locks. He had fat pink hands and a startled expression caused by the fact that his eyebrows were scantily defined. The other man, by contrast, had raven black brows and a savage hawk's face, which was pitted and scarred by the ravages of smallpox. His eyes were dark and as John stared he turned a look on the Apothecary which made John start at its ferocity and quickly turn his head away. He made his way inside the inn without glancing back.

Within it was all comfort as the landlord, used, no doubt, to coaches arriving at this ungodly hour of the morning, had produced a fine bill of fare. A large ham jostled a side of beef and from the kitchen came the reassuring smell of eggs being fried to a crisp. John took his place at the large trestle table which had been set for the occasion and bowed Mrs Silverwood into her place. Behind him he could hear a commotion and, turning slightly, saw that it was the hawk-like man insisting on dining in a private parlour. The landlord, looking put out, was somewhat reluctantly showing him to a snug leading off the passageway.

John turned to the second woman who had travelled on the roof and whose face was so familiar to him.

'Forgive me, Madam, but I feel that perhaps we have met before. Do you recall where that could have been?'

She turned on him a beaming smile and said in a broad Welsh accent, 'No, Sir, we have never met but I expect you might have seen me in the theatre. My name is Paulina Gower. Not that I am in the first rank of actresses, mark you. I expect 'tis more likely that you have seen me playing a maid or some such thing.'

John lit up. 'Of course. I was – many years ago I might add – a friend of Coralie Clive's, though I believe that she has now retired completely. Unlike yourself?' he added, a slight question in his voice.

Mrs Gower looked sad and knowing simultaneously. 'I wish that I had married well – as did she – though I learn she is now widowed, poor soul. But yet to give up the stage entirely would be difficult indeed.' She sighed. 'However I'm afraid that I do not have the choice. I must continue to work in order to survive.'

John pulled a sympathetic face. 'We live in hard times, I fear.'

Cuthbert Simms spoke up from across the table. 'Indeed we do, Sir. At my age I am still forced to teach to make ends meet.'

'But surely,' said John, addressing the two of them, 'you both love what you do and to continue it is no hardship.'

But he never heard their answers because at that moment the breakfast party was rudely interrupted by the arrival of the German woman who was shrieking at the top of her voice.

'Ach, but some of mein luggage is missing. There is a thief here. Vere is the coachman?'

'Having his breakfast as you should be, Madam,' somebody answered rudely.

She glared in their direction, unable to identify who it was who had spoken.

'I can eat nuzzink. I am fit to vomit with all this jigging about.'

'Well don't do it in here,' the same voice replied.

The Fraulein – at least John presumed she was such – gave another basilisk stare, turned on her heel and marched into the interior of the inn, clearly to find the driver and twist his ear. There was a general sigh of relief as she left.

Thirty minutes later they were clambering back on board. Most of the men – with the exception of Cuthbert Simms who claimed fear of the rheumatics – had taken their seats on the roof so that the two ladies could have some respite from the elements. John noticed that the man with the hawkish face had also gone within and had huddled down in his cloak to sleep. The German woman, hurrying up at the last minute, having rechecked the basket and deciding that all her luggage was complete after all, got inside with bad grace and a grumpy expression. The coachman cracked his whip.

'Next stop Marlborough, ladies and gents.'

And they set off.

John found himself sitting next to the man with scant eyebrows who turned out to be a pleasant fellow, a country solicitor with a practice in Exeter, returning home from a visit to an elderly sister who dwelt in London. Having exchanged courtesies and names – his was Martin Meadows – they chatted nonsense to one another until eventually the solicitor said, 'Tell me, do you treat many patients with delusions?'

John stared at him. 'Of what kind do you mean, Sir?'

'Well, those who think people are plotting against them. That type of thing.'

The Apothecary regarded him seriously. 'No, Sir. To be honest I can't say that I have. Why?'

Meadows looked non-committal. 'Oh, no reason really. I just wondered.'

They relapsed into silence but John, staring out at the tints of autumn, the first hints of which were just starting to emblazon the trees, wondered what was behind the question. He shot a sideways look at Martin Meadows and saw that his face was giving away nothing as he too gazed out at the ever-changing landscape.

John had always loved the county of Wiltshire, found it mystic, a dark and brooding landscape containing some of the country's most ancient and mysterious artifacts. The riddle of what Silbury Hill actually was; the looming question of the purpose of Stonehenge; the standing stones at Avebury. All these things intrigued him and he had often, when working alone in his compounding room, puzzled over them.

And now in the early morning light he breathed in the freshness of the air, looked around him at the magnificent rolling countryside, and fell quietly asleep.

Two

John was awoken by the sound of shouting and looking down saw that hostlers were running to give assistance as the coach pulled into the yard of The Castle and Ball in Marlborough. Looking round him he noticed that the Black Pyramid and Nathaniel Broome were standing up in preparation for descending and that Mr Meadows was clambering to his feet. Hastily adjusting his hat which had slipped down over one eye, John also rose.

The inn, which was extremely old, was comfortable inside and having made use of its facilities the Apothecary settled himself in a quiet corner and indulged in his favourite hobby of observing. Needless to say the German woman was complaining bitterly about something or other – John did not strain his ears sufficiently to discover what – and was being soothed down by Lucinda Silverwood. Paulina Gower, by contrast, was laughing merrily with the dark young lady, Jemima Lovell. He noticed that once again the man with the hawk's face had vanished and that Martin Meadows was also absent. Following a whim, the Apothecary made his way to the back of the inn where the private snugs were situated.

'. . . I tell you, Sir, that one or two faces are familiar to me,' a harsh voice was saying quite loudly.

John could not help but listen, standing quietly outside the door.

'Are you certain, Sir? Surely it could be a trick of your imagination.'

'It's the black man. There could not be two like him around.'

Martin Meadows answered, clearly trying to soothe the speaker down. 'Oh come. He is a type. A bare-knuckle fighter. I have seen several people like him in my time.'

'Have you indeed? And all black?'

'Well, no,' came the reply. 'Not all of them.'

There was silence and John decided that this was his moment to make an entrance. Grinning cheerfully, he gave a rat-tat on the door and walked into the room.

Meadows and the hawkish man were sitting round a table in deep discussion. They looked up as the Apothecary went in, the solicitor giving a smile of relief, the other glaring fiercely. John ignored him.

'Well, gentlemen, I hope I'm not interrupting. Can't find a seat in the other bar so I thought I would try in here.'

'Come in, come in, Mr Rawlings, take a chair, do,' said Meadows. 'May I present Mr Gorringe to you? Mr Gorringe, this is Mr Rawlings.'

John gave an effusive bow. 'A pleasure, Sir,' he said in an affected voice. 'Truly a great pleasure.'

Gorringe half rose, still looking furious, and gave the curtest of salutes back. 'Actually Meadows and I were having a private conversation.'

'But we have finished that,' said the solicitor hastily. 'Indeed we were looking for some young company.'

'Then come into the taproom,' John answered, laughing merrily over nothing. 'There's a goodly crowd in there. That is if you don't mind standing.'

'If you'll excuse me,' said Gorringe, and getting to his feet he left them abruptly, swirling his dark cloak as he went.

John looked at Martin Meadows. 'What a strange character.'

The solicitor motioned him to sit down. 'Indeed, indeed,' he sighed. 'He is under the strong conviction that he has met the black man before somewhere.'

'And what of it?' said the Apothecary, pretending carelessness.

'God knows, my dear friend. He is the type of man who sees a plot in everything. It is my belief that he suffers from some kind of mania.'

John would have replied but was prevented from so doing by a call of, 'All aboard the Exeter coach, Ladies and Gentlemen.' He and the solicitor made their way out to discover that Gorringe was already sitting on the roof and had produced a book which he was studying assiduously. He merely grunted as John and Martin took their places above. Below them, however, a scene was going on.

'My luggage. Zere is vun piece missing,' the German lady was screaming.

'I can assure you, Madam . . .' the guard was answering her patiently.

Behind her the Black Pyramid loomed suddenly and un-expectedly.

'Be silent, my good woman. I suggest that you spend the next few hours checking and rechecking everything you own.'

And with that he leant over into the basket and removed all her bags and an unwieldy-looking box and dumped them on the ground at her feet.

'But . . .' she protested.

'No buts, Madam. No buts, merely baggage.' And he climbed into the coach.

'Sir,' the driver called down urgently, 'we are due to leave immediately.'

The black man stuck his head out of the window. 'Then do so,' he instructed.

'But the lady . . .'

'I shall have ze law on you if you go vizout me!' she shouted, shaking her fist.

'My card,' said the Black Pyramid nonchalantly, and with the enormous reach of his arms handed her one as the coachman cracked his whip and the new team of horses led them outwards.

That evening they spent the night at Bath, clattering into the courtyard of The Katherine Wheel some hours later. Accommodation was limited and they were all forced to share their rooms with at least one other person. John found himself in company with Cuthbert Simms, while Mrs Silverwood doubled up with young Jemima and Paulina Gower. Lucinda and Jemima were informed that they would have to share a bed but they took this news cheerfully enough. The Black Pyramid – pleased as punch that he had got rid of the German woman, whose name turned out to be Fraulein Schmitt – took a bottle of brandy to the room he was allocated with Nathaniel Broome. That left the peculiar Mr Gorringe who, yet again, seemed to be paired with Martin Meadows.

John, remembering his previous visits to Bath and the many adventures he had had in that city, went to bed late. It seemed to him, sitting alone in a snug with a bottle of wine before he retired, that the ghosts of the past came back to haunt him. He saw Coralie as she once had been – young and fresh, vigorous and full of life, longing to taste it all, eager to build her reputation on the stage. How bitterly it all had treated her, he thought. And thinking of Coralie brought back memories of himself as a young man, relishing everything and treating the world as a huge plaything. Yet, he considered, there was no point in looking back. The secret of a successful life must surely be the ability to go forward. Then he thought of that great beau, Orlando, a doyen of Bath, who had sacrificed so much in order that others may move on and live in peace.

John sighed and taking a candle went up to his room and crept inside, careful not to wake Cuthbert who slept like a little child, his breathing light and fast, his small frame barely making a bulge in the bedclothes. Thankful that there were two beds in the chamber, John undressed and climbed in, instantly falling asleep, lulled by the wine.

He woke some hours later, listening intently, certain that he had heard a voice. Then quite distinctly somebody close to him said, 'Take care, Fulke Bassett, take great care.' This remark was followed by a laugh, so sinister that it made the Apothecary's blood run cold. Reaching for the candle John struck a tinder and lit it. He looked round. The room was empty, other than for the sleeping Cuthbert Simms, who had turned over and was facing the wall. After several minutes spent sitting up in bed, gazing around him, John blew the candle out and tried to sleep. But this time it did not come easily and he lay awake in the darkness, wondering whether he had dreamt the entire incident or whether a voice had actually spoken those strange words and laughed that terrible laugh.

They set off early the next morning, before breakfast – much to the Apothecary's chagrin – heading for Wells. Arriving there some three hours later they had a thirty minute stop and time to settle down to some serious eating. John found himself seated next to Cuthbert and felt tempted to mention to him the strange event of the previous night. Eventually he did so.

'Did you sleep well, Mr Simms? I did not disturb you when I came to bed?'

Cuthbert turned on him a jovial little face. 'Not at all, my dear chap, to answer your second question. As to the first, I slept soundly, though I dreamt rather a great deal.'

'Oh really? What about?'

Simms gave a piping laugh. 'Dashed if I can remember. By the way, did I tell you that I am heading for Lady Sidmouth's place, just outside Exeter? I was attached to her household some years ago, but only for a short while.'

'No, you didn't. May I ask the purpose of your visit?'

'Indeed you may. She has engaged me professionally, don't you know, based on her past experience of my work. I am attempting to teach the dance to her grandchildren, one of whom is a great lumpkin of a fellow – or so I am told.'

'I am sure you will manage splendidly,' John replied gallantly. He paused, then said, 'Tell me, did you hear anyone speaking in the night?'

Cuthbert gazed at him blankly. 'Speaking? What do you mean?'

'I don't quite know what I mean. It's just that I woke to hear a voice – I could have sworn it was in the room – saying something. Then the man laughed.'

'What did it – he – say?'

'Watch your step Fulke Bassett, or something like that.'

There was a fraction's silence before Cuthbert said, 'I think you must have dreamt it, my friend, because I heard nothing.'

'Perhaps it was you talking in your sleep.'

Cuthbert adjusted his cuffs. 'It might well have been,' he answered lightly. 'I told you I had a night of dreams.'

The conversation had reached a natural halt and John was trying to think of something trivial to say when a familiar voice boomed out, 'Are, zere you are. I have found you at last.' And with a gusty sigh Fraulein Schmitt dropped heavily into the empty seat opposite his having caught them up in record time. John remembered his manners and rose to make her a small bow, as did Cuthbert Simms. Looking down the table he saw that the others had not noticed her arrival – or at least were pretending not to do so.

She glared about her. 'It vas very vicked of zat black man to drive off vizout me.'

Hearing a reference to himself, Jack Beef turned round and stared at her with a certain amount of foreboding. Somewhat to John's surprise she waved a waggish finger at him and said, 'You are a naughty, naughty boy.'

He stood up and came towards her. Then he took her hand and kissed it in what the Apothecary could only think of as an extremely theatrical manner.

'Madam, I crave your pardon. It was very wrong of me to do what I did.'

She fluttered at him, all smiles and eyelashes. 'I vill forgive you if you vill buy me breakfast.'

'Nothing would give me greater pleasure.'

John was frankly astonished, firstly that she should have forgiven the Black Pyramid at all, let alone so easily. And secondly that he should have given in without saying a word in his own defence. For the journey made without her nagging presence had been peaceful and harmonious indeed. Puzzled, he looked at Cuthbert, but the little man was busily tucking into ham and eggs and did not return his gaze.

Half an hour later the coachman called them and they set off for the final leg of their journey. This took them through the rest of Somerset and finally into the mysterious county of Devon where he had spent his memorable honeymoon and had also met Elizabeth di Lorenzi for the first time.

John, sitting on the roof once more, studied the landscape and wondered for the umpteenth time why Elizabeth had sent for him. He would have thought – in view of their frank discussions on the last occasion they had met – that their relationship had sadly reached its ultimate conclusion. But obviously he was wrong. Suddenly John wanted to reach Exeter in a hurry and give thought to his future, whether it would include the Marchesa or whether he must continue on his own.

After stopping at Taunton and Collumpton – where they dined – they finally arrived in Exeter some thirteen hours after leaving Bath. Their journey ended at The Half Moon in High Street. John, miserable as the place made him, was too weary to book himself in anywhere else. For the inn brought back cruel memories of his honeymoon and Emilia's sweet warmth and comforting presence. Yet he gallantly strode in with the others and asked for a room for the night.

Almost the entire party was present. Mrs Silverwood, as charming and capable as ever, leading Jemima by the hand; Paulina following with Fraulein Schmitt, very subdued and not questioning her luggage once. The Black Pyramid and his manager strolling in, laughing at some private joke. This left John to walk in with Cuthbert Simms and Martin Meadows. Of that strange character Mr Gorringe there was no sign.

Having secured a room – on his own he was delighted to say – John made his way to the taproom determined to raise his spirits. Mr Simms and Mr Meadows were there before him, the little man sipping a glass of port while the solicitor was imbibing a cognac. Asking if he might join them, John sat down. The dancing master was in full flow.

'. . . oh yes, I was quite the talk of the town in my day. Everyone came to me – members of the nobility and even a crowned head or two. But then alas,' He sighed, 'fashions changed and Italian dance teachers became quite the thing. But I was delighted to say that I was taken into the household of a great merchant, to teach his offspring the Terpsichorean art. One of them was outstanding and a great beauty as well. Indeed I miss my little Helen so much.' He sighed again and John found himself thinking that the man was very slightly tipsy. 'She was the belle of the neighbourhood – and of London as well. And as for Bath, let me tell you that she took the place by storm. But she had other ideas and her father threatened to turn her out of the house.'

Meadows looked shocked. 'What an unpleasant thing to do.'

'Yes. It was.'

'What happened to her?' This from John.

'She died, alas.'

'How very sad.'

'Oh, yes it was. A tragedy in fact.'

Cuthbert Simms sighed for the third time and stared into the dregs remaining in his glass.

'Allow me to get you another port,' said the Apothecary, standing up.

'Just a wee one perhaps.'

As John crossed the floor to attract the attention of the potboy his eye was caught by the late arrival of Gorringe, the reception area being clearly visible to his left. The man strode in and shouted at a maid who happened to be standing in the hallway at the time. She bolted off and a few minutes later the landlord appeared. Unfortunately, the Apothecary could not hear a word of what was being said but he guessed that the hawk-faced man had gone to look for alternative accommodation but had been unable to find any at this hour of the night. Now he had returned and was demanding a room. Rather hoping that the landlord would refuse, John's hopes were dashed as a key was produced and Gorringe was shown upstairs.

The potboy was at his elbow. 'Yes, Sir?'

'Two cognacs and a glass of port at that table, if you please.'

'Very good, Sir.'

'You'll never guess who has just arrived and been given a room,' John said, rejoining the other two.

Martin laughed. 'William Gorringe – and he hasn't just arrived. He was first out of the coach and booked a room for himself before the rest of us had a chance to stir. Didn't you see him?'

'Frankly, no I didn't. I wonder where he wandered off to instead of coming in to have a drink?'

Cuthbert Simms gave an exquisite little shrug. 'La, who cares? I think he's a horrid man and not worth the discussion.'

John laughed. 'You're right. Let's talk of something else.'

But the dancing master downed his port and stood up, wobbling just the slightest bit. He made a perfect bow however.

'Gentlemen, if you will excuse me. I am afraid I am not used to so much alcohol. I must take to my bed immediately. Goodnight to you.'

And he went out using tiny precise steps. John turned to Martin Meadows.

'Do you have a room to yourself?'

'Yes, fortunately. The landlord was expecting our coach and had accommodation ready for several of us. And you?'

'Yes, I also.'

They finished their drinks then, having collected candles, made their way upstairs. John led the way and eventually found his room high up on the third floor. It was rather cramped but it had a clean and comfortable bed in it and he took off his clothes and crawled into the sheets. Contrary to his expectations, he slept fitfully, dreaming wildly and waking at least once an hour. Checking the time by his travelling clock he saw that it grew late and still he had not achieved a proper rest. Reluctantly he got out of bed and made his way to the bedroom door, thinking of going downstairs and getting himself a glass of water. And it was while he was standing there that he heard a noise from the floor below. Slowly, and somehow stealthily, he heard a door open and close.

Wondering why the sound should have made him so uneasy, John peered over the banisters and down the stairwell. He saw a figure – quite unrecognizable – moving swiftly along the landing, holding a candle aloft. Looking to see whether it was a man or a woman – for the figure was wearing a floor-length cloak – it vanished before he had time to come to any conclusion. John went slowly back to his room, deciding to forget the glass of water.

He sat down on his bed, thinking. Then he concluded that perhaps it had been a secret tryst and that it was no business of his to enquire further. And it was with this thought uppermost in his mind that he finally fell into a deep and dreamless sleep.

Three

John woke late, so late that for a second he thought he must have missed the coach. And then he recalled that his journey was over, that all that remained now was to hire a horse from a livery stable and make his way up to Elizabeth in her great house high above the river Exe.

He got out of bed and washed in cold water, scraping a razor over his chin as best he could. Then he went downstairs and into the guests' parlour to partake of his usual hearty fare. Somewhat to his surprise – it being a little after nine o'clock – he found that the only other person sitting there was Jemima Lovell. And on enquiring where the rest of their party were, was informed that most of them had left the inn on the final stages of their journey.

'I'm afraid that I overslept,' said John apologetically.

'I too. I did not sleep well the night before. Paulina Gower snores rather and it kept me awake.'

'Yes, of course. You were bundled into a room with two others. Did you have a place to yourself last night?'

'Yes, I did,' she answered.

John, remembering the strange person wandering on the landing of the floor below his, wondered if Jemima had heard anything but did not quite have the temerity to ask her.

'Tell me, where do you go from here?' he said instead.

'To Lady Sidmouth's house, not far from the small fishing village of Sidmouth. Do you know it?' Without waiting for his reply she plunged on, 'I am going there to make her a hat or two and some headdresses. I am a milliner, you see.'

'Isn't that where Cuthbert Simms was off to?'

'Yes. There is to be a huge assembly for her daughter's birthday. He is to prepare them all for the dances and I am to make their headgear.'

'How did he get there?'

'Lady Sidmouth sent a coach this morning and like a ninny I slept through its arrival. I shall have to make my way by whatever transport I can find.'

'Perhaps she will send it back for you.'

Jemima gave a delightful smile. 'I think not somehow. Once will be quite enough in Lady Sidmouth's opinion.'

'I see,' said John, and did.

They ate on in silence, the parlour almost empty except for a sprinkling of other guests who were partaking of their meal, their conversation sporadic. And then, quite distinctly from somewhere far above them, John heard a cry followed by the sudden pounding of feet.

'Whatever's that?' asked Jemima, startled, looking in the direction of the sound.

'I don't know,' John answered, but he half rose from his chair even while he spoke.

The noise of commotion grew nearer and the Apothecary stood up. Excusing himself to Jemima, he hurried into the hall.

The maid whom he had seen the night before being shouted at by William Gorringe was flying down the stairs at top speed, a jug in her hand, the contents of which was spilling out all the way down the staircase.

'Oh help!' she was shouting. 'Oh help! Somebody help.'

The landlord appeared from the area of the kitchen. 'What is it, my girl?'

'The gentleman in 103 . . .' she gasped out.

'What about him?'

'He's dead, Mr Tyler. Oh, Sir, it's horrible.'

John stepped forward. 'I'm an apothecary. Can I be of any assistance?'

Tyler looked him up and down. 'Do you have a medical bag with you?'

'No. I am here for social reasons. But I have one or two bottles of physic that I always carry.'

'Perhaps you had better bring them.'

'If the man is dead they won't do him a lot of good,' John replied shortly.

They climbed the staircase in silence, ascending to the second floor, the one below John's bedroom. The door to 103 stood ajar and the Apothecary realized with a start that it was the very door from which he had seen the mysterious cloaked figure emerge. He decided that for the moment he would keep the information to himself.

Inside it was still dark for the curtains were drawn. Crossing to them, John pulled them back and autumn sunlight, piercingly bright, flooded the room. He heard Tyler the landlord give an exclamation behind him and, wheeling round, saw the body for the first time.

William Gorringe lay on the bed in a sea of his own blood, a sea which had spattered onto the walls and even the ceiling. To say that he had been bludgeoned to death would have been an understatement. The man had received so many blows to the head that he was virtually unrecognizable, his face reduced to a lump of flesh, his eyes dislodged from their sockets by the severity of the beating he had sustained. Taking a deep breath John leant over the body and stared at what remained of the head.

The brains were oozing through in a mass of grey matter, hair sticking in it just to make the scene more unpleasant. Slowly, the Apothecary let his eyes wander downwards and saw that Gorringe had several blows, including one to the knees, which were bent up slightly as if the man had been asleep when the attack began. John made a mental note to ask the landlord – who was on the landing making the most terrible retching noises – about spare keys to the rooms.

He straightened up and crossed to the window, noticing that it was closed and that the catch had been slipped through on the inside. Staring downwards he saw that below him was the stabling yard. So it would have been possible for a man to have taken a ladder and made his way upwards and closed the window after he had come in. John's mind turned to the figure he had seen down the landing and he fervently wished that he had had both the time and the foresight to get a better look.

He turned once more to the body, thinking that Gorringe must have met his death at the hands of a madman or, at the very least, someone in an uncontrollable frenzy. He had a dozen or so separate wounds, the majority of which were to the upper regions. But his chest had also been viciously attacked and John wondered what implement could have been used. Possibly a heavy stick or a piece of piping. But a search of the room, albeit quick, revealed nothing. Whoever had killed William Gorringe had taken the weapon with them.

Outside in the corridor the landlord – very whey-faced – was waiting for him. John looked grim.

'We'll have to lock this door until the Constable comes. You have a spare key?'

'Yes, of course. The girl uses it in the morning when she goes in with the hot water.'

'And I presume that was what she was doing earlier?'

'Yes, poor soul. She walked in on that scene of carnage.'

It was a good description, John thought. Aloud he said, 'Where are the keys normally kept when they are not in use?'

'They hang on hooks in the kitchen. Why?'

'Because that could have been the way the murderer gained entry.'

'But that would suggest some prior knowledge, wouldn't it? They would have needed to know what room the victim was in.'

'Oh undoubtedly. This is hardly the work of a stranger. More that of a long-standing enemy.'

'I see.'

They walked down the stairs in silence to see a strained-looking group awaiting them at the bottom. There was the landlord's wife, who had her arms round the hysterical maid. There was Jemima, very pale and wide-eyed. There were one or two other guests, drawn by the terrible scream and the general commotion. They reached the bottom and John drew Jemima apart.

'Do you remember that man Gorringe from the journey?'

'Yes, indeed I do. He sat in the coach wrapped in his cloak and would speak to none of us.'

'I'm afraid he is dead, Miss Lovell.'

'But how? Did his heart give out?'

'The truth is that he has been cruelly murdered. A crime of passion if ever I saw one. Have you any idea at all where the rest of the coach party have departed to?'

Jemima slowly shook her head. 'No, only Mr Simms who, as I told you, has gone to Lady Sidmouth's.'

John pulled a face. 'I think they'll have to be found somehow.'

'Why? You don't believe that they could be connected with the crime, do you?'

The Apothecary looked at her. 'It's possible that one of them is a murderer.'

Jemima lowered her eyes. 'Oh dear, I hope not. They seemed such a pleasant crowd.'

'That,' answered John, 'is often the way.'

* * *

Two hours later he was free to leave the inn. The Constable had been; a lean blackbird of a fellow and a professional, in that he was hired by those whose turn it was to act as peacekeeper and had been in the position for some six years. Taciturn and dour, for all that John took to the man, for he clearly knew what he was doing and had organized everything very swiftly. William Gorringe had been removed from the room and dispatched to the mortuary awaiting the Coroner's verdict. The Apothecary had furnished the Constable with a list of names of the other travellers on the coach, told him of the strange cloaked figure he had seen, and the remaining guests in the inn had all been asked to give their particulars.

'Trouble is, Sir,' said the Constable, scratching his closely shaved chin and looking at John with a black-eyed glance, 'that it could have been a common thief. We've no proof that it was anyone that the victim knew.'

'Except that there were no signs of anything having been taken. Admittedly I didn't search the body but I did notice that the dead man wore a diamond ring upon his little finger and that it was still there this morning. Further, the room was left neatly and is it not the trademark of a robber that he always pulls the place apart?'

The dark eyes gleamed. 'You seem to know a lot about it if I might say so.'

John looked worldly. 'Merely facts that one picks up from reading the journals, don't you know.'

And now, having given the Constable both his London address and the address of the Marchesa – a fact which had left a good impression John could tell – he was off at last to see the woman who still held him in her thrall. Leaving the inn, the Apothecary walked to the nearest livery stable where he hired a large, sensible-looking grey horse – his experience with hired horses being none too favourable – and set off to ride out of Exeter. Before he had gone he had seen Jemima Lovell into a small trap that was making for Sidmouth and had negotiated the fee for taking her the extra miles to Lady Sidmouth's mansion. She said farewell with a sorrowful look in her brilliant eyes.

'Goodbye, Mr Rawlings. How sad that our journey should have ended so horribly.'

'*Au revoir*, Miss Lovell. Try not to think about it too much.'

'I'll do my best, Sir.' And giving his hand a squeeze, she had disappeared down the length of the High Street.

John, having been given a leg-up onto the grey horse, spoke to it as they rode out of the town.

'Now, my friend, I want a nice easy ride, do you understand. No funny tricks or rearing up. Just take me at a reasonable pace to Lady Elizabeth's and you shall be rewarded with a nice loose box and a bag of hay.'

The horse twitched its ears and plodded forward, leaving the city behind and following the line of the river Exe. John decided to go along the riverbank, which was pleasant in the September sunshine, but when it came to the high hill on the top of which Elizabeth's beautiful house was situated the horse refused to budge a step. In the end the Apothecary was forced to dismount and lead the beast upwards by its reins, puffing and panting as he did so. By the time he reached the lodge gates he was thoroughly out of breath and dishevelled into the bargain. Glad that he hadn't worn a wig and that his hair was tied back in a queue, John mopped his face.

The lodge keeper was new and looked at him with a certain suspicion. 'Can I help you, Sir?'

'I have come to see Lady Elizabeth di Lorenzi.'

'Do you have an appointment?'

'No, not exactly. She wrote and asked me to visit. I am an old friend.'

'I see. Well if you go up to the big house you can enquire there whether she is in.'

'Thank you,' John answered crisply, and feeling that he had done his duty by the horse, remounted and urged it up the curving, uphill drive.

As he rode the last few yards, the house now in sight, his throat went dry and he felt as nervous as a schoolboy. The last time he had been there had been in the spring of this year and Elizabeth had not been at home, gone to Bath for the sake of her health, or so he had been informed. He had taken that as her way of telling him that she had no further wish to see him. He recalled the time he had proposed to her and how she had turned to look at him, her long black hair blowing about her face. He also remembered her refusal, saying she preferred a life alone even though she was fond of him. She could hurt him, there was no doubting that. And yet out of a clear blue sky she had written to him, asking him to come to her, informing him that she had something of interest to tell him. Wondering what on earth it could be, John dismounted at the front door and handing the horse over to an hostler, mounted the six steps which led up to it.

A footman answered the bell and fortunately recognized John from the past.

'Ah, Mr Rawlings, Sir. Is my lady expecting you?'

'Yes and no. She wrote and asked me to visit her and here I am. But I didn't inform her of the date of my arrival.'

'I see. Would you like to wait in the parlour and I will see if she is at home.'

John stepped into the vast reception hall and gazed upwards. There, painted high above his head, was a representation of Britannia waving a spear. Smiling indulgently he traversed the large space, following the footman, and was shown into a small parlour leading off the Blue Drawing-room. His mind wandered over the difference in their stations in life. She had been born a daughter of the nobility, he the bastard child of one of the Rawlings family of Twickenham. She had married an Italian nobleman and had lived a wild and dangerous life. He had qualified as an apothecary and had found his excitement through working with Sir John Fielding. At that moment John realized with a horrible clarity that he could never offer Elizabeth the life to which she had been used and that he may as well leave now.

There was a noise in the doorway and John, turning, saw that the woman who filled his thoughts was standing there. He rose and bowed.

'Madam.'

She walked towards him, smiling her delicious smile. 'Sir,' she replied.

And then John looked at her properly and his heart plummeted before it rose again and started to beat wildly in his chest.

She laughed then, throwing her head back and chuckling.

'Don't look so shocked,' she said. 'As you can see, my dear, I am quite definitely with child.'

Four

John stood gaping at her, hardly able to take in what Elizabeth had just said to him. Then he realized several things simultaneously. Firstly that judging by the stage of her pregnancy – probably about four months in his professional opinion – he was undoubtedly the father. Secondly that she was dangerously old to be carrying a child. And thirdly, and most happily, that this event would surely draw them closer together once more. He cleared his throat and spoke.

'Elizabeth, my dear. I had no idea. Why did you not tell me before?'

She gave a careless laugh and sat down, motioning him to do likewise. 'I did not want to bother you with it.'

He leant across the distance between them and took her hand. 'That was wrong of you. It is my child as well. You should have written straight away.'

'Well, I didn't. In fact it went through my head to say nothing until after the birth. But then I thought how upset you would be and I changed my mind.'

'And thank God you did,' John answered fervently. He knelt down in front of her. 'My darling, is there anything I can do to help?'

She burst out laughing and he saw then that the forthcoming child had not changed her at all, that she was still as wild and free as she had always been.

'I think you've done that already, my friend,' she said, and laid a careless hand on her rounding.

John decided to match her mood. 'And very pleasurable it was too,' he said, and gave his lopsided grin.

She changed the subject. 'What time is it?'

John looked at his watch. 'Just gone three o'clock.'

'Then we shall have an early dinner. And now if you would be so good as to escort me I should like to walk in the gardens. I have forbidden myself riding – though only temporarily, I might add – so walking is my only form of exercise.'

He stood up, brushing at his knees, thinking to himself that she really was the most extraordinary woman he had ever met. Where the majority of her sex would be moaning and grumbling over an unwanted pregnancy she was treating the whole thing with immense *sang froid*. As they walked together out into the formally laid-out grounds with stunning views as far as the eye could see, he decided to challenge her. Leaning close to her he asked a question.

'Tell me, do you want to have this baby?'

Her lovely topaz eyes, on a level with his own, looked into his with a direct gaze.

'Yes, of course I do. You know that my son died, killed by that wretched group of young men who called themselves The Angels?'

'You have told me the story often.'

'Well, now that I can feel life growing inside me once more I long for the day when I can hold the child in my arms.'

John stopped walking. 'Elizabeth, will you marry me? I cannot bear the idea of our child being born a bastard.'

'Rather than a proposal you could have said that you love me desperately and have thought of no-one else in the months we have been apart.'

'Stop playing games with me,' the Apothecary said, very slightly irritable. 'You know I love you and you know how much. And if you don't you should. Besides, if you remember, I asked you to be my wife a long while ago.'

'Yes, I do remember,' she answered, her whole manner changing. 'And I know it is not just to give our child a name. But, my own dear John, I cannot say yes. I no longer wish for married life.'

'Not even for the sake of the child?'

'No, not even then.'

It was useless to argue further. John realized that if he wanted peace and harmony between them he must content himself with the fact that his second child would be born a bastasd. But then, he reflected, he had been illegitimate and had not had too bad a life of it. In fact, all things considered, it had been relatively happy if one discounted the tragedy of Emilia's end and the time when he had gone on the run. He sighed, and Elizabeth, mistaking the cause of it, took his hand and held it firmly.

'It is not that I don't love you in return, my friend. It is just that I love my freedom more.'

'And will you allow me to see my child? Am I to have access to her?'

'Or him.' Elizabeth said with a smile. 'Of course. You will be free to come and go as you please. As you always have been.'

'You have no wish to give the baby to me to bring up?'

She looked fractionally annoyed. 'No, no wish at all. This child will comfort me in my old age and give meaning and direction to my declining years.'

'I'm sure it will,' John answered, just a trifle sadly. 'Tell me, when is it due?'

'In February. It will come with the early lambs.'

'And may I be here?'

Elizabeth squeezed his hand. 'Of course. Please consider this house your second home.'

John gave up. There was no arguing with her. Most of the women he had known would face the thought of bringing a bastard into the world with shame and humility. Yet here was Elizabeth talking in the most rational way of bringing up her son or daughter by herself, regardless of gossip. The Apothecary had to come to terms with the fact that the Marchesa was entirely different from every one of his other acquaintances; that she stood alone.

They dined early and John, studying her, thought how this late pregnancy had enhanced her, rounded out her tendency to boniness, softened the contours of her face. Even the savage scar that ran down her cheek from her eye to her mouth seemed to have lost its cruelty and appeared like a gentle line.

'You are very beautiful,' he said down the length of the table and regardless of the hovering servants.

'In your eyes perhaps.'

'No, truly.' He was longing to tell her that forthcoming motherhood became her but did not like to mention it in the presence of the footmen waiting at table. Instead he said conversationally, 'Tell me, are you acquainted with Lady Sidmouth at all?'

'Yes, I know the old besom. Why?'

John rolled his eyes in the direction of the footmen and Elizabeth said, 'Thank you, Faulkener. You may tell the servants to withdraw. If you could return in a quarter of an hour or so that would be splendid.'

As soon as the room had cleared John got up and took his chair to sit beside her, taking her fingers in his hand and kissing each one individually.

'I love you,' he said.

She stroked his hair. 'And I love you. But you do understand that we cannot be together. Our lives are too different and I am too old for you.' He started to protest but she silenced him and said, 'You know that is true so don't deny it. But while you are here let us enjoy each other's company and have an amusing time.'

'Very well.' He sat up straight. 'Tell me about Lady Sidmouth.'

'I'll do better than that. You can meet her in person. I shall call on her tomorrow and take you with me. But why do you want to know about her?'

'There was an incident on my journey here.'

'What sort of incident?'

'A murder.'

Elizabeth raised her eyebrows. 'Tell me all about it.'

Filling both their glasses from the decanter that stood on the sideboard, John took a mouthful and then launched into the tale of how he caught the stagecoach at the last minute and of all the varied people he had got to know during the course of the journey.

'And so the unpleasant Mr Gorringe met his end in The Half Moon,' he ended lightly, though he shivered as he said the words, adding, 'Actually it was one of the most horrible crimes I have ever witnessed.'

'Why?'

'Because the poor devil had been bludgeoned to death in the most brutal manner. It was a truly terrible sight to see.'

Elizabeth remained silent, her profile etched against the light thrown by the fire. She said, 'Tell me more about the Black Pyramid. He interests me.'

'Do you believe he is the murderer?'

'Quite possibly. Did you not say that Gorringe recognized him?'

'Yes, I believe he did.'

'Then they have a past connection. And as the motive was not robbery you must look to the past, John. For that is where the answer will lie.'

'You sound like Sir John Fielding.'

Elizabeth pealed with laughter. 'Do I really? Is that my attraction for you? That I remind you of the man you work for?'

John raised a svelte eyebrow. 'Hardly that, my darling. I cannot imagine getting into bed with the revered magistrate.'

'I should hope not indeed.' She raised her wine glass. 'I should like to drink to you, John. Thank you for everything you have done for me.' She put her hand to her body. 'And thank you for the child. Now that I am *enceinte* I realize that it is something I should have considered years ago.'

'But then I would not have been the father.'

Elizabeth smiled enigmatically. 'No, I suppose not,' she said.

They went to bed shortly after the meal was cleared away, both in high spirits, though the awful sight he had seen that morning slightly tempered John's relief that he and Elizabeth had been reunited. However, she was clearly not suffering from any such inhibitions and burst into song, leaning against the upright pillows and sipping a glass of wine. Just for a second John thought about the servants, wondering whether they could hear her or not. Then he threw caution to the winds and joined in, singing lustily, clinking glasses with her and generally having a good time until eventually both of them fell asleep.

Five

The ride from Exeter to Sidmouth came back to John with horrible clarity the next morning as he and Elizabeth set off to visit Lady Sidmouth, travelling in her second-best carriage. He recalled the scrubland where long ago on his honeymoon he had seen a headless coachman driving a coach full of phantoms. This had later turned out to be a sinister deception but it had shaken him and frightened Emilia at the time. And because of those memories he was glad to leave that particular piece of coutryside and emerge onto the wooded headland that led down to the sea.

The bay of Sidmouth was surrounded on either side by land that protruded into the water. As one faced the ocean a long green promontory stuck out like a finger to the right. But the left-hand side was dominated by red cliffs, above which lay green pastures and in the midst of these was set the home of the redoubtable Lady Sidmouth. As the carriage turned into the drive John could see the house and put it down as having been built in the reign of Queen Anne.

It was of mellow red brick and in a niche above the front door stood a life-size statue of Demeter. The rest of the building flowed round this central point in becoming lines and the Apothecary found himself liking the harmonious whole enormously. The coachman dropped them at the main entrance and drove round to the stables on the right, while Elizabeth pealed the bell. John stood back and was astonished when the door was answered by a little woman wearing an apron.

'Wretched footmen,' she said by way of greeting. 'Never around when they are needed. Come in, my dear, come in. And who is your friend?'

'Lady Sidmouth, may I present John Rawlings to you. John, this is Lady Sidmouth.'

John bowed handsomely, then kissed the lady's hand.

'My goodness,' she said, 'what an elegant young man. Pray follow me.'

They did so, entering a large hallway and proceeding from there through a series of rooms until they came to one at the end of the house that overlooked the sea. John stared out of the large window to the undulating swell below him and remembered distant times that had been so full of joy.

He turned round to see that Lady Sidmouth was ushering him towards a seat.

'Come and sit opposite me, Mr Rawlings. I wish to look at you.'

She was one of the most extraordinary women that John had ever seen. She had very large upper lids which closed half her eye, revealing a pair of dark brown orbs beneath, which glinted like those of a harvest mouse. But this was not her most peculiar feature, for Lady Sidmouth appeared to have no lips at all. The Apothecary had never seen such a tiny and inverted mouth. When she spoke she did so without moving it and he peered to see if she had any teeth, and was rewarded with a glimpse of minute white seeds. To crown it all she had wispy brown hair which she had screwed up into a bun beneath a very ordinary work a day mob-cap.

'Well now, I think it is time for a little sherry, don't you?' And without waiting for a reply she rang a small bell that stood on a table. She turned her attention to Elizabeth. 'And tell me, my dear, how are you getting on?'

The Marchesa shot her an amused glance and said, 'I am *enceinte*, in case you hadn't noticed.'

Lady Sidmouth did not turn a hair. Instead she asked, 'And who is the father, may I ask?'

'I am,' John answered. 'And in case you are wondering I have repeatedly asked Elizabeth to marry me but she will have none of it.'

'Very wise too. My husband gave me ten children, ranging in ages from thirty to eleven, and then he died. Worn out I expect.'

John looked at her with new interest. She might be a peculiar-looking little creature but she was as outspoken as the Marchesa herself.

'Very probably,' he said, and smiled, at which Lady Sidmouth threw her apron over her face and laughed long and loud.

A footman entered the room and seemed to take the situation entirely as normal. 'You rang, my Lady?' he said, remaining utterly straight-faced.

'Of course I did, Hopkins. Who else would have done it? Can

you bring a decanter of the dry sherry and three glasses, please? Oh, and some of those sweet little biscuits that I like.'

'Very good, my Lady.'

A memory was stirring in John's mind, of a Robin Sidmouth he had once met in Bath. He turned to his hostess.

'Do you by any chance know a Robin Sidmouth? I met him once, some years ago.'

'Of course I know him. He's my eldest son. He's inherited the title now his father is dead.'

John turned to Elizabeth, who said, 'The Earl of Sidmouth. That's Robin.'

The Apothecary, who had always wondered about Robin's doubtful sexuality, asked, 'Is he married?'

'Of course,' his mother snorted, 'to a dull, lifeless girl called Maud. They've been wed two years and have had two children. Mind you he went kicking and screaming to the altar. I've always thought he was a Miss Molly myself.'

John, remembering, said, 'Who knows?'

To which she replied, 'Pish. I should have thought it perfectly obvious.'

Lady Sidmouth poured out the sherry and handed round the plate of biscuits which Hopkins had placed before her. 'You must excuse my wearing an apron,' she said. 'Fact is I've been in the kitchen making plum jam. Our fruit trees were laden this year.' She fixed a piercing glance on Elizabeth. 'Was there another reason for your coming to see me? Or was it merely to announce that you were with child?'

'No, there was another reason, my dear Dorothy. My friend John travelled down in a stagecoach with two people whom you are currently employing. One was a dancing master, the other a milliner. You know of whom I speak?'

'Yes, I know them very well. One is Simms, getting on in years but none the less a fine master of the Terpsichorean art. The other is Lovell, a dark-complexioned girl but for all that something of a beauty. They are both currently under my roof.' She turned to John, her tiny eyes gleaming with curiosity. 'Why do you want to know?'

The Apothecary hesitated, wondering whether or not to tell her about the murder of William Gorringe. He decided to be truthful only after another glance at her assured him that she would ferret the facts out of him one way or the other.

'Actually, a fellow passenger was murdered in the inn on the night before last. Jemima Lovell knew of it but Mr Simms did not. I wondered whether he should be informed before the Constable comes calling.'

'Will he come calling?' Lady Sidmouth responded.

'He might well. The hunt is on to find the missing passengers.'

'Then go and talk to him, Mr Rawlings. He is teaching even while we speak. You will find him in the ballroom. Hopkins can show you where it is.' And she rang the bell again.

But as he mounted the stairs behind Hopkins's stoutly stockinged legs the Apothecary thought that he had small need of directions. For from a room on the first floor there came a great deal of noise – cries of 'No, no. Do it like this,' followed by the strains of a frantic violin and a great deal of heavy-footed thumping. With a majestic gesture Hopkins threw open the door and John gazed within.

Children of assorted ages and sizes – a dozen of them – were ranged in ranks before a red-faced Cuthbert Simms, who had the traditional violin tucked beneath his chin and was presently haranguing them about not getting a step correctly. Eager young virgins of seventeen languished at the back while in the front were younger sprigs, one in particular looking horribly like Robin Sidmouth, all pouting mouth and high heels.

John stepped into the ballroom and every head turned in his direction. The dancing lesson ground to a halt.

'Mr Rawlings,' said Cuthbert in tones of great surprise. 'Whatever are you doing here?'

'I have come to speak to you, actually.'

'Very well. Ladies and gentlemen, you may take a short break during which you will practice the steps I have been endeavouring to teach you this morning.'

There were various squeals of protest but Cuthbert looked firm and clapped his hands, after which there were one or two half-hearted attempts made to obey his instructions.

'Well, my dear Sir,' he said, drawing John to one side. 'This is most certainly a surprise.'

'Indeed it is, Sir. But truth to tell there was a fatality at The Half Moon which had not been discovered at the time you left. I thought it only fair to warn you that the Constable might come to interview you.'

'Me?' exclaimed Cuthbert. 'Whatever for? I know nothing about it. What fatality?'

'William Gorringe was murdered in his bed during the night,' answered John, looking mild and honest – an expression he had been working on for some time.

'Gorringe, you say? Oh dear me, whoever could have done that I wonder?'

He turned away, wiping his sweating face with a large handkerchief and John could see that even the back of Cuthbert's neck had turned bright red.

'I've no idea. The matter is – as I said – in the hands of the Constable. We shall have to await developments.'

The dancing master was clearly flustered because he clapped his hands together and said, 'Ladies and gentlemen, you may have the rest of this morning off. I shall see you here at two o'clock sharply.'

There was a loud shout of delight and a charge towards the door. Cuthbert sighed. 'No matter how hard I try they behave like little hoydens.'

'Boys will be boys, I suppose,' John answered cheerfully. His gaze fell on two young ladies walking neatly towards the exit. 'Now that couple do you credit. Who are they?'

'The Lady Felicity Sidmouth – the Earl's sister. And the Honourable Miranda Tremayne. She's some sort of cousin and stays here as a guest.'

'I see.'

As they drew level the pair dropped neat bobs and John made an effusive bow in return. Miranda gave him a saucy glance and as she went through the door turned to look at him over her shoulder.

'My goodness, she's going to grow up a beauty.'

'She already is,' sighed Cuthbert. 'She has half the young men in the county calling on her. She is also my favourite pupil, being anxious to learn every dance there is.'

He was clearly relaxing now that the subject of Gorringe had been dropped but John felt it was his duty to persevere.

'Did you know William Gorringe before the journey to Exeter?' he asked casually.

The colour swept back into Cuthbert's cheeks and he answered very swiftly, 'No. No indeed. The man was a complete stranger to me until we met on the coach.'

He was just a little too emphatic John thought. But he felt he could question the dancing master no further. He got up from the chair to which Cuthbert had motioned him.

'Well, my friend, I'll bid you *adieu*. I just thought I ought to warn you before the Constable descends on you.'

He watched the little man suddenly drain of colour. 'When will that be, do you know?'

John shook his head. 'I'm afraid that I have no idea. But come I think he will.'

'Well, I can tell him nothing,' Cuthbert answered, and turned away.

John found the ladies in the kitchens, stirring large saucepans of jam. They looked up as he entered the room.

'Ah, there you are,' said Elizabeth, gesturing with her wooden spoon.

John leaned over to sniff the jam. 'Smells good.' He straightened and looked at Lady Sidmouth. 'Would it be too much trouble to have a word with Miss Lovell?'

'The dark beauty? Yes, by all means. She is upstairs in the sewing room. I'll take you to her myself.'

'And I'll go too,' said Elizabeth. 'I must have a look at this wondrous creature.'

I do believe she's jealous, thought John, and was intensely pleased with himself.

They went up the main staircase then ascended the wooden spiral used by the servants to get to the top floor. And it was here, sitting in a room that could easily become dark on a gloomy day, that Jemima Lovell sat, accompanied by a girl of about fourteen who was stitching a pile of shirts of varying sizes. Jemima looked up as the trio entered. She got to her feet and gave a hasty curtsey, while the girl did likewise.

'Lady Sidmouth, how nice to see you.' Her eyes widened. 'And Mr Rawlings. How do you do, sir?'

Elizabeth spoke up. 'What is that you are working on, my dear?'

'A headdress, Ma'am.' And Jemima passed it to Elizabeth, carefully removing the needle before she did so.

'Why, it's beautiful. What a clever girl you are. Where did you find her, Dorothy?'

John's conviction that Elizabeth was green about the eye redoubled.

Lady Sidmouth snorted. 'In London, of course. The place that you shun, my girl.'

'I prefer the country, it's true.' She turned her attention to Jemima. 'And whereabouts do you work, my dear?'

'In Greek Street, Ma'am. At Madame Sophie's. She is French and came over with the Huguenots. Or at least her family did.'

Elizabeth gave a deep sigh. 'I obviously miss much by keeping myself away from the capital.'

'I can lend her to you,' said Lady Sidmouth, somewhat patronizingly.

'I don't think that will be possible, Lady Sidmouth,' Jemima answered, sweet but firm. 'Madame Sophie is expecting me back in two weeks and I have a great deal of work to do here.' She turned to John. 'It was nice to see you again, Mr Rawlings.'

'And you, Miss Lovell.' He lowered his voice to a whisper. 'May I have a word with you in private?'

'Yes, by all means. When and where?'

But he never got the chance to answer her. Elizabeth was at his side, dark hair gleaming and eyes lit from within.

'Come along, my dear,' she said. 'We really must be getting back.'

'I've a question to put to Miss Lovell first. I was going to ask her in private but as we are so short of time I will have to forgo that.'

Jemima stood her ground. 'Ask me then, Sir.'

'It's this: Had you met anyone on the coach before you started your journey?'

'Yes,' she answered, somewhat surprisingly. 'I knew the actress, Paulina Gower. She buys hats from Madame Sophie. We had met before.'

'And that was all?'

Jemima lowered her eyes. 'Yes, that was all. The rest were complete strangers to me.'

Why did John get the strong impression that the girl was lying?

Going back in the carriage John knew a moment of intense happiness as he thought that just for once he had the better of Elizabeth. This was followed by instant shame that he should be so childish. Yet nothing could take away his delight that she had actually appeared jealous of Jemima Lovell, who admittedly was an attractive young creature. He glanced across at the Marchesa and impulsively took her hand. She turned to him and smiled and in that instant he suddenly feared for her. She looked tired and it occurred to John that this pregnancy, coming so late in her life, was going to be a great ordeal, culminating in a labour that surely would not be easy for her.

'My darling,' he said, 'you must retire to bed as soon as we get back.'

'Nonsense,' Elizabeth answered roundly. 'It is the height of the day. I shall dine as usual. Indeed I am quite hungry.'

'Promise me that you will retire early then.'

'My God, John. You are not going to turn into a grandmother are you? I really could not abide being nursemaided. I warn you that I shall continue to live my life as usual until the last possible moment.'

The Apothecary gave a rueful smile. 'And when will that be? When you go into travail I suppose.'

She smiled and squeezed his fingers. 'Maybe a week before,' she answered. And John knew that even if he remained with her for the rest of his life she would eventually be capable of winning every point.

Six

John woke early the next morning. Beside him Elizabeth slept quietly, her dark hair spread over the pillow, one hand curling up delicately, like a water lily. She was turned away from him and did not stir as he rose and crossed to the window, drawing the curtains back slightly to look out over the early daylight vista. Below him the river Exe wound its serpentine way through the valley and looking to his right he could see the city of Exeter dominated by its great cathedral. Standing there silently John knew that he must go there today and seek out the Constable, that he could not let the matter of the murder of William Gorringe drop as any other citizen would. That all his years of working with Sir John Fielding and Joe Jago had altered his thinking indelibly. With a sigh at his own folly, John went into the dressing room and put on his clothes.

Having breakfasted alone he went back to the bedroom to find the Marchesa awake but looking slightly pale.

'How are you today, Madam?' he asked, and kissed her hand.

'To be perfectly honest I feel a little unwell. I think I shall stay here awhile.'

'I told you yesterday you looked tired.'

'And I told you that I will not be nursemaided.'

John looked at Elizabeth very seriously. 'You do want to carry this baby to term, don't you?'

She gave him a beautiful smile and instantly seemed young and fresh again. 'Of course I do. I longed for another child when my son died and now to have one by an attractive and clever man is more than I could have hoped for.'

'Then take the pregnancy with care, sweetheart. Allow me to go to an apothecary in Exeter and get you some physic.'

She took his hand. 'I am sorry if I sounded ungracious just now – and yesterday as well. It is just that I cannot bear fuss. But you are right. I am old indeed to be having a child and I must take that into consideration. I will do as you say, Apothecary, and rest.'

John thought that he had never known her so compliant and decided to utilize his advantage. Leaning over, he kissed her.

'I will order the servants to bring you your breakfast in bed. And I shall go into Exeter if I may borrow one of your horses.'

She burst out laughing. 'I knew there was method in your madness. Choose any beast you like. By the way your hired mount has been returned by one of my grooms.'

'Thank you for that. I won't be long,' he said, heading for the door.

'And you ought to pay your respects to Sir Clovelly Lovell while you are in town.'

'I shall make a point of it.'

'And you are to give him my kindest regards.'

'Of course.'

A quarter of an hour later and he was in the saddle and heading for Exeter at a brisk trot, wondering just how best to organize what seemed like a very busy time ahead. He decided to leave his visit to Sir Clovelly till last and to make his pursuit of the Constable his first priority. But as fate would have it his entire plan had to be shelved because on entering Exeter one of the first things John saw was a hand bill advertising a prizefight between Gentleman Jack McAra and the Black Pyramid. Fascinated, he drew nearer and saw that the bout was to take place that very afternoon. Knowing instantly who would love to accompany him, John turned his horse in the direction of The Close and the home of that dear little fat man of whom the Apothecary had grown extremely fond over the years.

He found Sir Clovelly at home, sitting in his garden in the September sunshine and partaking of a little cordial and some sweetmeats. He looked up as John was shown in by a servant, his face registering anger at being disturbed, followed by a quick rush of recognition and joy.

'My dear boy,' he said, attempting to struggle to his feet, an attempt that John quickly stopped. 'I cannot believe my eyes. What are you doing here? What an incredibly pleasant surprise.'

John bowed with deference. 'As it is for me, Sir. And to answer your question, I am here visting the Marchesa but made it one of my first priorities to call on you.'

'And how delighted I am that you did so. Sit down, John, and have a sherry, do. I do not receive company as often as I once used.'

The apothecary's heart bled for him as he saw a lonely old man peering out of his fat, jolly face.

'I was wondering if you would accompany me to a prizefight this afternoon, Sir,' he said, making his voice sound excessively cheerful. 'Truth to tell I am on my own and would be honoured if you would consider accompanying me.'

Sir Clovelly visibly perked up. 'A fight, eh? I love a good mill. When is it to take place?'

'At two o'clock.'

'Ah, just time for a little light luncheon beforehand.'

'Then I take it you will come?'

'I shall be glad of an outing, my dear John. And I thank you for inviting me.'

'It is entirely my pleasure.'

Sir Clovelly's idea of a light meal was what other people would regard as a small banquet. John, who had breakfasted well, found himself refusing several courses leading to the inevitable questions as to why he was off his food.

'I am not, Sir, I can assure you. It is just that I am not used to eating at this hour of the day. I prefer to dine at night.'

'Oh, I do that as well, don't you know. Of course the damn doctors tell me to cut down but I find food such a great consolation, eating such an enjoyable pastime.'

Once again the Apothecary was struck by the pathos of the man and he determined at that moment to ask Sir Clovelly if he would stand as godparent to the unborn child. But how to broach the subject? John cleared his throat.

'Sir, I wonder if I might ask you a favour?'

Sir Clovelly paused, a wing of fowl halfway to his mouth.

'Certainly, my boy. Ask away.'

John hedged. 'Have you seen the Marchesa recently?'

'No, can't say that I have. I really must call. How is the dear girl?'

'Actually that is what I want to talk to you about.'

'Why? She ain't ill, is she?'

John actually blushed, a deep uncomfortable red. 'No, she's perfectly alright. The fact of the matter is that she is with child.'

Sir Clovelly put down the piece of chicken and gazed at John with small twinkling eyes.

'And I'll wager she still won't marry you.'

There was a momentary silence, during which the two men stared at one another, Sir Clovelly brimming with bonhomie. It was too much for the Apothecary who felt the start of a smile twitch at his lips. The next second he was grinning like a schoolboy caught committing a prank.

'You're quite correct,' he said. 'She won't. Society will surely close its doors to her as a result.'

'Now there you are wrong,' Sir Clovelly answered, resuming his consumption of food. 'Elizabeth is too powerful in her own right to merit such treatment. She is rich and she is charming. Maybe one or two of the more stuffy families will cut her but the rest of her friends will remain loyal, you mark my words.'

'I hope you are right.'

'Of course I am right.' Sir Clovelly finished his piece of chicken and wiped his hands. 'And, my dear boy, can you imagine Elizabeth in London? Can you imagine her as the wife of – forgive me – an apothecary? She is too free a spirit, too wild a soul, to be so constrained. The best thing you can do is to accept the fact of your forthcoming fatherhood with joy and see your child as often as is possible.'

John nodded. 'It's a bitter pill to swallow but I agree with you. I know that she would never settle down in the capital. But yet I had a glimmer of hope . . .'

'Best forgotten,' interrupted Sir Clovelly. He looked at his watch, fishing for it in a lower pocket of his coat which strained at bursting point over his extremely ample stomach. 'What time did you say this bout was?'

'At two o'clock, Sir.'

'Then we'd best depart.' And with a great deal of effort Sir Clovelly struggled to his feet.

The fight was scheduled to take place in a field slightly west of the High Street. John, entering the arena, felt quite overcome with excitement for the place was alive with every kind of trader, every booth, every hawker, that it was possible to imagine.

It seemed that the whole of Exeter – or at least a goodly proportion of its citizens – had decided to make this event a holiday, for the field was packed with people. Tall men of Devon walked with their round, rosy wives while children, shouting excitedly, played games of catch and blindman's-buff. There were stalls selling household goods, trinkets and sweetmeats, to say nothing of gloves, haberdashery, and one devoted entirely to ribbons and trimmings. There was delicious marchpane together with sugar cakes on sale, one of which Sir Clovelly bought, munching it with much relish and smacking of lips.

'Is it good?' asked John, smiling at him fondly.

'It's made of rose water and oranges. I think I'll take some home. They are very light and enjoyable.'

In the middle of the field a piece had been cordoned off and it was here that the two men were going to fight. But there was another quarter of an hour before the bout was scheduled. The Apothecary, his spirits raised high by the general buzz and excitement, wandered to a booth in front of which children sat on the grass, watching marionettes acting out a story of knights and dragons. In his fond imaginings he could see Rose sitting with a little sister – or could it possibly be a brother? – beside her, watching with large eyes and a toss of flame-coloured hair as a very realistic dragon roared at a brave knight. Happily, he wandered on. And then he stopped dead in his tracks because coming towards him was that Exeter solicitor, Martin Meadows with, of all people, the sensible Lucinda Silverwood. Standing directly in their path, John gave a fulsome bow.

'Good afternoon. What a surprise to see you both. Greetings, Madam, I trust your daughter is well?'

Looking slightly flustered, Lucinda curtseyed. 'She has not yet had her child, thank you Mr Rawlings. I thought I would have some time to myself while I could.'

Meadows gave a laugh that to John's ears sounded somewhat guilty. 'We met here by chance and I asked Mrs Silverwood if she would accompany me.'

'Quite so,' the Apothecary replied smoothly. 'I take it you have both heard the news of Gorringe's murder?'

'Indeed we have. The Constable called at my office this morning.'

'And he tracked me down yesterday evening. My daughter was quite alarmed, I can tell you.'

'I wonder if he has been so lucky finding the rest of the travellers.'

'I wonder indeed,' said Meadows, looking a little bleak.

There was a call from the area in the middle of the field. 'My lords, ladies and gentlemen, the fight will begin in three minutes.'

Excusing himself, John went to stand with Sir Clovelly amongst the crowd of onlookers. Glancing round, the Apothecary could not help but notice the young blades of Exeter packed in little groups on either side of the home-made ring. Dressed very finely, their breeches tight and their coats cut back, displaying excellent thighs and interesting bulges, they all had stylish tricornes on their heads and many sported diamond pins in the folds of their cravats. Thinking that he must pay some attention to his wardrobe when he returned to London, John saw that Mrs Silverwood stood several rows back beside the mild-mannered Martin Meadows.

Nathaniel Broome stepped into the ring and announced in a surprisingly loud voice, 'Ladies and gentlemen, may I present to you the Black Pyramid.'

'Indeed you may,' shouted one young beau and during the ensuing rumble of laughter, the Negro climbed into the arena.

He was stripped to the waist and wearing only a pair of black tights, and John gazed in frank admiration at the beauty of the man's body. He gleamed like polished oak, in fact he seemed almost incandescent as he flexed his muscles, his torso rippling like a waterfall. His shoulders were so broad and strong that he resembled a dark god that had come down from Mount Olympus to play amongst the mortals. John could not remember ever seeing such a healthy specimen. Yet the Black Pyramid was not young, probably about forty or maybe a year or two older.

A roar went up from the crowd as he walked round the ring with his arms raised aloft. Then another man, very bald and somewhat rat-faced, stepped up beside him.

'My lords, ladies and gentlemen, pray welcome Gentleman Jack McAra.'

There was an even louder cheer as Gentleman Jack leapt into the ring in a sprightly fashion and cavorted before the crowd. Looking at him through narrowed eyes John decided to place a bet on the Black Pyramid, for McAra was frankly running to fat and appeared generally out of condition. He turned to Sir Clovelly.

'Do you fancy a wager, Sir?'

'I do indeed. I'll put a guinea on Gentleman Jack.'

'And I'll see you. I think the Black Pyramid is going to win. Will you take the bet?'

'I most certainly will,' answered Sir Clovelly, and rubbed his chubby hands together.

There were clearly a great many wagers changing hands for it seemed that McAra was known in the neighbourhood and had a particularly lethal punch. But John, surveying both candidates, felt certain that he had made the right choice and smiled to himself, ready to be entertained.

The fight opened with a flurry of blows to the black man's head, all of which he seemed to shake off as if a fly was buzzing round him. He stretched out his magnificent long arms and landed several buffets to McAra's body which, John imagined, must have hurt tremendously. And so it went on. The two men straining and crunching their naked, bony fists into the body of the other, protecting their heads but unable to avoid the hits that were coming towards them.

It seemed to the Apothecary that McAra was getting the worst of it, for though he admittedly had a cruel punch he was getting more and more out of breath and was sweating profusely.

The Black Pyramid glistened with perspiration which he wiped off during the interval between rounds. John, observing him closely, saw that he had a faraway look in his eyes and realized that the black man was in a world of his own, that nothing mattered to him except finishing off his opponent. That, in that sense, he was a born fighter.

The end came swiftly. Gentleman Jack threw a splintering punch, so loud that one could hear his fingers cracking on the Black Pyramid's head. This clearly hurt the black man for with a roar he turned on his assailant and swung a blow to his jaw which made him drop in his tracks. The man in charge counted Jack out swiftly and raised a long black arm to the public. The Pyramid had won.

John turned to Sir Clovelly Lovell who was looking slightly downcast.

'I think you owe me a guinea, Sir.'

'Yes, my boy, I believe I do.'

'Thank you. Now, would you mind excusing me for a moment? There are some people I must talk to.'

John hurried over to where Mrs Silverwood and Mr Martin were wandering away round the fair. He bowed.

'An excellent fight, was it not?'

'It was indeed.'

John addressed himself to the solicitor. 'My dear sir, if you should recall anything further that the late Mr Gorringe said to you I wonder if you would be good enough to contact me. I am staying at present with Lady Elizabeth di Lorenzi.'

'Oh yes. She lives in the big house above the river Exe, does she not?'

'Indeed she does.'

Mrs Silverwood's face looked suddenly pointed. 'Why?' she said. 'What is your interest in the dead man may I ask?'

'The answer is, madam, that I work occasionally for Sir John Fielding of Bow Street and nowadays I cannot come across a case of murder without investigating a little. Please forgive me.'

Was it his imagination or had the pair of them gone suddenly quiet?

'I see,' Mrs Silverwood answered softly. 'Well, good day to you, Sir.'

'Good day, Madam,' John replied, bowed, and went back to join Sir Clovelly Lovell.

Seven

Any hopes the Apothecary might have had of questioning the Black Pyramid after the bout were swiftly dashed. The fighter was instantly surrounded by a large crowd of Exeter rips – who had obviously wagered deep on his winning – and was carried out of the field, shoulder-high. Hurrying behind him was Nathaniel Broome together with various hangers-on and assistants. Scurrying along, John managed to detain the manager just as he was leaving the field. Broome looked at him in some surprise.

'Hello, Mr Rawlings. I didn't expect to see you here.'

'I saw an advertisement stating that the Black Pyramid was fighting so I came with the express purpose of watching him.'

Nathaniel gestured to the crowd ahead. 'As you can see he is rather taken up.' He roared with laughter at his own joke, his small gingery face creasing.

'So I observe. Tell me, my friend, did you know that William Gorringe was killed during the night we all stayed at The Half Moon?'

'Yes. Terrible business. The Constable caught up with us at our current hostelry and informed us of same. The Pyramid was quite shaken I can tell you.'

John thought that the Blind Beak could do with this particular Constable as a Runner. As a paid employee of those whose turn it was to act in the hated job, he was turning out to be splendid.

'I'm sure he was utterly shocked. Was he able to throw any light on the case?'

The pale blue eyes – set too closely, giving Nathaniel a some-what pathetic air – held his own. 'No. Why do you ask?'

'No reason. I just wondered,' John answered somewhat lamely.

'Well, he told the man that we never set eyes on Mr Gorringe until that coach ride. And there the matter rests, Mr Rawlings. There the matter rests.' Nathaniel drew a watch from his waist-coat pocket. 'Gracious me. I'm running late. I must be off. I hope we meet again one day.' He gave a slight bow. '*Adieu.*'

And he was gone, scuttling along behind the Black Pyramid

who was still shoulder-high and being transported rapidly towards the town.

John stood still for a moment, trying to assemble his thoughts. But the impression he had most strongly was that today several people had stated quite baldly that they had no knowledge of William Gorringe – and that he had believed none of them.

Having deposited Sir Clovelly Lovell back at his home, John Rawlings remounted his horse and set off in search of that remarkable fellow, the Exeter Constable. Having no idea at all where the man lived, the Apothecary decided to make enquiries in a tavern and being near the West Gate entered The Blackamore's Head, an inn he remembered from his honeymoon.

It was quiet inside, there being only one or two old codgers staring moodily into their pots of ale. They looked up as John entered but, having eyed him, soon lost interest and went back to contemplating their drinks. At the back of the bar a lanky potboy was whistling tunelessly beneath his breath and made his way in a slow and somewhat unwilling way to where John was sitting.

'What be you drinking then?'

'I'll have some ale, please.' The Apothecary produced a coin which he held between his thumb and forefinger. 'Can you give me some information?'

'Depends.'

'Do you know the local Constable?'

'Why, you in trouble then?'

Without moving from his seat, John gripped the boy's ear and twisted it. 'That will be enough of your backchat. Answer me. Do you know the local officer of the law?'

'Yes, I knows him,' the boy answered, rubbing the side of his face and grimacing.

'Well, can you tell me where I can find him?'

'All you have to do is go to his house.'

John was getting angry. 'If I knew where that was I would.' He gripped the ear again. 'Do you want this coin or don't you?'

'Yessir. I wants it. He lives halfway up the High Street in a two-storey cottage. I don't know the number – and I swear that's the truth, Sir.'

'Very well.' John let go of the ear and handed over the coin. 'Now I'll have the ale if you please.'

He sat consuming it, trying to plan what he should do next. He had seen all the men who had travelled down to Exeter with him – namely the Black Pyramid, Nathaniel Broome, Cuthbert Simms and Martin Meadows – and two of the women. But Paulina Gower and Fraulein Schmitt still eluded him. He vaguely recalled that Paulina had mentioned the theatre in Exeter and determined to take Elizabeth there soon. But that left the abominable German woman. Where was she and who could possibly be putting her up? Or perhaps, indeed, she lived here. Steeling himself against the thought of trying to question her, John finished his ale.

And then there was one of those extraordinary twists of fate that people say never happen. The door of the inn opened and in walked the Constable himself. He ran his eyes swiftly over the people within and John felt them coming to rest on him. He had the impression of a small, dark bird-like man with a pair of black eyes that could possibly be very frightening indeed, and then the constable made his way towards him.

'Well, well. We meet again, sir. How have you been keeping?'

'Very fine, thank you.' He motioned the man to sit down. 'I'm glad you've come in because I was just about to call on you.'

'Oh really? And why would that be?'

John thought rapidly and decided to reveal his interest to the intelligent being sitting opposite him. 'Have you heard of Sir John Fielding?' he asked.

'Would that be the magistrate in Bow Street? The blind one?'

'It would indeed.'

'Ah,' said the constable, and relapsed into an expectant silence.

'Years ago,' stated John, 'there was a murder in Vaux Hall Gardens. I was a suspect but somehow I managed to convince Sir John – he was plain Mr Fielding in those days – of my innocence. Indeed he asked me to help him solve that case. And I have been working with him on and off ever since. To be honest with you I enjoy the challenge.'

The Constable shot him a look of wry amusement. 'I doubt you would if you were at it day in and day out, Sir.'

'You have a point there. But regardless of that there is something I have to tell you about the murder of William Gorringe.'

'Oh? And what might that be?'

'That he feared some fellow passengers on the coach. He told Mr Meadows that he felt threatened.'

'By whom?'

'The Black Pyramid, the bare-knuckle fighter, for one.'

The Constable sat silently for a moment or two, then he said, 'That is very interesting indeed, Sir. It corroborates Meadows's statement to me.'

'At the time he believed that the man was suffering from delusions, in fact he asked me about the condition. But now it appears that Gorringe was speaking the truth.'

'So it would seem. I have made some enquiries about him and it seems that he is not from round these parts.'

The potboy appeared, somewhat late in the day, and grinned rather sheepishly at John.

'This is the Constable, Sir. May I get you another pot of ale?'

John turned to the man.

'If it is all the same to you, Sir, I'll take a small glass of canary.'

'Of course. And I will have a refill.' He held his empty tankard out to the boy. 'I am Tobias Miller. Known to the world in general as Toby.'

He grinned in a friendly manner but the Apothecary had the feeling that behind the smiles lay a brain like a vice. Nor were the dark eyes readable, completely shuttered from all outside penetration.

The drinks arrived and the Constable downed the glass of bright yellow liquid. 'And now, sir, I'd like to ask you a few questions.'

'Certainly.'

'You say that you had never met Mr Gorringe before?'

'Definitely not. In fact I did not see him until we stopped for breakfast at some unearthly hour in the morning.'

'I see.' There was another long silence, then Toby said, 'So is it your belief, Sir, that one of the fellow passengers did away with him?'

'It certainly looks that way. That would be my instinct.'

'I think you're probably right. The man had no friends or relatives in the West Country that I have so far discovered. But if that were the case – that he was murdered by another passenger – it would suggest a certain amount of premeditation.'

'It occurs to me that they must have discovered which coach he was travelling on – which is practically impossible.'

Yet again Toby was silent, then he said, 'Not if someone tipped the killer, or killers, off.'

'That he was travelling to Exeter on a particular day at a particular time.'

'Precisely.' The Constable got to his feet. 'Well, I must be off, Sir. It has been very pleasant meeting you. Where can I contact you again should I need to speak to you.'

'At the home of Lady Elizabeth di Lorenzi. You know where that is?'

'Indeed I do. Well, goodnight, Sir.'

And so saying Toby tipped his hat and walked out into the early evening.

As John rode home the sun was lowering in the heavens in a truly dramatic fashion. The sky had turned the colour of dragon's blood and was drenching the clouds with the same vibrancy. Vivid tinctures coloured the earth and as John trotted forward he found himself looking round with a sense of awe. And then he saw a scarlet ribbon winding its way across the land and for a moment was startled before he realized it was a stream meandering down to join the Exe.

The Apothecary dismounted and knelt down by the water to drink, leading his horse to do likewise. As he scooped up a handful and drank it down he noticed that the stream was full of bubbles and his mind turned again to some experiments he had been doing on combining gases with water to produce a carbonated effect. Aware that there was another Englishman interested in the same principal, one Joseph Priestley, John determined that this winter he would work on his experiments tirelessly until he had discovered the secret of carbonating water. Refreshed, he remounted and made his way up the steep valley to where the house stood on the summit.

He was surprised to discover that Elizabeth had not only risen from her sickbed but was waiting impatiently for him in the blue drawing-room.

'Ah, there you are,' she said. 'I am so glad you are back because I have arranged with Lady Thackeray to meet her at the theatre tonight. You have just time to change before we set off.'

'What about dining?'

'That will have to be a supper at home after the play, I'm afraid. Are you hungry? Because, if so, I can get some bread and cheese and pie sent up from the kitchen.'

'No, I can hang on. I had rather a large luncheon with Sir Clovelly Lovell as it happens.'

'Why am I not surprised by that remark?'

'Because you are clever,' said John, and kissed the top of her head as he made his way upstairs.

Half an hour later and they were stepping into Elizabeth's finest coach and heading once more for Exeter. Leaning back against the beautifully cushioned interior John was vividly reminded of the minimum of comfort he had received on his journey down, particularly with Fraulein Schmitt moaning and groaning almost without cease. And this set his mind off at a tangent, wondering about the mysterious woman and where she had got to. He had meant to ask the Constable if he had had any luck in tracing her but somehow the conversation hadn't gone down that path. Yet Tobias Miller was a bright and intelligent man and if anybody could locate the wretched creature it would be him.

The play being performed was Shakespeare's tragedy *Macbeth* and John was astonished to see that Paulina Gower was playing the Lady herself. Thinking she had had scant time for rehearsal, he realized that Paulina must have studied the part before and come down to Exeter almost at the last moment, which made him wonder whether she was a stand-in who had been called upon at the very end.

Taking his seat in a box, sitting between Elizabeth and Lady Thackeray, John looked at the Playbill programme which informed him that the part of Macbeth was to be played by Thomas Roundell, rather a mediocre actor in the Apothecary's opinion. The rest of the cast were unknown to him but John had the feeling that he was about to see a performance that was slightly under par. Yet Paulina surprised him, making him literally quiver with fear in her spellbinding mad scene. In fact he clapped enthusiastically when the curtain, raised and lowered only at the beginning and end of the performance, finally came down.

John turned to the two ladies. 'Lady Thackeray, Elizabeth, would you forgive me if I absent myself for a few minutes. I would like to call on Paulina Gower and congratulate her.'

Lady Thacheray raised a large quizzing glass which snuggled comfortably on her voluptuous bosom and peered at him through it. This magnified one of her eyes to four times its size so that John had a momentary illusion that he was being regarded by a Cyclops.

'Do you know her?' she boomed.

'I met her in the coach travelling to Devon.'

'A somewhat superficial acquaintanceship.'

'Be that as it may,' John replied evenly, 'I think I will go and pay my respects.'

Elizabeth waved an airy hand. 'I will await you in the coach.'

Realizing that he had little time the Apothecary hurried through the audience as best he could and out into Water Beer Street, then turned down into a little alleyway that ran beside the theatre. But here he enountered a problem. A crowd had already gathered and if he were to linger and speak to Paulina he would keep Elizabeth and her formidable companion waiting an unconscionable amount of time. Searching in his pockets for a piece of paper he found an old bill and scribbled on the back of it, 'Dear Miss Gower, I thoroughly enjoyed your performance. Do you remember me from our coach journey to Devon? I would like to talk to you about an important matter. Please meet me tomorrow morning at ten . . .' John scratched that out and wrote eleven. '. . . o'clock at The White Swan in High Street.' He added his signature and, pushing his way through the throng, handed it to the stage door keeper. That done he scurried round to the front of the building and joined Elizabeth in her coach, Lady Thackeray already having left.

'Did you see her?' Elizabeth asked.

'No, the company was too great. I would have kept you waiting.'

In the darkness the Marchesa took his hand. 'You are going to investigate that murder, aren't you? The one that happened in the inn.'

John raised her fingers to his lips. 'I am doing so already,' he answered with a smile.

Eight

Paulina Gower was wearing far more face paint that John remembered. With her carmined lips and her cheeks painted a becoming pink, to say nothing of the kohl applied to her eyes, she looked very charming and quite different from the pallid creature who had been travelling in the Exeter coach.

'Madam, may I compliment you on your appearance,' John said gallantly, and rising from his chair kissed her hand as she sat down opposite him.

'Thank you. But you said you wanted to see me on a matter of some urgency and I am afraid I have little time,' she answered, her Welsh accent audible once more, though it had been greatly modified during her performance.

'I understand. But first of all allow me to get you a drink. What would you care for?'

She gave a half smile. 'Well, as I am not acting tonight I will have a small, dry sherry.'

'You do not drink when you are appearing on stage?'

'Never,' she answered. And at that moment John had a glimpse of a highly disciplined woman who kept everything, particularly her emotions, under tight control. He summoned a potboy – a great deal friendlier than the one of the previous evening – and as soon as he was gone, Paulina turned to the Apothecary.

'What is it you have to say to me?'

He came straight to the point. 'Did you know that William Gorringe – one of our fellow passengers – was murdered during the night at The Half Moon?'

'Yes. The Constable came to see me in the theatre last evening. It quite unnerved me I can tell you.'

'I see.' And the Apothecary thought for the twentieth time what a fantastic fellow the constable was to have located them all with very little help. 'What did he ask you?'

'If I was acquainted with Mr Gorringe. If I could think of any reason why anybody should want to do away with him. That sort of thing.'

'And what did you reply?'

Paulina gave him a wide-eyed stare. 'That I had never seen the man before in my life. Naturally. And now may I ask you a question?'

'Certainly.'

'What is your interest in the affair and what gives you the right to question everybody else? Are you someone special or is it just your native curiosity?'

John put on his important face. 'The fact of the matter is, Miss Gower, that I work for Sir John Fielding. I am investigating the matter on his behalf.'

It was a half-truth but it gained the right results. Paulina looked suitably impressed. But she was an actress, John thought with slight chagrin.

'Really?' Paulina said. 'I met his brother, Henry, you know. Years ago in Glastonbury. He had gone there to take the waters from the Chalice spring, as had my father. I was just a slip of a girl but I can distinctly remember Mr Fielding because he was so tall. I believe the Blind Beak is as well, though I confess I have only seen him from above, as it were. I have been to his courthouse in Bow Street several times.'

She spoke the words lightly but the Apothecary felt that they contained a slight criticism, as if he should have been present in court as well.

'I act as an occasional investigator for him,' he said, and the explanation sounded lame.

'Really?' she said again. 'How interesting.'

Now there could be no doubt. Her voice was decidedly sarcastic.

John leaned forward on the table that separated them. 'So, Miss Gower, there is absolutely no need for you to listen to or answer one word I say. I would like to make that quite clear.'

'In that case,' she said, standing up, 'I'll save you the trouble of proceeding.' And she swept from the snug in which they had been sitting.

John stared after her, feeling annoyed. The interview had been highly unsuccessful and he had been quite definitely challenged over his role in the affair. All he had learned from it was that Paulina had some acquaintance with the Fielding family and that she had – according to her at least – no knowledge of William Gorringe.

But was that true he asked himself. Or was the talented actress merely putting on a performance for his benefit?

Half an hour later found him in the apothecary's shop discussing the merits of an infusion of raspberry leaves in both pregnancy and childbirth.

'It is excellent, Sir. My wife drank it constantly throughout her eight confinements.'

'Good heavens, did she really,' said John, trying valiantly not to laugh. 'Actually I do know about it. I am an apothecary myself.' And he handed the man a card.

'Oh, you're from London town, Sir. You must see some strange people in that place.'

'Yes, quite a few. But I imagine that you do too. After all, ailments are ailments wherever one comes from.'

'That's true enough. But I have always thought that London must be a sink of iniquity.'

John smiled. 'Perhaps it is. Anyway, I'll take two bottles of the infusion, if you please.'

'Certainly, Sir. And I hope that your wife will have an easy labour. Is this her first child?'

'No, her second,' John answered, and wondered at himself for adopting the role of Elizabeth's husband with quite so much ease.

Stepping out into the street he paused for a moment to stare into the window of the apothecary's shop, fascinated, as always, by the great glass bottles full of bright blue liquid. And he was standing thus, thinking of nothing in particular, when from across the street he heard a horribly familiar voice.

'Vere is mein canary bird?' it was shouting ridiculously. 'Oh, mein Gott. I must have left him in ze market.'

And a moment later, allowing John just the merest glimpse of her, Fraulein Schmitt hurled herself into a hackney coach and vanished from view. Disconsolately, John walked along High Street, thinking that the wretched woman must live in Exeter or its environs. Then, without really looking where he was going, the Apothecary suddenly found himself outside The Half Moon. And there in the courtyard, almost ready to depart, was the London coach, polished up and with fresh horses in the traces but the same driver and guard standing beside it. Immediately John went in to greet them.

'Good morning to you.'

'Good day, Sir. And how are you?' answered the driver.

'Very well, thank you. Not quite ready to leave for London, however.'

'Enjoying life in Devon then?'

'Indeed I am.' John produced a guinea from his pocket. 'May I speak to you in confidence?'

'You certainly can, Sir,' said the guard, and seeing the flash of coin, came closer as he echoed, 'Certainly.'

'It's about the murder the other night. Tell me, did you know the murdered man at all?'

'Mr Gorringe? Well, strangely enough I had seen him a few times before,' the coachman replied.

'Oh? When and where was that?'

'It was on another run that I do from time to time, London to Shoreham via Lewes and Brighthelmstone. He used to come on that quite regular.'

'You're sure it was him?'

'Positive, Sir. He had a very arresting face, if you know what I mean. A cruel face really. I'm not surprised somebody had it in for him.'

'Can you remember where he got off on this other run?'

'Lewes, Sir. And he always had a coach waiting to pick him up.'

'Strange he didn't travel in that.'

'Well, he didn't. And there's another funny thing as well.'

'What was that?'

'He used to call himself something different. I know because I heard his coachman use the name.'

'And what was it?'

'That's the devil of it, I can't remember.' The coachman turned to the guard. 'Can you?'

'Sorry to say I never even heard it, Sir.'

John handed over the coin. 'Thank you for the information. It was very interesting.' He turned to the driver one more time. 'You are certain it was him?'

'Either that or his twin brother, Sir.'

'I see.'

John nodded and went on his way, very puzzled indeed by what he had just heard. It would seem that Gorringe – or whatever he had called himself in the past – had been a man of some means and had either lived near Lewes or had visited somebody regularly in that particular vicinity. At this moment, disgruntled as he was, John would have put his money on Paulina Gower as the murderess, assisted by the German woman. But that was only his present mood. He was actually, to quote the guard, totally bewildered by the whole affair.

Stepping into The White Swan he sat turning his wine glass in his hand, staring fixedly into its depths as though it could tell him the answers. And so he was sitting, not really seeing anyone as he tried to make some sort of sense of what he had just heard, when he felt a movement at his side. Looking up, John saw that Martin Meadows was standing by his table, looking earnest. He half rose.

'Mr Meadows. I'm so sorry. I was deep in thought.'

'That's perfectly all right. May I join you? There is something I would like to discuss.'

'Please do. Would you like to share my bottle? I have to ride back and I must keep my wits about me so I can't possibly drink it all.'

'That would be very kind. But I, too, am returning to work and therefore one glass will suffice.'

Having procured another vessel from the serving maid, John turned his attention to the solicitor who today was looking far less startled, his eyebrows seeming fuller and his wig – very new and curly but once again brown – sitting sedately upon his head.

'What is it you wish to discuss with me?' the Apothecary asked.

'I have been thinking over the coach journey down – in fact I can think of little else – and I keep remembering how worried Gorringe was. At the time, as you know, I put it down to mental disorder, but now I realize that the man was telling the truth.'

'What was it he said exactly?'

'That the Black Pyramid reminded him of a slave he had once had, though he could not be certain as so many years had passed. The other person he kept talking about was none other than our little dancing master friend, Cuthbert Simms.'

'Good gracious,' said John, totally startled. 'Of all the mild-mannered men.'

'That is precisely what I said at the time. But Gorringe insisted that he had employed the fellow as dancing master to his children and that his appearance on the coach was decidedly sinister.'

The Apothecary downed his wine and said, 'But why? I frequently meet people I know and nothing could be further from my thoughts than a threat to my safety.'

Martin sighed. 'That is what I told him. But as things have turned out it seems that he was right all along. I can tell you now that I went to that fight yesterday to get a closer look at the black man.'

'And what did you think of him?'

'A magnificent specimen. But as to his character, who knows?'

John looked thoughtful. 'I heard something interesting today.' And he launched forth with the tale told him by the coachman.

Martin Meadows behaved in a particularly professional manner, folding his hands and listening intently. Then, when John finally grew silent, he spoke.

'So if the coachman is to be believed it would seem that Gorringe had another life and another name. How very odd. I wonder what it was.'

'That's what I would like to know.'

'It certainly gives one food for thought.'

'Indeed it does.'

Shortly afterwards the two men parted company. John going to fetch his horse, which was tethered nearby, Meadows returning to his office. As he rode back to join Elizabeth for dinner the apothecary found his head full of the case and he wished that he had the Blind Beak to consult and, even more useful, the incredible Joe Jago to help him sift the matter through.

After they had dined and were sitting in the Blue Drawing Room Elizabeth turned to him with a beautiful smile.

'Sweetheart, it is Lady Sidmouth's ball next week and knowing what cutting fashions you besport I wondered whether you would like to order a new set of night clothes from the tailor in Exeter.'

The Apothecary collected himself and looked at her, nodding.

'You have a definite point. The suits I brought do look rather tired. How quick is the fellow?'

'I believe he takes a few days only.'

John got up and took a seat beside her, putting his arm round her gently expanding waist. 'Tell me truly, do I appear like last year's model?'

She took his face between her two hands. 'My darling, you positively sparkle and I would be proud to be seen anywhere with you. It's just that I know you well and wondered if you would prefer something new in which to display yourself to the entire county.'

He kissed her fingers. 'You have read my character utterly. I shall visit the tailor tomorrow.'

'Good. Now tell me, how are you getting on with your investigation?'

'Not well.' And John proceeded to inform her of the latest twists and turns.

When he had finished she said, 'You are sure that he was murdered by someone on the coach? It could not have been done by someone he met by arrangement in Exeter?'

'That's the devil of it. I can't be sure of anything. The case is as nebulous as a waterfall.'

'The Constable sounds good.'

'He is a very useful man. Sir John could do with him as a Runner.'

'Can't you make an appointment to see him when you are in Exeter tomorrow?'

'Now that is a very sound idea. I shall go to his house and do so.'

'Clever Mr Rawlings,' said Elizabeth, and patted his hand.

It seemed a pity, thought John, to be in Exeter and not call on Sir Clovelly Lovell. So on arriving in the city for the third day running, he made his way to The Close determined to waylay the little fat man in his den. But to his disappointment he was informed that Sir Clovelly was out. Turning away determinedly John headed for High Street and for the home of Toby Miller, that most efficient officer of the law. Surprisingly enough the man was at home and John found himself ushered into a very small study where Toby sat behind a mound of papers. On the end of his nose a pair of spectacles without sides was perched, relying entirely on their grip on the human proboscis to stay upright. He took them off with a slight sigh of relief as John came into the room.

'Greetings, Mr Rawlings,' he said, rising from his chair. 'How may I help you?'

'I just wondered how you were getting on with the case.'

'I take it you mean the enquiry into the death of William Gorringe?'

'Yes I do. I hope that perhaps you wouldn't mind sharing information with me – as I am Attached to the office of Sir John Fielding. Quite unofficially, of course.'

'There is little to report, Sir. Mr Martin Meadows came to see me and told me that the dead man had also mentioned one Cuthbert Simms as someone who was familiar to him. But I have yet to see that gentleman. He is giving dancing lessons at Lady Sidmouth's, I believe.'

'Yes, but not for much longer. Her ball is next week and then his employment will be over.'

'I'll be sure to catch him before he leaves.'

John put his elbows on the table that separated the two men and said in a low voice, though there was nobody else to overhear a word, 'But I have something which might be important to tell you.' And he proceeded to recount the conversation he had had with the driver and the guard of the London coach.

Tobias listened in silence then replaced his spectacles on his nose. 'How very interesting, Sir. Indeed what an extraordinary tale. I feel that one of us should follow it up.'

And he looked at John Rawlings in a very pointed manner indeed.

The Apothecary spent the next hour at the shop of the tailor that Elizabeth had recommended, glorying in the latest fabrics from France and falling in love with one, of the finest satin, in a vivid shade of crimson,decorated all over with a million little silver butterflies. Having been measured and explained that he needed the suit within a week, John retired to The Green Dragon and found Sir Clovelly Lovell, sitting in a corner imbibing a bottle of claret and partaking of a small snack to keep him going.

'Sir Clovelly!'exclaimed John and seeing the little man's jolly eyes light up went to sit opposite him.

'Damn trouble is,' stated Sir Clovelly without further ado, 'that I couldn't stand my wife when she was alive but I miss her nagging now that she has gone. The house is so dashed quiet, don't you know.'

'Perhaps you need to remarry, Sir,' said John, jesting. But Sir Clovelly took him seriously.

'I don't think so, dear boy. I mean who would have me for a start? And then if I found some eager young virgin I don't think I would have the energy to cope. As for a widow woman I reckon she'd have a thousand screaming children and I would be driven to distraction. No, I think I'll stay as I am and bore all my friends with my troubles.'

'You could never do that, Sir,' John answered gallantly. And leaning across the table he gave his fat friend a hug of pure affection.

Nine

The following morning was a truly golden one. The late September sunshine awakened the Apothecary and as he got out of bed Elizabeth woke as well and they fell to kissing and laughing before he went to his own room to dress. He was longing to get out of doors, to get the last burst of summer into his lungs before the grip of autumn took hold. So − Elizabeth taking her time about getting herself prepared − he strolled outside as soon as he had consumed his usual breakfast.

It was a glorious day. As far as the eye could see everything was sparkling and fresh, washed by a shower which had occurred during the night. The colours of the season were everywhere; trees lifted their heads proudly, displaying shimmerings of gold and flame and occasionally dropping a leaf which crunched beneath the feet of horses and passers-by. The pastures were green, cattle and sheep grazed placidly; the sky above was a deep blue, the colour of sloes. The Exe reflected its light and wound through the valley like a swathe of flax flowers. A wildness ran through John, a sensation that he had experienced from time to time over the years. He knew that the changing seasons were being echoed by something within himself, something that spoke of eternal youth and immortality. Yet that was only a part of it, the rest of the emotion was inexplicable.

Without him hearing Elizabeth came out onto the terrace and spoke his name. He turned and looked at her as if he were observing her for the first time. In that bright autumn light in which you could see a bird fly at a great distance, he realized that she had changed. There were silver hairs amongst the raven black and the great dark eyes had more tiny lines around them. The disfiguring scar which was so ugly yet at the same time made her brilliantly attractive, stood out in the pitiless light. But she stood tall and straight, the four month rounding just beginning to make itself known beneath the folds of her dress. And then she put her hand to her abdomen and drew a breath.

'It's moving, John. The child has quickened.'

He ran to her side and placed his hand beside hers, but she laughed and shook her head.

'A butterfly opened its wings, that is all. You will not be able to feel it yet.'

He laughed, realizing as he did so that he sounded like a youth, not a mature man. 'I think this is one of the most exciting moments of my life.'

'But you have experienced it before. With Emilia.'

At the mention of the past the Apothecary felt some of his earlier mood dissipate. He looked at Elizabeth solemnly

'Yes, indeed I have. But you and Emilia are very different people. I feel that I have been fortunate, and honoured too, to have had the pleasure of loving you both.'

She must have sensed the sudden seriousness in him for she put out her hand and took his. 'Just as I am honoured to be carrying your child. Come on, sweetheart. Let us enjoy the beauty of the day. Shall we go for a carriage ride?'

'I would like to travel beside you on horseback if that is all right.'

'I am very pleased to hear it. We shall make a horseman of you yet.'

Half an hour later they were setting off, heading towards the coast and the high cliffs. As they neared their objective John could see the town of Exmouth below and the meeting of the mighty Exe with its mother ocean. He turned his head to the right and there, dark and stark in the autumn sunshine stood the ruin of Wildtor Grange, the house in which he had first set eyes on Elizabeth. He tapped on the carriage side with his riding crop and the Marchesa stuck her head out.

'There's the Grange.'

'I know. Do you want to go and look?'

'Yes, I think so,' John answered.

But inside he felt somewhat apprehensive. It was true that he had first seen Elizabeth within those decaying walls, but at that time he had been on honeymoon with Emilia. So the mansion contained memories of both women and he was not sure that he wanted to revive such thoughts.

They were approaching the house from the top of the cliffs and from this angle the windows – or rather the one or two that had survived – were glittering in the sunlight. The illusion was extraordinary, as if the place were still lived in, as if the glow came from within, cast by crackling log fires. On Elizabeth's instruction the coachman began to circle the mansion, looking for somewhere to draw up the carriage, while John followed slowly, gazing up at the formidable ruin with a kind of terrible fascination.

The coach eventually stopped in the stable block. John looked at the place with a shudder, remembering the Society of Angels who had once terrorized Exeter and who had hidden their carriage there. But they were all gone now and were scarce remembered by the younger generation. He dismounted at the block just in time to hand the Marchesa down from her carriage. She shivered as she looked round her.

'I don't know why I said to come to this accursed house.'

'I take it you no longer keep up your rooms here?'

For Elizabeth had once upon a time kept a private apartment in the heart of the ruin where she had hidden out when it had been necessary.

'I have not visited the place for about two years.' She turned to the house with determination. 'I think I shall go and look at them now.'

And she marched off towards the spot where they had long ago found entry through a low window without glass. John followed more slowly, his good mood of earlier now totally gone. He was riven with memories, some so sweet, some less so, and it seemed to him that Emilia was not very far away from him as he followed in the Marchesa's wake.

The elements had done much to harm Wildtor Grange he thought as he stepped through the window. Leaves, long dead, had blown in and there were signs that wild animals had made the house their own. The sad and melancholy atmosphere had grown even more oppressive, the Apothecary considered, as he strode through the echoing reception hall. Ahead of him he could see the Marchesa's indomitable figure heading up that huge and monstrous staircase which reared to the floors above. With reluctant footsteps, John followed in her wake.

She must have been moving very fast for she was out of sight by the time he reached the top, where the staircase branched into two, each fork leading in opposite directions. John was just about to proceed along the left-hand corridor when he paused. From downstairs, far below, he could hear the distant sound of voices.

His flesh crawled on his body as every thought of supernatural phenomenon set his nerves jarring. The concept that he might be listening to a long-dead conversation from the defunct Thornes – the family who once had lived in the Grange – filled him with horror. Yet somehow he steeled himself to creep back down that great gothic staircase to the huge hall below. Whoever or what-ever it was that was speaking was in one of those ghastly side rooms, full of rotting furniture, that led off the reception hall, but which one it was John had no idea. Following the sound of that unearthly whispering, he crept along.

It was a man and a woman conversing, of that much he was sure. Edging into one of those empty, decaying suites he drew closer to the sound until eventually, after passing through cavernous and deserted rooms, he found himself in earshot. John crouched down beside a sofa that must once have been the height of elegance, and listened.

'. . . but what of my father?' the woman was saying.

'He's perfectly safe, my dear,' came the reply. 'Don't worry about that.'

'But he is bound to be suspected.'

'As will we all.'

There was a pause then the young woman – or at least John judged her to be so by her tone – said, 'But the Constable is far from stupid I am told.'

The Apothecary strained his ears.

'Remember that everyone is innocent until proved guilty.'

She gave a humourless laugh. 'That is what worries me.'

John moved forward a fraction, afraid of missing a word, and then loud and clear from the floor above came Elizabeth's voice, 'Where are you, my dear? You must come and see this. John, where have you vanished to?'

There was a horrified silence from the next room and then the Apothecary heard two pairs of feet running for dear life as the speakers rushed from the room as fast as they could. He sprang up and sprinted into the now deserted salon in which they had been speaking. They were gone and by a different route from the one that he and Elizabeth had employed to gain entry. Nonetheless John chased after the sound of their departure until he came to a French window in a far drawing-room. All the glass had gone but the door hung open on creaking hinges. Peering out he saw two riders leaving the Grange and going hell for leather. He stared, wishing that he had his telescope, but they were already too far away to identify with the naked eye. He turned as he heard foot-steps behind him. Elizabeth stood there.

'What on earth are you doing?'

He faced her, fractionally annoyed. 'There were two people in here. They were talking about something which I have a strong suspicion was connected with the murder case. When they heard your voice they ran for their lives. And who can blame them?'

Elizabeth looked contrite. 'I'm sorry, my dear. I had no idea.'

'It wasn't your fault,' he said.

'I should have guessed something was up when you disappeared so suddenly.'

'Yes.' John sighed. 'Now what was it you wanted to show me?'

'Oh, it was just a silly little thing. There's a handkerchief of yours still in my drawing-room.'

John thought back to the last time he had been in Wildtor Grange and felt somewhat embarrassed. But he couldn't help but dwell on the fact that for something so trivial Elizabeth had inter-rupted a most important conversation. His mood of youthful exuberance totally vanished, John now felt middle-aged and serious.

Elizabeth came closer to him. 'Do you want to pursue them? I presume they have gone?' she added as an afterthought.

'They've gone all right and I would imagine that they are halfway across Devon from the speed they were riding.'

'Well, in that case you must set off at once. I shall follow in a more sedate fashion in the coach.'

John swiftly picked up her hand and kissed it, then, without saying a word, sped out through the tattered French window. Five minutes later he was mounted and thundering over the cobbles. As he left the Grange behind him, heading up towards the cliffs, he saw the two riders ahead of him, not going towards Exmouth as he had imagined but instead turning towards the fishing village of Sidmouth. He increased his pace but one of them – the woman – looked over her shoulder and must have said something to her companion. A moment later and the pair had plunged into the dense trees that grew on the lower ground above the village. John knew at that moment that he had lost them so he reined in and waited for Elizabeth to catch him up.

But who were the riders and where had they been heading? That was the question that puzzled him for the rest of that day.

That late afternoon brought a surprise visitor to Elizabeth's house, none other than the Constable of Exeter himself. An hour before the time to dine John was sitting in the red salon, perusing the newspaper, when the head footman entered.

'There is a personage here to see you, Sir. He says that he is Constable Tobias Miller. He also says that he is from Exeter.'

John looked up. 'Send him in, Perkins. I can assure you that he is perfectly genuine.'

Toby came into the room walking solemnly behind the footman, his bright eyes darting round the room and all its magnificent furnishings.

'Good evening Mr Rawlings,' he said, and gave a bow of the head.

John stood up. 'My dear Mr Miller, this is an unexpected surprise.'

'Forgive me calling without an appointment, Sir, but I just wanted to inform you that I have now seen most of the people who travelled on the coach that night.'

John motioned the man to sit down and poured a dry sherry which he handed to him. Tobias sipped it like a connoisseur.

'And how were they?'

'All very charming, Sir. I must say I took to Mr Simms.'

'When did you see him?'

'I called at Lady Sidmouth's this afternoon. Mr Simms had had a day off and had just come in from a ride.'

'Really?' said John thoughtfully.

'Yes. We talked awhile. A very polite gentleman, he was.' Tobias leant forward confidentially. 'Now, about that business we were discussing the other day, Sir.'

'Yes?'

'Believe me, if I had the time and the resources I would investigate that. But here I am, a professional Constable, and as busy as a bee as a result.'

'You really think the answer might lie there?'

'God's boddikins, Sir. We have nothing else to go on at all. I think Mr Gorringe's past is the only hope we have.'

'That's something Sir John Fielding always says.'

'Well, I never,' said the Constable, and made a pleased mouth.

'So you want me to look into it?' John asked.

'If you do, Sir, it would be greatly appreciated.'

'Then I will. But not just yet.'

'I don't know how to express my thanks.'

'Think nothing of it,' John said, taking Tobias's glass and refilling it. 'Changing the subject, did you by any chance manage to locate the German woman, Fraulein Schmitt?'

The Constable sighed and shook his head. 'Now that is the one person I cannot find at all.'

'Then tomorrow I'll go and search for her,' the Apothecary answered, and even as he said it felt that he had set himself some monumental tasks of which Elizabeth might not altogether approve.

That night the Apothecary slept by himself and dreamed that he was alone in Wildtor Grange, climbing that enormous staircase, terrified out of his mind. A figure stood motionless at the top and John approached it with a feeling of dread, a pounding of his heart and a feeling of sickness in his throat. The figure had its back to him and the Apothecary longed to turn and run but, in the way of dreams, his legs were powerless and refused to move.

'Who are you?' he called – and his voice came out as a mere whisper.

The figure stood there, silent and unmoving, and then it turned. John gazed in horror at the face of William Gorringe, hideously maimed by his appalling injuries. Behind him a voice said, 'Can't catch me,' and the Apothecary woke drenched with sweat and wondering what meaning the dream could possibly have.

Ten

Proceeding into town early the next morning, John left Elizabeth's carriage at the habit makers – where she was being fitted for several new gowns to see her through to the end of her pregnancy – before she went to dine with Lady Sedgewick and her family. Then he went on foot to the market place. For there he knew he would find a man selling caged birds who might just remember selling one to a German woman several days before.

The market thronged with life. Glove makers jostled fishermen, who had brought their latest catch in to be sold, including live lobsters and crabs. Stalls selling haberdashery stood beside those selling farming implements. A gypsy fortune-teller had erected a small tent and was giving bashful young maidens advice on their love lives. And next to her, with canaries and linnets chirruping in cages which John considered too small, was a dark, swarthy pedlar plying his trade. John went up to him and pretended to examine the birds.

'May I interest you in a songbird, Sir? A pretty canary for your pretty lady?'

John looked pensive. 'Alas my lady is a keeper of cats. I do not fancy the bird's chances greatly. But perhaps you could furnish me with some information.'

The man's eyes grew wary. 'Oh, and what might that be, Sir?'

John produced a coin and held it beneath the pedlar's nose. 'I wondered if you could give me some tidings of a customer I believe you had recently.'

'I have many customers, Sir. How would I know this particular one?'

'I don't think you would forget her. She was a German woman, large and loud-voiced. She would have come to your stall several days ago.'

'Oh yes, I do recall someone. She argued with me over the price.'

John handed over the coin. 'Yes, that would be her. Do you know where she comes from by any chance?'

The man scratched his stubbly chin. 'Said she was buying the bird as a gift for her sister.'

John winced at the thought of there being two such women.

'Have you any idea where her sister lives?'

'Sorry to be unhelpful, Sir, but I don't. It's not the sort of thing I discuss with my customers. Why do you ask? Has she done something wrong?'

'I'm not sure,' John answered enigmatically, and gave the man another coin.

He walked away, thinking what a bore everything was. And then he had another idea. Fraulein Schmitt had taken a hackney coach from the stand opposite the apothecary's shop. With quickening footsteps John made his way there.

As luck would have it the coach she had taken was just pulling in to the place reserved, John recognizing it by its faded woodwork. He immediately went up to it and the driver looked pleased.

'Where to, Sir?'

John put on his authoritative face. 'Tell me, my good man, do you remember a fare you took the other day? It was a large German woman who had mislaid her canary bird and got into your hackney to take her back to the market.'

'Yes, I remember her, indeed I do.'

Yet again John produced a coin. 'Did she ask you to drive her home once she had rescued the bird?'

'Yes. And I took her. She's staying with her sister in Porch House in Sidford, not far from the bridge.'

'Take me there,' said John, 'and you'll get double this.' And he threw the coin to the driver as he leapt into the coach and rumbled out of Exeter's cobbled streets.

On his honeymoon and during his earlier adventures in Sidmouth, John had never visited Sidford. Now as he drove along its narrow – and only – street he found himself staring at it with a certain admiration for its rural aspect. Heavily lined with trees, the dust-covered way wound downwards, culminating in a rustic packhorse bridge which spanned the River Sid. A sheep and a cow, quite unattended, were making a slow way across it, the only living creatures in sight.

John called up to the driver. 'Porch House, you said?'

'Aye, Sir. That's it there.'

The Apothecary followed the line of his pointing whip and saw a Tudor building, standing in its own well laid-out gardens. At that moment he wondered what on earth he was going to say to the German woman and to her sister, who, he imagined, would be equally formidable.

A maid, dressed in mob-cap and apron, answered the front door. 'Yes, Sir?' she asked anxiously.

John gave her a kindly smile. 'Would it be possible to speak to Miss Schmitt?' he said.

'The ladies are in the garden, Sir. I don't like to disturb them.'

'You may tell them that an old friend wishes to have a brief word with them. I have come all the way from Exeter especially.'

He gave her the most winsome smile of which he was capable. She looked confused.

'I'll go and see, Sir. Would you like to step inside.'

John did so and was overwhelmed by the general comfort of the place. From where he stood a central flagstoned floor led straight through the house to the back door, down which the maid was running in a frantic sort of way. Off this led low-ceilinged pannelled rooms with a fire blazing in an inglenook despite the warmth of the day, and a cat dozing sleepily in front of it. A profusion of autumnal flowers stood in brightly polished copper jugs and from the kitchen area came a smell of good, plain, country fare. John almost wished they would invite him to dinner until he remembered the Marchesa and his promise to join her later.

The garden door, which the maid had closed behind her, opened again and there, entirely at odds with the genial atmosphere of the house, stood Fraulein Schmitt. She glared at John ferociously.

'Vot is the meaning of zis intrusion? Vye have you come here?'

John bowed. 'I have come to inform you, Madam, that Mr William Gorringe has been murdered most foully,' he boomed in theatrical tones. 'Furthermore, the Constable of Exeter is seeking your whereabouts and wishes to ask you questions.'

She flew into a rage though John could not help but notice that her face had completely drained of colour.

'How dare you come here and threaten me,' she shouted, waving her arms in the air.

'Madam, I . . .' he began, and then the garden door opened again and a little fat woman, no more that four foot eleven and round as a hoop, entered.

'Augusta,' she shouted, 'why are you making so much noise? Be silent I pray you and allow the young man to speak.'

Fraulein Schmitt turned to her. 'But he is trying to threaten me.'

'Nonsense, dear. He looks far too pleasant to do any such thing.'

John gave the newcomer a beatific smile and inched a step forward. 'Madam, I come only to give your sister a warning that the Constable of Exeter is looking for her.'

'I see. Now would you like to take a seat and tell me the whole story.'

'Vait a moment . . .' protested Augusta, but her sister made a silencing motion and indicated that the Apothecary should sit down in a chair opposite hers. He gratefully accepted.

'Let me just explain that I am English by marriage,' the little woman said. 'Years ago, long before the Seven Years War, my husband, John Mitchell, came to Dusseldorf on business. We married within a few months and I returned to Devon with him. Our parents being dead my sister Augusta left home some while later and went to work in Sussex as a teacher of French and German. But she always visited me from time to time and that is what she is doing at this very moment. So I suppose it is about the unfortunate murder of the man she travelled with that the Constable wants to question her. Yes?'

She put her head on one side and looked at John with bright eyes, reminding him vividly of a robin, even to her shape.

'Yes, Mrs Mitchell, you are quite right. You see indications are that the murdered man knew his killer and that it was more than likely somebody who was travelling on the same coach.'

'I must protest,' Augusta said loudly, 'vye should the Constable think it is me?'

'I don't know that he does,' John answered mildly. 'He just wishes to talk to you, that is all.'

Fraulein Schmitt burst into a noisy and showy fit of weeping. 'I am being persecuted,' she sobbed. 'It is not fair. It is cruel. Ach, Matilda, vot have I done to deserve such treatment?'

Her sister had obviously learned long ago how to control such outbursts.

'Now hush Augusta, do. Mr . . .?' She gave John a docile smile.

'Rawlings, Madam. John Rawlings.'

'. . . Rawlings might think you are guilty of something if you continue.'

Augusta turned a horrible colour, a cross between putty and curds, but stopped moaning. 'Of vot could I be accused?' she asked.

John merely smiled, thinking that the draining of colour was probably caused by panic. Yet for all that his instinctive dislike of Augusta Schmitt made him rule nothing out. He turned to the woman.

'If I were you, Madam, I would come to Exeter tomorrow and go to see the Constable voluntarily. I am sure he would appreciate it.'

'That is a very good idea,' said Matilda Mitchell firmly. 'I could drive you there in the trap.'

John stood up, addressing himself to his hostess. 'Madam, if you will forgive me. My hackney is waiting outside and I fear the fare will be enormous. I must make haste.'

'Of course. It was nice of you to call, Mr Rawlings.'

The Apothecary bowed. 'A pleasure to meet you, Ma'am.' He made another, more formal, bow in the direction of the Fraulein. 'Good day, Miss Schmitt.'

She growled something inaudible in return and John made his way out thinking how different the two sisters were not only in looks but also in personality.

Elizabeth, as usual, had not realized how long he had been and was happily dining with Lady Sedgewick and her family. Milady had a large modern house built close to the cathedral but standing in its own pleasant grounds. John, feeling that he looked like a tramp, made his way on foot to the imposing front door and was greeted by a black footman standing well over six feet in height.

'I've come to collect the Marchesa di Lorenzi,' John said, staring up at him. 'She is expecting me.'

'Very good, Sah. If you wouldn't mind waiting.'

The footman strolled off nonchalantly, ushering John into a small reception room before he went. He returned after a few minutes, a great smile adorning his features.

'This way, if you please, Sah.' And he bowed John into a magnificent dining-room where Elizabeth sat with a youngish, attractive woman and children of assorted ages and sizes gathered around the dining-table.

They all looked up as John entered. Feeling decidedly ill-dressed

and as if he smelt of the country, he took a seat where Lady
Sedgewick indicated. She raised a lorgnette and looked at him.

'So *this* is the young man!' she said.

The Apothecary felt terrible, just like a boy who has been caught
out committing some major schoolboy sin. He stood up and bowed
ornately.

'Allow me to present myself, Madam. I am John Rawlings,
apothecary of Shug Lane.'

'What a quaint name,' said Lady Sedgewick, though whether
she was referring to him or his address John could not be certain.

'Isn't it,' Elizabeth answered carelessly. 'Though there is nothing
quaint about young John.' She laughed. 'Though on second
thoughts . . .'

The eldest boy and girl, aged about eighteen and sixteen respect-
ively, giggled wildly, while their mother laughed aloud.

'Hush, there,' she said when she had calmed herself. 'We are embar-
rassing the poor fellow. Grevil, Dorinda, be silent. We have finished
dining but are currently on the port, Mr Rawlings. As my eldest boy
is but a sprig we have dispensed with the formality of withdrawing.'
She smiled at the Apothecary, rather too broadly for his liking.

He turned a somewhat cold look in Elizabeth's direction. 'I take
it you have enjoyed yourself, madam.'

'Very greatly,' she said, and flickered her eyelid at him.

The apothecary was thoroughly discomfited imagining that the
Marchesa had told Lady Sedgewick of her pregnancy. He could
almost hear them.

'And who is the father, my dear? Anyone from round here?'

'No, my friend, it is an apothecary from London.'

'Gracious me. He must have mixed a rare potion!'

And he could picture the older children, standing outside the
door and craning forward to listen as they collapsed in heaps of
uncontrollable giggles. The port bottle came round to the left and
John was sufficiently perturbed to pour himself a glassful which
he immediately downed.

'Would you like another, Sir?' asked the girl called Dorinda.

'Yes, I would.'

'Then help yourself.'

John did so before passing the bottle to the left. And then, having
swallowed the further drink, he took control of himself once more.
If they were all making fun of him – and this went for Elizabeth

as well – he would act the role of the rake from hell. He slouched back in his chair and addressed the boy called Grevil.

'D'you know London at all?'

'No, sir. I have never visited the city.'

'Ah well, you must ask your mama for permission to do so. It's a wild place indeed and truly suitable for a young buck like yourself.' John lowered his voice to an audible whisper. 'There are girls ripe for the taking.' And he winked his eye.

Lady Sedgewick, who was a fine-looking woman with a mass of dark hair, large luminous eyes and an expression like a well-bred horse, tutted disapprovingly. Elizabeth, who had immediately read John's motives, gave him an amused smile.

'Grevil shall go to the capital when he is a little older, Mr Rawlings. I consider him too young at present to venture forth unattended,' said his mother.

'But I could attend him, Ma'am.'

'Thank you, Mr Rawlings but I must decline your kind offer. I think a tutor would be a better kind of escort.' She cleared her throat. 'Tell me, Elizabeth, are you going to Lady Sidmouth's ball?'

'Indeed I am. Nothing could prevent me. This morning I ordered a new gown especially.'

'As have I. The children are taking dancing lessons and Grevil and Dorinda have received personal invitations.'

'Then I will have the pleasure of inviting your daughter to dance,' said John, his tone exceptionally warm.

'We shall have to see about that,' answered Lady Sedgewick, giving him a dark and extremely reproving look.

Going home in the carriage afterwards, Elizabeth said, 'Why did you behave so badly?'

'Because they were all giggling and laughing, making snide jokes about me fathering your child.'

'Oh come now, what an infantile attitude. You're a poor creature if you cannot take a jest made at your expense.'

John turned his head to look at her. 'How can you be so insensitive? I love you and I love the forthcoming baby. I do not find it a fitting subject for tomfoolery.'

Elizabeth sighed. 'No, you are right. It is a serious matter.' She fixed him with a gaze that held various emotions in its depths. 'We love each other, you and I, and yet we can never be together.'

John knew that he should argue, that he should protest, but suddenly he felt at the end of that particular road. He sighed.

'You're correct, Elizabeth. We are too different. Tomorrow I shall leave you.'

'I see,' she answered stiffly. 'And do you intend to come back?'

'If you wish me to.'

'Of course I wish it. John, do not tease me. I am vulnerable at the moment.'

'I could never depart unless you wanted me to,' he answered solemnly, a feeling of great gloom descending on him.

'I think a few days apart would do neither of us any harm. But promise me to return in time for Lady Sidmouth's ball.'

'I promise,' the Apothecary answered solemnly, and stared out of the window at the wild countryside just beginning to fade into darkness.

Eleven

In contrast to the day he had left London for Devon, this morning was fine and fair. The words 'Golden October' ran through the Apothecary's mind as he climbed aboard the London-bound stage-coach in company with a thin nervous lady whom he helped into her seat. Somewhat to his surprise he saw that sitting directly opposite him was Lucinda Silverwood. He half rose and bowed to her.

'Good day, Madam. How nice to be travelling with you. I take it your daughter has had her child?'

She smiled. 'Yes, indeed. A healthy boy. So my job is now done and I am going home.'

'Which is where?' the Apothecary enquired.

'In Sussex. I live just outside Lewes.'

'What a coincidence. That is where I am heading.'

An infinitesimal look of anxiety crossed her face to be rapidly replaced by her usual serene expression. 'How delightful. I shall have a travelling companion.'

'It will be entirely my pleasure.'

They relapsed into silence and John thought about his meeting with the Constable earlier that morning when they both had to admit that they were no further forward with the case.

'It's the very devil, Sir. I've interviewed them all bar the German woman and you say that she is coming to see me this morning.'

'I am certain she will. Her sister is very different from her and she is driving Fraulein Schmitt in in a trap, so I have no reason to doubt it.'

'Well, though none of them has an alibi, they seem a fairly straightforward bunch to me.'

Straightforward would have hardly been the word he would have used to describe such a diverse mixture of people considered John. But he had said nothing. Instead he had offered the information that he was on his way to Sussex to discover as much as he could about William Gorringe's past.

'Well, I wish you luck, Sir. But don't be too disappointed if you come away empty-handed.'

And with that comforting thought the Apothecary had left to go to The Half Moon to catch the stagecoach. As he had gone he had spotted a trap in the distance being driven by the redoubtable Matilda Mitchell and had given a small sigh of relief.

Now he sat in the coach while the horses were backed into the traces amidst a certain amount of encouragement and swearing from the hostlers and the horsekeeper. Looking out of the window he saw with a certain amount of surprise that the Black Pyramid and Nathaniel Broome had come into the yard. Then he noticed they were carrying luggage and realized that they were going to travel with him as well. He watched as the great black man swung himself up onto the roof and put down a mighty hand to pull Nathaniel up to sit beside him.

'All aboard, ladies and gentlemen?' called the driver.

'Wait for me,' shouted an elderly man, puffing into the inn yard at the last minute. He was hauled up by unseen hands and the coachman cracked his whip.

'Well, we're away,' said Mrs Silverwood, wiping a tear from her eye.

'You will miss your daughter no doubt,' John answered her.

'Oh yes, I shall. She is my only child, alas. And Nicholas my only grandchild.'

'So far,' the Apothecary said cheerfully, and brought a smile to her lips.

The journey to London was a repetition of the excursion down but done in reverse. Having left Exeter at nine in the morning – as opposed to mid-evening – they stayed once again in Bath. During their first break John, having gallantly handed the ladies out and assisted a clergyman to descend, found himself face-to-face with Jack Beef, alias the Black Pyramid.

The black man had swept him a fulsome bow. 'My word. So we meet again. How delightful to see you Mr Rawlings.'

'The pleasure is entirely mine,' the Apothecary answered, returning the compliment.

There was a great flash of white teeth. 'I take it that you are returning to London?'

'Actually I am travelling on further. What about yourself?'

'I am going to a fight in Islington. At Stokes's Amphitheatre to be precise.'

'Oh, I like that place. I went there years ago and saw a female boxing match.'

'Well, now it's Jack's turn,' said Nathaniel, coming round the corner and tipping his hat in the direction of the Apothecary.

'Did you do well from your bout in Exeter?' John asked conversationally.

'Extremely well. In addition to my purse I got a reward from some young blade who had wagered a great deal on my winning. It was a most enjoyable trip.'

'But marred by the murder of William Gorringe no doubt.'

The black man straightened his face while Nathaniel swept his hat from his head.

'That was an unfortunate business. Both Nat and I have seen the Constable but we found it hard to give him any information. I imagine it was some burglar who crept in and was surprised during the robbery.'

'I think not,' John answered briefly.

'Oh? Why do you say that?'

'The man was attacked with unbelievable savagery. All the evidence points to him being killed by somebody who really hated him.'

The Black Pyramid looked grim, his face tautening into deep lines and dark furrows. 'Must have been someone from his past,' he said.

'And that,' replied John, 'is precisely what I am about to investigate.'

He raised his hat to the pair, who stood staring at him, astonished, and proceeded into the inn to partake of a light repast.

They reached the Gloucester Coffee House late the next night, having raced back from Bath only stopping to allow the passengers food and comfort. John had tried to sleep as darkness fell but he had found his brain too full of thoughts to allow him to doze. Opposite him Mrs Silverwood had slept deeply, so deeply that John had been forced to wake her when they arrived in London. He had gone immediately into The Gloucester Hotel to book himself a room for the night; Lucinda had followed him, yawning. The Black Pyramid and Nathaniel Broome, however, had hired a hackney coach and had disappeared into the night without further ado.

The only room left had been one for two persons and John had turned to Mrs Silverwood.

'Do you object to sharing with me, Madam? I promise that I will not embarrass you in any way.'

'I would share with anyone tonight,' she had answered, her voice sounding exhausted.

So John had signed them in as Mr and Mrs Rawlings and they had been shown to a small attic dwelling at the very top of the house.

Without false modesty Lucinda had removed her upper and outer garments and had lain down in the bed in her stays, shift and under-petticoat. She had immediately fallen asleep. John longed to take off his breeches but did not dare strip down to his drawers. Instead he removed his shoes and stockings, his coat and waist-coat, and also dived into bed, making sure that he kept a good distance between himself and the slumbering Mrs Silverwood.

He, too, must have slept deeply because he awoke the next morning to find her missing. He sat up in bed, slightly annoyed that she hadn't woken him to go to breakfast, where he presumed she was. But having made his way downstairs he was informed that his wife had already left the inn and further had settled the account for the two of them. Grateful but for all that puzzled, John ate a somewhat indifferent breakfast, then made enquires about coaches leaving for Lewes.

'They leave from The Borough, Sir. From The White Swan.'

John recalled with a mixture of mirth and misery his memories of the place at which he had stayed when he had been on his way to the Romney Marsh.

'Thank you very much. You are quite sure Mrs . . . er . . . Rawlings has paid the bill?'

'Positive, Sir,' answered the man, and gave John a lewd wink.

Not feeling in the least like walking, John hired a hackney coach and proceeded in this conveyance to the busy part of London known as The Borough, crossing the Thames by means of a slow progress over London Bridge. When he eventually arrived he found that a stagecoach was leaving for Brighthelmstone at eight o'clock and felt a great sense of relief that he only had to wait ten minutes before it departed. Hurrying, he managed to secure a place on the roof in a rather precarious seat at the very back. As he scaled the coach's side he realized that he was probably on a fool's errand.

'First stop is Croydon,' called the guard and with a turn of wheels and a crack of the whip, John set off on this extremely nebulous adventure.

They reached Lewes approximately nine and a half hours later having stopped at Croydon, Godstone, East Grinstead and Uckfield before they reached their destination. Dropping John and another woman, large and grumpy and wearing eyebrow wigs made of mouse fur, at an establishment named The White Hart, the Apothecary decided to book himself a room for the night and afterwards go into the taproom to pick up any local gossip.

But first he must dine, feeling very empty and decidedly in need of a good glass of claret. He made his way to the dining parlour which was totally devoid of people and addressed an ancient waiter.

'Good evening. I have just arrived off the stagecoach. Am I too late to get a bite of supper?'

'Provided you take what the cook has to offer, Sir, no, you are not.'

'Then fetch me some pottage and pie and I'll be happy.'

'And what would you like to drink?'

'Some wine, if you please.'

'Certainly, Sir.'

The waiter left the room and John was just starting to read a newspaper when the woman with the eyebrow wigs, which John regarded as quite the most monstrous fashion, came in and sat down at a table adjacent to his.

'Where's the serving man?' she enquired abruptly.

'He's just gone out to put in my order,' John answered, lowering the paper.

'Well I hope he hurries back. I'm starving to death after that journey.'

As she looked as far from her demise as was humanly possible the Apothecary merely smiled and started to read once more.

'Well, how did you fare whilst travelling, Sir?'

'I have been on the road for some days,' John answered pleasantly. 'I have come from Exeter.'

'Goodness me. That's a fair way to travel. What brings you to this part of the world?'

'Business. Just business.'

At that point the waiter came in and after grumbling that there was nothing decent left to eat the woman ordered an immense amount of food and a bottle of wine. John's claret had arrived by this time and he politely offered the woman a glass as she was still waiting.

'Very kind of you, Mr . . .'

'Rawlings, Ma'am.'

'I'll accept.'

He poured it out and saw her get the look in her eye of someone who was longing to talk.

With a mental sigh he relinquished the newspaper.

'I've come to visit my daughter,' she started. 'She lives close by but, alas, has too many children to warrant my staying with her, every bedroom being taken if you follow my meaning.'

John nodded.

'Of course, I am a native of these parts. I was actually born in Lewes but shortly after my arrival my father got employment on the Vinehurst estate – he was assistant gamekeeper, don't you know, and rose to become the head man. Anyway, my mother and I – there were just the three of us in the family at that time – moved to a tied cottage. When I was old enough I became a maid in the big house but I was courted by a very pleasant gentleman – he was the son of the jewellers, you know, Ludden's of Lewes they are called to this day.'

John's pottage arrived and he started to eat it but the woman continued regardless.

'Of course that marriage gave me the start in life I had always wanted. Deep inside me I had always had the craving to be something else, a woman of importance, a creature of note.'

John supped his soup and nodded, hoping her food would arrive soon and there would be a merciful silence.

'Well, I achieved my ambition. I went to London and was accepted for small parts at the Theatre Royal, Drury Lane.'

The Apothecary wondered whether to mention Coralie Clive but realized he wouldn't get a word in anyway.

'I had to leave my husband behind me, alas. But when I was rising up the ladder . . .'

John grinned wildly at the thought.

'. . . he was taken ill, poor soul, and so I left my career and returned to nurse him. I had two daughters by him, you know, and then I lost him.'

John longed to ask where, but forbore.

'Oh, that was a sad day. But I gave him a splendid funeral. We had the most magnificent lying in state, I can tell you. The whole of Lewes came to pay their respects. Anyway as I had no son the jewellery company passed to his younger brother, which was most unfortunate. Still, he left me well provided for and . . .'

At that moment the woman's meal arrived and she dug in with relish. There was total silence and John gave a sigh of relief as he ate his pie in comparative comfort. But no sooner had she consumed her pottage than she started once more.

'Of course, I am a lady of leisure these days.' She looked at John from under her mouse fur brows and he felt a sinking of his heart.

'My congratulations,' he murmured.

'But I do find it lonely, being on my own. It is so difficult to meet any gentleman with whom one has anything in common. I may have been born in humble circumstances but I played with the Bassett children as a young girl, I'll have you know. And now I am a woman of means. So I am looking for a husband,' she concluded archly. 'Do you know anyone, Sir?'

'Unfortunately not off-hand, Madam. Why don't you place an advertisement in a newspaper?'

'Now that,' she said, digging into her chicken with gusto, 'is a very good idea.'

John had been too tired to visit the taproom and so had gone straight to bed. But during the night he had awoken from a dream and sat bolt upright. Something the woman had said earlier had come back to him while he slept, and now he turned it over in his brain. She had mentioned the name Bassett and the Apothecary began to puzzle where he had heard it before.

And then he remembered. He had been sharing a room with Cuthbert Simms and had heard a disembodied voice say, 'Take care, Fulke Bassett. Take great care.'

As he put his head back on the pillow, John Rawlings determined to ask the woman exactly to whom she had been referring – at the risk of being considered an interested suitor.

Twelve

There was no sign of the talkative woman at breakfast the following morning and John gave a crooked smile at the thought that both the females with whom he had recently spent the evening had vanished by daylight. However, the same old waiter was serving and John called him over to the table.

'Good morning, my friend. Has the lady been down to breakfast yet?'

'No, Sir. I expect she be still abed. Shall I tell her you were asking for her?'

'No, I'd rather you didn't,' John answered hastily. He helped himself to beef and bread. 'Tell me, does the name Bassett mean anything to you?'

'Of course, Sir. They'm be the big family round here. Made a lot of money in the City, did the old great grandfather, and built him a grand house called Vinehurst Place. That was before the tragedy, you see.'

John sat bolt upright and put down his newspaper. 'What tragedy was that?'

'The shooting, Sir. The great grandson – who inherited the house – shot his daughter dead. Seems that he wanted her to marry some old Marquis – a real old beast of a fellow who had already had three wives – and she objected. It seems she had already given her heart elsewhere, though she would tell no-one who her lover was. Anyway, to cut to the point, on the eve of her wedding they had a most terrible argument and he shot her dead.'

'Good heavens. What happened to him?'

'He ran from the house and was never seen again.'

John could scarcely believe it. 'You mean he escaped the law?'

'Completely and utterly. He just took off into the night and has not been heard of from that day to this.'

The Apothecary could hardly eat his breakfast. 'So what happened to the house?'

'That was left to Master Richard – he was the old man's son. Apparently he ran to his sister's side and held her while she was dying. Then, once the funeral was over, he moved away to London where he now resides. Vinehurst Place is kept clean by a handful of servants but nobody goes there anymore.'

'Where is it? I'd like to go and have a look at the place.'

'It's easy enough to find. Leave Lewes on the Brighthelmstone road, then take the first turning left at the crossroads. Follow a narrow path and you will come upon the house from the back. It should take no more than an half hour to reach.'

'Thank you so much for the information. I shall set off as soon as I have finished my repast.'

The waiter shook his head sadly. 'It do seem tragic to me that the old place that was once so full of life and fun should stand so empty and lonely.'

John asked on a whim, 'Is it haunted?'

'They say the dead girl, Miss Helen, goes weeping along the corridor. The servants often hear her.'

Despite the fact that it was a warm day and John had reached the stage of toast and marmalade, he gave a shiver.

'What a terrible tale. Thank you for telling me.'

'You be'm more than welcome, Sir.'

It was a good half hour's walk, John thought, as he strode out on another particularly beautiful day. The sky above was the deep blue of ripening grapes, with wisps of cloud the colour of angel's wings. The trees were in high drama, ranging in shade from pale gold to wild and fiery russet. There was a mysterious scent in the air. A combination of woodsmoke, leaves and dark, damp earth. The Apothecary breathed in deeply and felt a leap of his spirits, a joyousness in being alive and well. He felt glad that Elizabeth was bringing his child into the world to share in the marvellous experience of being part of it.

His thoughts turned to his daughter, Rose, and he had a sudden longing to see her again. To see her childish beauty crowned by her mop of red hair. He pictured her walking along with Sir Gabriel, his tall figure leaning heavily upon his great stick, his three-storey wig white as ivory, bending to examine a flower that his granddaughter was pointing out. He considered that if he left Lewes tomorrow morning he would have time to hurry back to them and maybe stay a day or two before returning to Devon for Lady Sidmouth's ball.

Ahead of him loomed the crossroads and John, turning, saw behind

him the small town he had just left with its great and gloomy castle
rearing high above, perched on a hill overlooking the river. He
turned again and took the left fork, proceeding down a narrow lane
until the way before him opened up and he found himself before
a tall pair of cast-iron gates. Peering through them he saw a long
green sward – about a mile in length – leading to a house that
seemed to him to be the epitome of graceful design and elegant
construction. John pushed at the gates which swung open with an
almighty creak. Looking guiltily round to see if anybody else had
heard the noise, the apothecary eased his way between them.

The moment he set his eyes on Vinehurst Place he felt almost
mesmerized by it, as if the house had him in its thrall. And yet as
John drew nearer he saw that the place was lifeless. No smoke rose
from the chimneys, no head peered out from one of the many
windows, there was no sound of any kind. It was just as if the
place had been deserted on the night of the murder and nobody
had set foot in it since.

The Apothecary drew nearer, his eye taking in with admiration
the rose-pink brickwork and the clever way in which the builder
had curved the cornice below the great attic storey, giving a false
but pleasing perspective. The windows had delightful arches above
them while the garden door had a span with a design. John strained
to see what it was but at that moment a figure appeared from
nowhere and stood motionless watching him. It was its very stillness that frightened the Apothecary who, after stopping in his tracks
and staring for a moment or two, turned on his heels and walked
rapidly away. There was no shout and no sound of running feet
and when he glanced over his shoulder he saw that the figure still
stood there, immobile as a statue, its motionless head staring in his
direction. Frightened out of his wits, yet for no good reason, John
ran the rest of the way and, squeezing through the gates, hared
down the lane that lay beyond.

Afterwards when he had regained his breath and his equilibrium John walked slowly back to Lewes, wondering why he had
been so afraid. The figure had been real enough, there had been
no doubt about that. Yet it was the fact that it made no move
towards him that had scared him so much. Telling himself that he
was being foolish the Apothecary reached the small town and
headed into an hostelry to have a reviving drink.

★   ★   ★

That evening he went for a walk – or rather a climb – for he plodded up the hill to the castle and stood there beside its menacing hulk watching a fog come up from the sea and blow along the course of the river. He observed it slowly wrap its tendrils round the little town and knew that as soon as he descended from the castle's heights he would find himself immersed in it. It was at that moment that he decided to go back to London the next morning to reunite himself with Sir Gabriel and Rose. Elizabeth had made it clear that he was to return to Devon to escort her to the ball but after that – who knew? Shivering slightly, John descended the hill and found himself plunged into the mist.

It was thicker in the town than he had imagined and what scant lighting there was came mostly from the fronts of shops. John plunged on in the direction of The White Hart – or what he imagined the direction to be – and had just crossed the street when two women suddenly appeared out of the fog and walked quite close to him. Normally he wouldn't have given them a second glance but there was something in the way that they carried themselves that attracted his attention. John sunk back into a shop doorway as a breath of their conversation reached his ears.

'. . . glad to be out of it I can tell you.'

'I'm sure you are, my dear. But don't dwell. It's all over now.'

'Yes, thank God. Poor Charles. His guts saved him from a terrible ordeal.'

'Yes, indeed.'

They were alongside the Apothecary, just passing him, and the light from a shoemaker's shop shone directly on them. John gave an audible gasp. He was astonished to see the dark little milliner, Jemima Lovell, and walking beside her was none other than the woman who had travelled back from Devon with him, Lucinda Silverwood herself.

Thirteen

The hackney coach dropped him next afternoon at the corner of Gerrard Street, and the Apothecary practically ran the rest of the way to Nassau Street. Dashing up the few steps to the front door he inserted his key in the lock only to feel the door being pulled from the other side and to hear a little voice saying, 'Papa, is that you?'

He practically flew into the reception hall. 'Sweetheart, how did you know?'

'She has been telling me for the last two days that you were coming,' said Sir Gabriel Kent, making his way out of the library, walking slowly and leaning heavily on his cane. John turned to him and just for a minute saw his father quite clearly.

Sir Gabriel was now eighty-three years of age and as spare of frame as ever. But time was at last taking its toll on him and he no longer stood straight and tall but was starting to stoop, while lines of wisdom had cut deep into his countenance. His skin had become the colour of parchment, matching his amazing white wig, and his hands were covered with the brown marks that some people called death spots. But his eyes were still bright and golden and looked at John with the same clarity that they had always held.

'My dearest boy,' he said, and embraced his son warmly. 'Rose has a gift indeed for she has been informing me all day yesterday and most of today that you were on your way to see us.'

John smiled a secret smile at his daughter, knowing full well that she had been born with ancient magic. However, the child's next question disturbed him slightly.

'How is Mrs Elizabeth?' she asked.

'Very well, thank you,' answered her father, somewhat nonplussed.

'Come, my son, let us repair to the library,' said Sir Gabriel, then turning to Rose he added, 'Dearest, I wish to speak to your father privately. You may join us in thirty minutes.'

The red hair flew as she tossed her head but she trotted away to her nursemaid obediently enough. John stared after her.

'Does she miss her companion Octavia?'

Sir Gabriel straightened his shoulders. 'Well, I think she does somewhat. But most of all, John, she misses you.'

He led the way into the library and the Apothecary sat down opposite him and allowed his adopted father to pour him a small sherry. He stared at the great old man as he passed him his glass.

'Father, there is something I have to tell you.'

'Oh yes?' And Sir Gabriel gave him a glance which held a great deal of amusement in its depths.

John, for no reason, felt awkward. 'It's about Elizabeth di Lorenzi.'

The golden eyes gleamed. 'Something to do with the reason she wanted to see you, no doubt.'

'Yes. Sir, you are going to be a grandfather once more.'

Sir Gabriel's face creased. 'I see that you didn't waste your time in Devon then.'

John felt himself blush. 'Well, I . . .'

His father interrupted him. 'There is no need to explain to me, my son. You have been a widower for some years and I know that at the time you were very much in love with the Marchesa di Lorenzi. Tell me, are you still?'

'Yes, yes I am. But she will not marry me, Sir, despite the fact that she is carrying my child.'

'So she intends to give birth to a bastard?'

'Yes, I fear she does. But don't worry about her position in society. She is rich and she is powerful. Only a few people will abandon her.'

'But what of you, John?'

'I am resigned to my fate. But even if I could marry her it would mean giving everything up and going to live in Devon, for she would never come to London.'

'Why not?'

'She loves the countryside and the whole way of life. She cannot bear the thought of being a mindless town belle of fashion with nothing to do all day but play cards and gossip.'

'And could you not open a shop in Exeter?'

The Apothecary smiled ruefully. 'I don't know that I could manage it. Remember that I have been brought up in the city and am used to the noise and the stinks. Besides, even if I were to go to her cap in hand she still would not have me. She is fiercely independent.'

'As are you, my boy. And therein lies the problem I believe.'

'What do you mean?'

'Two proud people love each other but can never give up their way of life.' Sir Gabriel steepled his long fingers. 'But I have said enough. We will discuss the matter no further. Let us drink a toast to my forthcoming grandchild.'

He pulled a long bell cord and when a servant appeared ordered some champagne to be sent up from the cellar. They were in the middle of drinking it when Rose reappeared.

'Can I speak to Papa now, Grandfather?'

'Yes, my darling, you certainly can.'

With his daughter perched on his knee and drinking a toast to the child that was to come, John felt totally happy. But then he thought of the mystery of seeing Jemima and Lucinda walking along together and tried to find a logical explanation for it. What had Miss Lovell been doing in Lewes? Admittedly Mrs Silverwood had said she lived in that area but the dark young lady had given no such reason. It was a great puzzle which was possibly connected with the murder of William Gorringe.

Rose said, 'You're very quiet, Papa. Are you thinking something?'

'Yes, I am.'

'What about?'

'About something that happened while I was away. I am sorry that I can't discuss it with you but one day I will talk to you about everything.'

'When will that be?'

'When you are sixteen,' John answered, plucking a figure out of the air.

She counted on her fingers. 'Another eleven years to wait.'

'Yes, I'm afraid so.'

She turned an enquiring face to him. 'Tell me about Mrs Elizabeth, Papa.'

He hesitated, wondering what to say, but it was Sir Gabriel who stated in a perfectly normal voice, 'She is going to have a baby, Rose. A little brother or sister for you.'

The child looked surprised. 'I don't quite understand.'

John wished that his father had not started going down this particular path, determining not to tell Rose any more than she could comprehend.

'I am the baby's father, sweetheart. That is how it will be your brother or sister.'

'I see,' she answered, though it was clear that she did not really. 'When will he be coming?'

'In February,' John answered, 'though we cannot be certain that it is a boy.'

'I think it is,' she answered, and gave John a smile which had such traces of his late wife in it that it tore at his heart.

Rose got to the ground. 'I shall go and prepare a painting for him.'

'How very thoughtful of you,' Sir Gabriel answered.

'He will be delighted with that,' John added, but when she had left the room he turned to his father, 'Why did you have to tell her that, Papa?'

'What precisely?'

'That Elizabeth is going to have a baby.'

'My dear child, should Rose see the lady – at Christmas-time or whatever – she will notice at once. One cannot keep such things from young and bright minds like that with which my grandchild has been blessed.'

John grinned. 'You're right, of course. And perhaps we will all keep Christmas in Devon, including you, Sir.'

Sir Gabriel looked pleased. 'I am delighted that at last I shall have the chance of meeting the woman who has had so profound an effect on you. And I shall also have the opportunity of visiting my old friend Sir Clovelly Lovell. Thank you for including me.'

John nodded, hoping madly that Elizabeth would agree to them descending on her at the festive season. Then he changed the subject.

'I haven't told you this before but there was trouble on the journey down.'

'Of what nature?'

'A murder,' John answered succinctly, and proceeded to relate to his father the whole story, including his recent visit to Lewes, his sighting of the amazing Vinehurst Place and the spellbinding effect it had had upon him, and finally his seeing the two women – whom he had not realized were even connected to one another – walking through the fog together.

Sir Gabriel sat in silence for a moment, then said, 'Perhaps they formed a friendship through the coach journey and arranged to see each other again.'

'I suppose it is possible but it is also highly unlikely.'

'Why?'

'Because Miss Lovell was working at Lady Sidmouth's making hats and headdresses for the ball which she is about to give. And Mrs Silverwood was at her daughter's helping with the birth of her first grandchild.'

'So not much chance to communicate, eh?'

'None at all I would say.'

'Then I agree with you. It's damnable odd. Are you going to see John Fielding about it?'

'Yes, I shall go tomorrow. And on the following day I must leave once more. I promised Elizabeth that I would return in time for Lady Sidmouth's rout.'

'Why don't you take Rose with you?'

'I would like to but I feel it would be wrong of me without seeking the Marchesa's permission first.'

'A good reply. Now, my son, let us stretch our legs a little before the hour to dine. Where shall we walk to?'

'To Shug Lane, if it is not too great a step for you, Sir.'

'My dear child, I shall go there with ease. And, of course, the assistance of my cane.'

In his absence and now that Nicholas Dawkins, his former apprentice, had married and gone to live in the delightful village of Chelsea, John had appointed a retired apothecary to come and run his shop for him. And as John entered the premises in Shug Lane the other man came from the compounding room, a slight frown upon his face. His name was Jeremiah de Prycke and as soon as he saw who it was he changed his expression to one of a somewhat forced grin. That is his facial muscles contorted leaving his eyes unsmiling, a pale china blue and slightly bolting. He wore a long black gown and a hat, even though the day was warm, and he bowed low on seeing John.

'Mr Rawlings. How are you? I was not expecting you back quite so soon.'

'I am very well, thank you Mr de Prycke. And how has young Gideon been behaving himself?'

Behind Jeremiah's back John's apprentice could be seen pulling the most terrible faces and making an obscene gesture.

'Oh, well enough,' Jeremiah answered in a voice that suggested that Gideon had conducted himself appallingly.

Sir Gabriel said drily, 'What excellent news. I am delighted to hear it.'

Jeremiah who, most unfortunately, had far more hair upon his chin than on his head, waggled his straggly white beard.

'Oh well, taking into consideration his youth, you know.'

'Mr Rawlings,' protested Gideon, 'I am eighteen years old. And I have been out adminstering all the clysters which Mr de Prycke considers not his province. I truly can say that I have behaved to the best of my ability.'

Jeremiah turned on him pettishly. 'Did I not say so, you silly boy.'

John intervened. 'Have you been called out a good deal, Mr de Prycke?'

'Quite a lot, yes. Mostly by people with imaginary ailments. Time wasters all.'

'Really? You do surprise me. The majority of patients I tend are genuinely in need.'

Sir Gabriel sat down in a chair that Gideon brought for him. 'I can honestly declare, John, that it is a pleasure to be in your shop again. It has such a calming atmosphere. Would you not agree, Mr de Prycke?'

'To be honest with you, Sir, I prefer the country. There are far too many people in London for my liking. As you know, I live quietly in Islington. But even that is not far enough away for me.'

'You should go to an island in the Atlantic ocean,' Gideon muttered to himself.

'What was that?'

'I said London is noisy and full of commotion.'

Mr de Prycke looked annoyed and his hat slipped sideways slightly revealing a few straggles of wispy white hair and a completely bald pate. He turned to John.

'Are you back permanently, Sir? Are my days with you finished?'

'No, I'm afraid not. I must return to Devon and will probably be away another two weeks . . .'

Behind Jeremiah's back Gideon mimed hanging himself.

'. . . so if it is no trouble I would ask you to continue covering for me.'

'I shall enquire of my landlady whether she can continue to rent me a room. It is far too far to travel in from Islington every day, you see.'

'I do hope that I am not causing you any trouble.'

Mr de Prycke looked winsome, or at least made an effort to do so by drawing his mouth in tightly and forcing a roguish expression into his eyes.

'Not at all, Sir. Not at all.'

When the Apothecary considered how much he was paying him, he did not feel quite so guilty. In fact he did not feel guilty in the least when he studied the expression on Gideon's face. He addressed himself to his apprentice.

'I would like you to take as many calls as you can, Gideon. It will be excellent practice for you. Do you not agree, Mr de Prycke?'

'Well, there are certain commissions . . .'

'Certain, yes. But I want the boy to get as much experience as possible. Besides it will get him out from under your feet.'

'There will be some advantages admittedly.'

'Then I am sure you will pursue them,' said John vigorously. He motioned to Sir Gabriel. 'Are you ready to return home, Sir?'

'I am, my son.' The old man made a slight bow in Mr de Prycke's direction and was rewarded with a salutation that set Jeremiah's gown billowing like a sail.

'So delighted to meet you, Sir Gabriel.'

'Indeed.'

Out in the street Sir Gabriel turned to John. 'What a beastly creature. I do hope that he is not upsetting Gideon too much.'

'Yes, I know what you mean. He reminds me of something that one would see peering at one from deep in the sea.'

'A crab?'

'Possibly. I was thinking more on the lines of a squid.'

'Good gracious. Well, I shall keep an eye on young Purle and make sure that he is not suffering too greatly.'

'Thank you, Father. Please write to me if there is any trouble.'

'I will most certainly.'

That night John went to bed early and fell into a deep sleep. But he woke in the small hours and thought of how he had once shared this bed with Emilia. And even though he now loved Elizabeth he knew that Emilia held a very special place in his heart. In the darkness he spoke to her.

'My darling, I miss you. I know you will understand me falling in love again. But be assured that you are and always will be very special to me.'

Was it his imagination or did he feel himself suddenly grow warmer as if a pair of loving arms had enfolded him? Whatever it was, the Apothecary felt strangely comforted and slept peacefully once more.

Fourteen

John thought that if he had been given a guinea for every time he had visited Sir John Fielding's salon on the first floor of the tall, thin house in Bow Street, he would be a wealthy man by now. As he climbed the twisting staircase he felt that he knew every stair and every turn. It was dark and the Beak Runner in the Public Office had given him a candle the better to see his way up but as he approached the door it was flung open and the figure of Joe Jago, silhouetted against the brightness of the room behind, stood waiting for him.

'My very dear Joe,' said John, 'how wonderful to see you again.'

'And you too, Sir,' said the other man, and welcomed him into the salon.

Inside it was all cheer and brightness – the curtains drawn, the fire blazing, the light of many candletrees illuminating the polished furniture. The only thing missing was the Blind Beak himself.

'He's still in court, Sir,' said Joe. 'Finishing off a difficult case. He shouldn't be too long.'

John hovered. 'May I sit down?'

'Of course you can. Goodness me. You're almost one of the family.'

'And where are Lady Fielding and Mary Anne?'

'They are out visiting friends. May I offer you some refreshment, Sir?'

John had dined only an hour before, taking the meal early in order to eat with Rose, who had a very long face about her as it was her father's last night in London.

'I promise I will be back in two weeks' time, sweetheart,' the Apothecary had said in order to reassure her.

'I wish you didn't have to go, Papa.'

'I must say goodbye to Mrs Elizabeth, darling.'

'I see.'

Sir Gabriel had interrupted. 'Would you rather be driven by Irish Tom, John? I am sure that Rose and I can manage without him for a fortnight or so.'

'No, Sir. I know you use him daily. Besides I will try and get a flying coach this time. It should be quicker.'

'As you wish, my boy.'

Now the Apothecary looked up at Joe. 'I dined recently so a small port would be very welcome.'

Jago poured out two glasses and sat down opposite John, noticeably leaving the Blind Beak's chair vacant.

'So how are things going with you, Sir?'

John peered into the depths of his glass. 'I am to be a father again, Joe.'

'Ah,' came the slightly nonplussed reply.

John looked up. 'The mother is Lady Elizabeth, the Marchesa di Lorenzi. I have repeatedly asked her to marry me but she refuses point blank.'

'Oh dear! I don't quite know what to say, Mr Rawlings. I am rather inexperienced in these matters.'

The Apothecary gave him a look of much fondness, thinking to himself that as far as he knew Joe Jago had never been married and had not had a great deal of contact with the opposite sex.

'It is an unusual situation I admit. But then Elizabeth is a highly unusual woman, Joe.'

'I agree with you there, Sir. But on the odd occasions I have met her I always found her pleasant enough. I'll never forget how kind she was to you at the time of Mrs Rawlings's death.'

'She was more than kind, Joe. I think she saved my life. That is, that you and she saved it between you.'

The clerk flushed beneath his red hair, ill concealed by an old and tired wig. 'I did what I could, Mr Rawlings. That is all.'

The Apothecary could have wept for the goodness of people around him but fortunately at that moment they heard a familiar heavy tread on the stairs and both men stood up. Joe went to the door and as it was thrown open, called out, 'Mr Rawlings is here to see you, Sir,' and the Blind Beak came into the room.

The man was now forty-six years old and stood well over six feet tall. As well as being of great height he was also well built so that his physical presence, to say nothing of his persona, filled the room. He wore a long and somewhat old-fashioned wig of curling white hair which hung to his shoulders, accentuating his nose and his full and passionate mouth. He had pushed up the black ribbon he always wore over his eyes so that they were exposed, closed as usual, beneath a pair of jet black, rather heavy, brows. But his hands – this evening carrying a cane to help him find his way – were beautiful, long and slender, almost feminine in their shape and delicacy. On his little finger the Magistrate wore a gold ring with an amethyst which glistened in the light.

As always John bowed. 'It is a pleasure to see you again, Sir.'

'My dear Mr Rawlings, how nice to hear your voice. Take a seat do.'

Because he knew the room so well, the blind man made his way without difficulty to the great chair which stood beside the fireplace. Lowering his frame into it, he turned his head to Joe.

'Jago, fetch me a drink, there's a good chap. I feel wretchedly depressed.'

'Why, Sir, if I may ask?' said John.

'Because I have news from my contact in Paris that that devil Wilkes is thinking of returning to England. He'll make trouble, mark my words.'

Into John's pictorial memory came a list of the members of the Hell-Fire Club with Wilkes's name prominent among them. That is until the man had fallen out with Sir Francis Dashwood, the founder, and had been barred from attending. Now he was in voluntary exile in France having been expelled from the House of Commons and convicted in the Court of King's Bench for printing and publishing issue Number 43 of the *North Briton* – in which he had libelled George III – together with Wilkes's pornographic 'Essay on Woman'. He had four years previously come face-to-face with Sir John Fielding and demanded that the Magistrate issue a warrant against the Secretaries of State for theft of papers from his house. The Blind Beak had denied the request, knowing full well that the papers had been officially seized.

'You refuse me, Sir,' Wilkes had shouted, 'then you too shall hear from me!'

It had been an empty threat but the news that the man was thinking of returning from France quite clearly made Sir John ill at ease.

'But let us not waste good conversation on that universal hound,' said the Magistrate now. 'A health to you, Mr Rawlings. Tell me, how is the world using you?'

'Sir, I have become involved in a murderous situation,' answered John.

'Tell me of it.' And Sir John Fielding sat back in his chair, put his head against the cushioned mat and listened while the Apothecary told him the story of his journey to Devon and all that had transpired since. Eventually he spoke.

'You say that you were told by the coach driver that he had driven the man Gorringe before but that he used a different name?'

'Yes, Sir. Yet my investigations in Lewes yielded up nothing, except for that strange business of seeing two of the women who travelled in the coach walking along together.'

'Quite so.' The Blind Beak sipped his drink. 'Surely not a coincidence?'

'I would hardly have thought so.'

There was silence in the room, a profound silence during which Joe winked at John. Meanwhile the Magistrate performed his usual trick of appearing to sleep, which meant, as the Apothecary knew, that he was thinking deeply.

'Tell me about the constable in Exeter,' he said at last.

'A professional, Sir. And quite efficient from what I've seen. But he has an enormous amount of work to do and quite an area to cover.'

'Um.' There was another long silence and then the Beak turned his head in the direction of Joe. 'Tell me, Jago, are you due for any leave?'

'No, Sir John.'

'Then in that case you must take some unofficially. I want you to go to Lewes with Mr Rawlings and then on to Devon. Assist in any way possible. But you must be back here within a fortnight. Is that understood?'

'But how will you manage, Sir?'

'It will give young Lucas a chance to get used to the court. I shall have to rely on him.'

'He is very inexperienced.'

The Blind Beak sighed. 'We all were that once upon a time.'

Joe nodded gravely. 'You're right there, Sir. I shall be glad to accompany you Mr Rawlings and help you by any means I can.'

'If it doesn't inconvenience Sir John then I'd be pleased to have your company.'

'When do we start, Sir?'

'Tomorrow morning,' John answered. He turned to the Magistrate who remained oblivious of the movement. 'I must return to Devon first, Sir. I promised the Marchesa that I would be back in time to escort her to a ball.'

'Very good. But I would suggest another visit to Lewes soon. I have a feeling that the answer might lie there. The key to the whole thing might well be Gorringe's former identity.'

'I shall go there after the rout, be assured of it.'

'Remember you will only have Jago's assistance for two weeks,' the Blind Beak answered.

'I will indeed, Sir John.'

'Well now, let us change the subject. Has anything of interest other than the murder taken place since last we met, Mr Rawlings?'

John coloured even more deeply. 'I am to be a father again, Sir. The Marchesa is with child.'

'Well bless my soul,' the Blind Beak answered, and laughed his deep melodious chuckle.

The following afternoon Joe Jago and the Apothecary set off by flying coach to Exeter. These conveyances were smaller than the stagecoach, carrying a maximum of four people, and were faster, having only to stop to change horses and give the travellers some rest. This particular coach halted for the night at Overton, having already traversed a distance of some sixty miles, and the two men, having seen by their watches that it was ten o'clock, went straight to bed, after consuming a hasty supper.

The next morning they set off at seven, stopped briefly at Blandford, dined at Dorchester, then pushed on through the darkness till their arrival in Exeter some three and a half hours later. John proceeded at once to The Half Moon, determined to show Joe the scene of the crime. Fortunately the room in which William Gorringe had met his grisly death had not been let to anyone else.

'Are you game to stay in it, Joe?'

'Indeed I am, Sir.'

So, rather wearily after so much intensive travelling, the two men climbed the stairs to the second floor and entered room seven. It had been scrubbed out and some sort of rosewater sprinkled about so that all traces and the smell of blood had disappeared. But even though the linen was fresh and clean, the bed upon which William Gorringe had met his terrible end was the same. John glanced at it somewhat fearfully, almost as if he expected the battered corpse to be lying there. He turned to Joe.

'This is where he was killed. He was lying on the bed, his head reduced to a pulp. I don't recollect ever having seen a corpse so badly beaten.'

'Does it worry you sleeping here?'

'No, not at all,' John answered with great bravado.

But secretly he felt a little dubious about getting into the big bed and deliberately chose the side where William Gorringe's body had not been. Joe, oblivious, removed his outer garments and got in beside him where he fell immediately into a deep and peaceful sleep. But John could not lose consciousness and now wished fervently that he had hired a horse and ridden on to Elizabeth's. Yet he knew full well that to have ridden through that dark and desolate landscape would have been asking for trouble from any highwaymen who might be roaming the road.

A groan jerked the Apothecary into full wakefulness and lighting a candle he peered fearfully into the dark corners of the room. But it was only Joe moaning a little as he turned over. Reluctantly John blew out the light and finally fell asleep.

He woke to find Joe whistling cheerfully as he shaved in delightfully hot water.

'Good morning, Mr Rawlings. Did you sleep well?'

'No, I didn't. I believe this room is haunted, Joe.'

'Oh I don't think so, Sir. It was just your imagination.'

'I'm not so certain. Remember it has witnessed a violent death.'

'I dare say a lot of other places have as well and they can't all be haunted.'

'Well, I'm glad I'm not staying here another night,' John answered defiantly. Then added, 'But what about you, Joe? I am sure that Lady Elizabeth would be glad to have you as a guest.'

'That's kind of you Mr Rawlings, but I feel I will be of more use staying behind in Exeter. But before we part company I'd be obliged if you would let me have a list of everyone travelling on the stagecoach with you. And, if possible, give me some address for them.'

'I'll do it as soon as I have had breakfast. But tell me, Joe, how do you intend to get around and about?'

'I shall hire an horse. A good sturdy beast that I can rely on.'

'An excellent idea.' John got out of bed. 'But be sure to call on me soon so that we can compare notes.'

'You can trust me to do that, Sir. Besides I'd like to get a look at the Marchesa's home.'

'I think that you will approve of it enormously.'

'I look forward to seeing it.'

And, that said, Joe continued with his shaving.

Fifteen

It was the night of Lady Sidmouth's ball. Outside the house and along the drive she had had flaming torches placed so that the entire area had taken on a mystic quality. As John alighted from the coach he heard far below him the seductive song of the sea and imagined mermaids chorusing as they rested on the rocks beneath, combing their long, flowing hair.

Elizabeth had dressed very beautifully in a deep lilac over-robe on top of a petticoat of white lace, which had bands of lilac crossing it at intervals. Down the sides of the gown she wore ruches of pleated silk interspersed with tiny imitation violets. At her throat she had a choker of ribbon and this, too, was decorated with little violets. Her neckline was square and low, her breasts rising above it in the most delightful way, while on her head she wore a high white wig built up over a frame. In this ensemble her pregnancy did not show and John thought her one of the loveliest creatures he had ever cast his eyes on.

He, too, had taken a great deal of trouble with his appearance, wearing the suit of crimson satin covered with silver butterflies made for him by the tailor in Exeter. His waistcoat, cut quite short, was of silver, fitting him snugly over the waist, which still remained slim despite the passing years. Over this his dramatic coat had a high stand collar and this, together with a new wig dressed away from the face with long sidecurls, made the Apothecary look interesting and handsome, something that he felt he did not always achieve.

They paused a moment as they descended from the coach. It was a calm night and although it was dark – or perhaps because of it – the house looked beautiful and fairy-like, set in its own parkland, with terraces sweeping down to gardens which, in their turn, swept to lawns which went down to the sea. The moon was out, casting a silvery light over the whole surroundings. The scent of the very last flowers of the season could be vaguely sniffed upon the air and John paused a moment, imagining this place in high summer, when the overwhelming perfume of the grounds met the high salt smell of the ocean and bathed one in an atmosphere soothing yet stimulating.

Inside, the house was decorated superbly. Lady Sidmouth, in her eccentric way, had ordered the gardeners to bring in garlands of greenery which hung between the pillars in the entrance hall. Indeed she had decorated the house almost as if she were preparing for a pagan festival. John, looking at Milady, garbed from head to toe in a violent shade of pink, a great wavering headdress of purple plumes upon her heavily wigged head, thought her more than capable of it. She stood in a receiving line of people, on one side of her the fat little boy whom John now knew to be the son of the Earl of Sidmouth, on the other his aunt, the sixteen-year-old Felicity Sidmouth. Further down the line was their cousin, the beauteous Miranda Tremayne. As the Apothecary drew level with her she gave him a special, secretive smile.

John and Elizabeth passed on and into the ballroom, where they discovered the frantic and tiny figure of Cuthbert Simms, who tonight was playing the part of Master of Ceremonies. Several footmen weaved their way amongst the crowded room with trays on which stood glasses of champagne. John took one as did the Marchesa.

'Ah, my dear Lady Elizabeth,' boomed a voice behind them, and a local woman, tall and handsome – the kind who would look good on a horse – started to engage the Marchesa in conversation. John looked around him and then let out a muffled cry of surprise. Emerging from the set, which had just come to an end amidst loud applause, was Joe Jago, smartly wigged and even more smartly dressed. The Apothecary shook his head in wonderment. Grinning broadly, the clerk approached him.

'God's life, Joe. You were the last person I expected to find here.'

'Ah well, Sir, I have a habit of popping up in strange places.'

'You do indeed. How did you manage to get invited?'

Joe looked modest. 'Lady Sidmouth asked me. I happened to see off a cut-purse who was attempting to rob her in Exeter. She was duly grateful and we have become quite friendly since.'

'And you have achieved this in scarcely any time.'

'We work fast in the Public Office, Mr Rawlings,' answered the clerk, and winked a bright blue eye.

John looked round the room. 'I wonder who else is here.'

'Several people who came down on the fateful coach trip I imagine.'

'Yes, so there are.'

The Apothecary waved and bowed to Martin Meadows, who was somewhat disastrously dressed in a topcoat of bright pea green which did not really become him, and to Fraulein Schmitt and her sister, the little round Matilda Mitchell, both dressed to kill in the fashion of five years previously.

'How strange that they should have been asked,' he whispered to Joe.

'And they are not all,' the clerk whispered back.

Paulina Gower, resplendent in a gown of dark blue with a lighter petticoat beneath, had just sailed into the ballroom and was presently looking round her to see who she could engage in conversation. She bore down on the Marchesa with a determined step.

'How do you do, Madam. Forgive me introducing myself but I have glimpsed you at the theatre. I am Paulina Gower.'

Elizabeth gave her a friendly smile. 'Of course. I saw you play Lady Macbeth. Quite one of the most chilling performances I have ever witnessed.'

The horse-like woman raised her quizzing glass. 'Ah, Miss Gower. I am *chawmed* to meet you. I have not seen you act as yet but it is an experience that I much look forward to. How long are you staying in Exeter?'

'I am booked to play the season, Ma'am. I shall be departing in March.'

'Then I must get tickets immediately.'

'How kind of you.' Paulina Gower turned her head and saw John and her look of benevolence – very much adopted by actors and writers when their work was being praised – changed to a cold glare.

'I did not expect to see you here, Sir,' she said acidly.

'You never know with me,' John answered, grinning inanely. He bowed to her. 'But it is always a pleasure to see you, Madam.'

She gave him a look and then swept on to speak to somebody else. John turned to Elizabeth. 'Marchesa, would you care to dance?'

'Indeed I would, Sir.'

A set was just ending and John led her out as Cuthbert Simms called out, 'Partners if you please, ladies and gentlemen, for Green Stockings.'

Deryn Lake

He was sweating profusely and looked rather depressed, clad as he was in a striped green and white ensemble with a huge cravat that concealed a large part of his face. John bowed and Elizabeth curtsied as they walked past him to take their places.

The Apothecary, at his most professional, could not help but worry as Elizabeth whirled and jigged and clapped her hands. And afterwards when he led her away he said as much.

'Sweetheart, was that dance too strenuous for you?'

'Gracious no,' she replied. 'Remember that this is my second child and I refuse to cut out all my pleasures.'

But there were small beads of perspiration on her upper lip and John was pleased when a break was called in the dancing and she went to speak to a group of people that she knew. This left him free momentarily and he seized the opportunity to attract the attention of Cuthbert Simms. Bowing ornately, the little man forced a smile.

'Ah, my dear Sir. How do I find you?'

'Very well,' John answered, 'but somewhat tired. I am heartily sick of coach travel.'

'And why is that may I ask?'

'I have been doing a great deal of it. Since we last spoke I have been to Lewes, via London. And that done I returned to Devon.'

The dancing master wiped his sweating brow. 'Oh, and what took you to Sussex may I ask?'

'I was following a lead in that still unsolved murder. I heard that the victim had taken the London stage there using another name.'

Cuthbert's cheeks went even pinker than they had been. 'Really? How interesting. And did you find any clues?'

John put on his innocent face. 'Not exactly. But can I tell you the most extraordinary thing?'

'Of course.'

'Well, while I was there I saw that little dark girl who worked here making hats and headdresses. What was her name now?'

'You don't mean Jemima Lovell?'

'That's right,' answered John, snapping his fingers. 'That was what she was called. Anyway I witnessed her proceeding along in Lewes and chatting animatedly to another passenger from our particular coach.'

The dancing master's face had turned from a roseate hue to one of immense pallor. 'And who might that have been?' he asked, his voice a rasp.

'Mrs Lucinda Silverwood, would you believe. I had not realized that the two of them had formed such a close association. Why, they were walking intimately as if they had known one another most of their lives.'

Cuthbert made a highly visible effort to pull himself together. 'They have clearly become friendly.'

'Clearly indeed,' John answered, bowed, and left the poor man.

The evening progressed well. Elizabeth danced twice more and then, somewhat to John's relief, sat and chatted to the other ladies. However, she encouraged him to join in and he found himself in a line of dancers opposite the delectable Miranda Tremayne, who gave him an incredibly naughty look as they joined gloved hands and passed one another. Fortunately the dance was rather too vigorous to encourage a great deal of conversation but as it ended Miranda curtsied and said, 'May I walk with you a little, Sir?'

'By all means but I am joining the Lady Elizabeth you know.'

'And which is she?' asked the minx, feigning ignorance.

'The dark-haired woman sitting next to Lady Sidmouth.'

'Oh,' said the reply, the very sound expressing surprise.

John raised a dark eyebrow. 'You know her?' he asked.

'No, Sir, we have never been introduced. I take it she is a friend of your mother's.'

He felt furious. 'Why do you say that?'

'Because she looks a little – mature.'

'She is also very beautiful and clever. Perhaps you will attain her standards when you reach her age.'

'Oh la,' said Miranda, with a wicked smile, 'I can't think about that now. That time is positively years away.'

'Then be sure to use the hours carefully,' the Apothecary answered, bowed, and walked off.

He was still seething when he joined the Marchesa and she, knowing him so well, detected a change in his manner.

'My dear, has somebody said something to annoy you? You look positively evil.'

'No, it was nothing. Somebody trod heavily on my foot, that's all.'

'Who was it? Surely not that very pretty girl you were dancing with?'

'It was some horrid old man. I'm not certain which.'

'Well, it is to be hoped that he falls over in the next set.'

Elizabeth laughed, tickled him under the chin with her feather fan and turned to talk to her neighbour. John stole a surreptitious glance at her. He now knew Miranda Tremayne to be a vicious little beast but still her remarks had stung him. For to him the Marchesa was the most beautiful and the most powerful woman he had ever met. Yet, if facts were faced, she was old indeed to bring a baby into the world. And suddenly John feared for her, feared that the child which he had given her might prove too much for her and end her glorious and vivid life. He stood up abruptly, bowed to the ladies, and made his way to the refreshment table.

Frau Schmitt bore down on him.

'Ach, mein friend. Have you got any nearer to solving this murder case?'

'No, no nearer I am afraid, Madam.'

'I vent to the Constable zat morning. Naturally he exonerated me of all guilt.'

By no stretch of the imagination could John envision the man doing such a thing but he merely smiled.

'That must have been a great relief to you.'

'Vye you say such a thing? I am completely innocent.'

'Madam, this affair is one of many strange depths. A man who called himself William Gorringe was murdered on the night we all stayed at The Half Moon. There was no robbery so clearly he was murdered by somebody he knew – unless it was the work of a total lunatic. Therefore it is perfectly reasonable for the Constable to assume that it was someone with whom Gorringe travelled. Until that person is brought to justice everyone – including myself – is under suspicion.'

'Zat is as may be but I can assure you zat I had nussink to do vith his death.'

For some reason that he could not pinpoint John had the peculiar sensation that Augusta was declaring her case too loudly, too emphatically. He almost felt as if he had stepped outside himself and was listening with a stranger's ears.

She was muttering on. 'I alvays say zat nobody can break down ze barrier of truth. In fact I used to teach zat to my pupils ven I was their German governess.'

John looked polite. 'Oh yes? And how long ago was that?'

'A good while. Almost twenty years. I vas vith a family, you see.'

'How interesting,' the Apothecary answered, his thoughts miles away.

'Of course I had become a companion more than anyzing. I mean my pupils had grown up. I had long since ceased to give zem formal lessons. In fact I voz an intimate friend of my employer's daughter.'

'Why did you leave?' asked John.

'Alas, poor Helen died in tragic circumstances. Zere vas no job left for me. I had to throw myself on ze mercies of fortune.'

'How very unfortunate.'

'It voz indeed. I miss Helen even to zis day.'

John looked at her and saw that the big fishy eyes had filled with tears and for the first time since he had met Miss Schmitt felt pity for the woman.

'I'm so sorry,' was all he could think of saying.

'Zank you, zank you. She meant a great deal to me as, indeed, did her brother.'

The Apothecary was filled with the idea that the German governess had been in love with her pupil when he had grown to manhood.

'It must have been terribly sad for you when you left.'

'It voz. Of course I got ozzer employment in ozzer homes but zey were nothing like the life I had enjoyed with Helen and Richard.'

Not really knowing why he did so John took hold of Augusta's large hand and squeezed it.

'But you are quite happy now, aren't you?'

'Yes, I am content. Zat is all I can say.'

Afterwards, going home in the coach through the moonlight of that autumn night, he started to tell Elizabeth the story. But her head had descended on to his shoulder and he realized that she was dozing. He sat in silence, smelling the rich Devon earth giving up its autumn smell. Soon it would be Christmas and he must ask the Marchesa if he and his family could visit her again. But tonight his mind was too busy to deal with thoughts of the festive season. They ran over and over the events of the evening: of Cuthbert Simms's strange fluctuations of colour, of Augusta Schmitt's sad story of a life lived in genteel poverty. Until she had met and fallen in love with Richard – for the Apothecary was sure that that was how it had been.

He closed his eyes but visions of the long-dead Helen flashed before them. He saw a lovely young girl dying of consumption, but somehow his mind could not agree with the picture. He started to wonder then precisely how she had died and determined that he would go and see the German governess and ask her exactly what happened. As he too dropped off to sleep, the Apothecary's thoughts were in turmoil.

Sixteen

It was at exactly three o'clock in the morning that John Rawlings sat bolt upright in bed. Beside him the face of his little clock in its leather case was bathed in a shaft of moonlight that had stolen in between the closed curtains. But it was not to this that the Apothecary's attention was drawn. In fact his brain, still somewhat dulled by recent sleep, was trying to remember something of vital importance which he had recalled as he was waking but had now forgotten again. Struggling to bring the thought back, the Apothecary looked round the room.

He was alone in one of the many guest beds, hung with drapery and exceedingly fine in proportion. Elizabeth had gone to sleep in her own suite, overtired as she was after the exertions of Lady Sidmouth's ball. Angry with himself that his memory had failed him, John got out of bed and walked slowly to the window, his feet cold upon the wooden floor. He paused a minute before throwing back the curtains to reveal a landscape bathed in the cold unearthly light of the full moon. Not a creature moved, not a leaf stirred. It was just as if he were gazing on a painted theatrical set.

He had a sudden desire to be out there, to be a part of that mysterious and strangely-lit whole. With this mood upon him John removed his nightshirt, put on a pair of drawers, fastening them with a string around the waist, and pulled on a pair of breeches. Rapidly finding a shirt and leaving the neck open, he put on a cloak and silently made his way downstairs. Creeping through the sleeping house like a shadow he made his way to the kitchens and out by the door at the back, afraid to swing open the huge front door because of the noise.

Once outside John started to walk briskly, the autumn air striking him with a sharp chill that penetrated his thick cloak and made him shiver. Yet he relished the exercise, hoping that it would stimulate his brain into remembering the vital information that had come to him in his sleep. He tried to recall the conversations of the night before. He had spoken to Lady Sidmouth, of course, and to Elizabeth, naturally. He had had a conversation with Cuthbert Simms, had passed the time of day with several other people, including Grevil and Dorinda Sedgewick, who had giggled more wildly than ever at the sight of him. Then had come the time he had spent with the evil-tongued Miranda Tremayne, the glacial Paulina Gower, and finally the large and fishy-eyed Fraulein Schmitt. One of those people must have said something that had triggered off the nocturnal thought processes. But what was it?

Far below him the River Exe glinted like a silver mirage in the unrelenting moonlight. John stared down at it feeling as if he were the only human being alive, that he had been transported into a strange fairy land where he was the only creature breathing.

Mentally he ran through the various conversations he had had. All pretty ordinary except for the nasty Miranda who had inferred that Elizabeth was old enough to be his mother. He changed his thought patterns abruptly, still shocked by the girl's innuendo. And then his mind turned to that last chat he had had with the formidable German woman. He recalled feeling sorry for her because of some incident in her past. He strained to recall exactly what it was she had said. And then it came to him. Surely she had told him of a Helen and Richard? Surely she had told him that Helen had died in tragic circumstances?

Where else had he heard this story? But the Apothecary knew the answer almost before he had asked himself the question. The girl who had been shot by her father had been called Helen and her brother, who had shut Vinehall Place up and moved to London after the terrible circumstance that had befallen them, was called Richard.

With a grim smile on his lips the Apothecary ceased walking and headed once more for the great house in which Elizabeth and her unborn child slumbered in peace.

'You are quite positive, Sir, that the names were the same?' asked Joe Jago, pensively sipping his ale.

'Completely and utterly,' answered John.

'I see,' said Sir John Fielding's clerk, and relapsed into thoughtful silence.

They were sitting in The Blackamore's Head in Exeter, having arranged to meet there at Lady Sidmouth's rout, where Joe had distinguished himself in the dances and whirled about with a great deal of elan. Now, though, the clerk looked grim-faced as he considered the import of the Apothecary's words.

'They are not uncommon names, Sir. It could be a mere coincidence.'

'It could indeed. But there is one sure way to find out.'

'Question the German lady further.'

'Not a task to which I look forward with relish,' John answered with a sigh.

'Would you care for me to do it?' Jago enquired.

'I would adore it but my belief is that she will take fright and start shouting at you.'

'She cannot go on shouting forever,' Joe commented reasonably.

'No, but she can do it for a mighty long while by which time you will be thoroughly worn out. No, Joe, much as I hate the thought I think the task befalls me.'

'Then I shall accompany you.'

But John's words of protest died on his lips as the doors to the tavern were swung open with a mighty thud and the Black Pyramid made a huge entrance, followed by the somewhat seedy figure of Nathaniel Broome, who sidled in behind him almost in an apologetic manner.

'Good gracious,' John hissed at Joe. 'It's the Black Pyramid himself. The fighter I was telling you about.'

'What's he doing here?' Jago muttered back.

'Heaven knows. But I'll soon find out.'

John rose, realizing as he did so that his head barely reached the black man's shoulder. 'My dear friend . . .' he began.

But the sentence was never finished as the Pyramid swung round and made a gloriously ostentatious bow.

'Why, if it isn't Mr Rawlings,' he said loudly, giving a brilliant display of flashing white teeth. He nudged his companion who gave a spluttering cough. 'Nathaniel, you recall the gentleman surely?'

'Oh yes, of course I do,' answered the other, wiping at his eyes with a brightly coloured but somewhat grimy handkerchief. 'Pleased to see you again, Sir.'

'Allow me to buy you a drink, Mr Rawlings. And what about your friend?'

'Joe Jago, at your service,' said the clerk, rising to his feet and giving a short bow.

The Black Pyramid looked at him with narrowed eye. 'I know your face from somewhere, Sir. No, don't tell me. I'll recall it sooner or later.' He turned back to John. 'Now, what are your orders, Mr Rawlings?'

Ten minutes later the four men were sitting round a table, each with a jug of ale before him, making idle conversation. But all the while John could glimpse the Black Pyramid eyeing Joe Jago in a speculative fashion. In the end he could no longer bear it. Wondering whether the former Jack Beef had guessed the truth, he asked, 'Have you solved the riddle of my friend's identity?'

'Yes, I think I have,' came the reply.

'And?'

'Well, Sir, it is either this gentleman or his brother that acts as clerk to Sir John Fielding and appears in court with him. Am I right?'

'Perfectly,' Joe answered promptly. 'It is not my brother it is myself. I take it you have observed me from the Public Gallery?'

'Of course. I have never been up before Sir John, though more by better luck than judgement.' The Black Pyramid chuckled softly to himself, a sound which made the other members of the group smile. 'I would have known you anywhere by your red hair which, as your wig slips often askew, is extremely recognizable.'

Joe snatched his wig from his head which he then scratched before saying, 'Then you can probably guess what I am doing in Exeter, gentlemen.'

Nathaniel turned his small-eyed gaze on him. 'No, I can't. What is your business here?'

'I have come to investigate the coach trip which ended in murder.'

There was a silence during which Nat Broome coughed loudly while the Pyramid continued to stare at Joe, his gaze virtually unblinking.

'I see,' he said eventually. 'On behalf of whom may I ask?'

'On behalf of myself,' Joe replied levelly.

'But surely Devon is beyond Sir John's or your jurisdiction,' said Nat, sliding his eyes round to look at Joe once more.

'Of course it is,' the clerk replied with a certain asperity. 'But I am down here for my own interest. I have known Mr Rawlings for many years, you see, and when he mentioned the strange affair in conversation I could not resist the temptation to take some leave and come to Devon and search for clues. Quite unofficially you understand.'

The Black Pyramid gave Joe an extremely odd glance. 'You did this just out of friendship?' His incredulity was audible.

'Most certainly,' Jago replied crisply. 'But anyway I needed an excuse to get out of London. The stinks are terrible, you know. Makes the whole air quite thick.'

The black man laughed, a warm seductive sound. 'You try boxing there in an indoor arena. The smell of sweat is positively acrid.'

'At least it's fresh,' John put in gloomily – and everyone chuckled.

'I've come down for a fight at Lord Lechdale's. That's to be tomorrow and held indoors. In his Great Hall I believe.'

'Well, I wish you luck, Sir.'

'I can get you an invitation if you so desire.'

Joe spoke at once. 'I should like that very much. I can think of nothing better than a good mill.'

'And I would like to go as well,' put in John.

'Tell me,' said Jago, having refilled everyone's tankard first, 'every-thing you know about the murdered man.'

Nathaniel let out a high-pitched laugh. 'Oh the investigation begins here, does it?'

'Most certainly.'

It was the Black Pyramid who answered him. 'I knew nothing of the dead man except that he seemed very irritable throughout the journey.'

John interrupted. 'But I thought he told Mr Meadows that he felt he knew you – had seen you before somewhere.'

The Pyramid raised a massive shoulder. 'My friend, I am a famous bare-knuckle fighter. Many, many people have seen me during the course of my career. I am hardly surprised the man thought he recognized me. It is a common occurrence.'

'I don't recall it being quite like that,' John answered quietly. 'You see I happened to come in on a conversation between the deceased and Martin Meadows in which Mr Gorringe swore he knew you.'

'So?' said the black man, a steely look in his eye.

Joe cleared his throat. 'So we must accept your explanation.'

Nathaniel was looking decidedly uncomfortable. 'I always said that that Gorringe would make trouble.'

Joe's eye caught John's for the briefest second then flickered away. He stood up.

'Gentlemen, it has been a great pleasure speaking to you.' He produced a watch from a pocket in his waistcoat. 'Goodness me, I am late for my next appointment. I must go forthwith.'

John got to his feet. 'I'll walk with you a bit of the way, Joe.' He bowed. 'Goodbye gentlemen.'

The two men rose and returned the salutation, then huddled over their ale, their heads close together.

Once outside the tavern John turned to Joe Jago. 'Well?'

'They were lying through their teeth, both of them.'

'I thought as much.'

'They knew William Gorringe and he knew them. What we must find out is when and how well.'

The village of Sidford lay quiet beneath the noonday sun and John, looking at the rustic bridge with its usual passengers of slow-moving cattle, thought what a delightful setting it was. He imagined himself owning a house here, far away from London and its wicked life. But even as the idea entered his mind he knew that he would be quite incapable of leaving the metropolis and its many and varying excitements. He thought of Vaux Hall and the Peerless Pool, he thought of Chelsea buns and the Theatre Royal, he thought of the Hercules Pillars inn and the Foundling Hospital, and was aware that he loved London life with all its ugliness and wild raw beauty too much to consider moving away.

And just for a second he felt as if he had entered Elizabeth's mind and knew that just as he was an avowed Londoner, so was she a born countrywoman. And that she, too, could no sooner leave Devon with all its magnificent scenery and that it was ridiculous to think of her ever doing so. He sighed then, wondering how often he would be able to see his child when it was born, and Joe must have heard him because he gave the Apothecary a strange look.

'Everything all right, Sir?'

'Yes, I'm fine.'

'You're sure?'

'Positive.'

'Then let's go and find the redoubtable German lady.'

But when they knocked at the door of the house only the little maid answered, bobbed a curtsy, and said, 'The ladies have gone away for a few days, Sirs. They felt that they needed a little holiday.'

'Where have they gone, do you know?'

'Cornwall, Sir. To the town of Padstow. Mrs Mitchell has a friend there and they have decided to call on her. Shall I say you came?'

'Please do. Do you know how long they are staying?'

'About a week, Sir.'

'How very unfortunate,' said John as they stepped back into the waiting trap, a mode of transport they had hired to get them around.

'It is indeed, Mr Rawlings. But I am sure we shall find ways of occupying our time.'

'How exactly?'

'By going to see the Black Pyramid fight for a start.'

John smiled crookedly. 'I can't think of a better way of spending an evening.'

As he said this he thought of Elizabeth and hoped that she would forgive him the minor falsehood.

Seventeen

The candles were being replaced by servants, the wine decanters too, and bets were being laid by the hordes of people present, which, somewhat to John's astonishment, included several members of the fair sex. And what women they were. Pretty, painted dolls – patched, powdered and pretentious – vied for attention along-side big, bosomy buttocks, with low-cut gowns and leering smiles, many of which displayed brown rotting teeth. John thought, running an interested eye over them, that they all looked like products of a Covent Garden whorehouse serving both ends of the social scale.

He and Joe Jago had arrived at the home of Lord Lechdale an hour earlier, driving along in the dying light of the sun. It had been an amazing experience to pass through a landscape from which the colour was slowly being bleached away, watching the trees and fields grow dark then black, with here and there a point of light where something caught the amber rays and was brilliantly reflected. As they had approached Wych Manor every window in the place had gleamed red, while the building itself had appeared gaunt and unreal. But as they drew nearer and the sun moved round they saw that it was after all a Tudor mansion house lit with nothing more than candles and that their eyes had been affected by the strange light of sunset.

The fight was to be held in the Great Hall which had at one time been the entire house, medieval in its origins, the rest of the building having been created by later members of the family. In this Hall Lord Lechdale had constructed an arena by dint of placing together a host of sturdy trestle tables and on this cordoning off a ring with rope. At the moment the ring stood empty as the guests mingled, drank and eyed up the women. John noticed an old fellow, wrinkled and gnarled as one of last Christmas's nuts, with a whore on each knee, caressing them both, while they, in their turn, each had a hand on his vital parts to his obvious great delight.

Joe grinned. 'Poor old dolly monger. He's having the time of his life.'

'And not only him,' answered John, and pointed to where the youthful Grevil Sedgewick was succumbing to the charms of a beauteous young whore.

'Oh dear, oh dear,' answered the clerk, scratching his head so that his wig sat askew. 'I hope someone has told him the facts of life.'

'Well, if they haven't he's on the point of finding out,' answered John, and held out his glass for a refill.

At that moment a thunderous voice called for silence and into the expectant hush came the announcement, 'My lords, ladies and gentlemen, may I present to you the Black Pyramid.'

Looking as if his body had been recently oiled the black man stepped into the ring, the ropes held up for him by Nathaniel Broome, and raised his hands above his head. There was a roar of approval from the crowd gathered, many of whom had seen him fight before and who had staked a great deal of money on him winning again.

'And now, gentlemen, Mighty John Elmwood.'

A man who lived up to his name clambered into the ring to receive a slightly less enthusiastic welcome. But for all that he was a marvellous sight, standing at least six feet five in height – a veritable giant – and packed with powerful muscles and enormous arms. Looking at him, John had a sinking feeling. He ran his eye over the man's heavy breasts, thick neck, and the tracery of black hair that encased his entire body, and silently said a prayer for the Black Pyramid.

Bets were being laid and men crowded round the ring. The whores watched idly, fanning themselves with affected boredom, except for those who had made a conquest and disappeared with their victims. The gnarled old man had sought a private chamber with both his women and young Sedgewick had disappeared in the company of his doxy, presumably to have the veils finally removed from before his eyes.

Lord Lechdale stood up and declared the bout about to begin but was drowned out by a great roar of cheering and shouting. Nat Broome whispered some final instructions to the Black Pyramid and stepped out of the ring. John drew a breath.

With a fleetness of foot that the Apothecary had not realized he possessed, the Black Pyramid began to circle his man, landing a punch now and then which the mighty fellow obviously considered no more than he would a fly settling on him. His tactic was clearly to land a punishing blow on the black man's jaw and send him flying to the floor. However he had some difficulty in achieving this because the Pyramid stayed just out of arms' reach, constantly dodging and weaving his way around the ring.

John turned to Joe. 'I've got a feeling he's going to lose.'

'He can't do that, Sir. I've just bet a guinea on him.'

The bell went for the end of round one and more bets were placed and a great deal more wine consumed.

'It's a good match though,' said the clerk, removing his wig and displaying to the world the thatch of red hair that lay beneath.

'I think we'll see some action now,' John answered.

He was right. Mighty John Elmwood put on a sudden turn of speed and rained blows down on the top of the Black Pyramid's head. Hurt, the black man punched at his opponent's chest and actually got into a clinch with him. The referee, a small neat man dressed entirely in white, circled them trying to break the hold but neither of the two fighters were listening to him. Instead they parted of their own accord and stared at one another menacingly. Then the Pyramid shot out a snake-like arm and landed a terrific blow on the point of Mighty John's chin. The great man rocked back on his feet but stood his ground, having first spat out a tooth with all the nonchalance of one disposing of a quid of tobacco. Then he thundered after the Black Pyramid at full pelt. There was a cry from the crowd as the black man fell to his knees.

'This is it,' shouted John, aware that he was about to lose two guineas.

'God's teeth but I think you're right,' answered Joe, jumping to his feet.

There was a huge roar as the white man, apparently forgetting that he was in a boxing tournament, picked up the hapless Black Pyramid and threw him clean out of the ring and flat on his back onto the stone floor. The referee raised one of Mighty John's huge arms, like the side of an ox, above his head and shouted, 'The winner'. The boxing match was over.

John got to his feet and was immediately surrounded by a crowd of pushing young men, some jubilant, some downcast, depending on whether they had lost or gained small fortunes. They were shouting excitedly at one another, refilling their wine glasses, and generally charging about. But the Apothecary was making for the figure lying motionless with only one person taking any notice of him at all, that being Nathaniel Broome. Feeling somewhat anxious, John knelt down beside the unconscious Black Pyramid and felt for his pulse. It was faint but it was there.

'Can you lift him?' he said to Nat. 'He'll get trampled to death in this melee.'

'If you can assist me, Sir.'

Together they lugged the massive frame to a side of the room, John taking the head end, Nat the feet. The black man was packed with muscle that weighed heavily, so much so that both men were gasping by the time they put the fighter down again.

'Has he been knocked out before?' John asked, dragging in breath.

'Oh yes. Once or twice. But this is the most severe beating he has ever had.'

'I'll try to bring him round. Go and fetch a damp cloth, there's a good chap.'

Joe Jago appeared at their side, squatting down and peering into the Black Pyramid's face.

'Still alive I see.'

'But in dire need of revival. Lift his head, Joe.'

Scrabbling round in his pocket the Apothecary located a small bottle of salts which he placed under the Black Pyramid's nostrils. The black man's eyelids twitched and his eyes opened, then rolled up in his head alarmingly. At that moment Nat reappeared with a grubby cloth which John put on the bare-knuckle fighter's head.

'What happened?' asked Jack Beef, rolling his eyes down again.

'You lost the fight,' Joe answered with a glint of icy humour.

The Black Pyramid gave a groan and gingerly shifted his shoulders. 'I'm in agony,' he said quietly. His eyes closed once more. 'I haven't had such a beating since the night Mr B . . .'

'Keep quiet,' admonished Nathaniel urgently. 'Don't talk. It's bad for you.'

'I think we should try to move you,' said John as the circle in which the black man lay began to grow smaller as the rips of Exeter crammed forward to claim their winnings. He looked at Joe and Nat. 'Help me get him to his feet.'

With a great deal of effort and cries of 'Heave', John and Joe managed to raise the Pyramid up, where he stood with buckled knees, lolling like a large dark doll, an arm round each of their shoulders. Nathaniel, meanwhile, propped him up from behind, sweating with the strain.

'Time to go I believe,' said John, and this said the party left the Great Hall, solemnly bowing their heads to their host who stared at them astonished as they passed by.

Once outside, the three men managed to haul the barely conscious fighter into the coach that Elizabeth had loaned John for the evening.

'Where are you staying?' the Apothecary asked Nathaniel.

There was a momentary pause. 'With friends in Exeter.'

'Then we'd best take you back there.'

It seemed to John, ministering to the Pyramid as best he could in the small space and the darkness, that the coach trundled its way through the night interminably. Lord Lechdale's mansion was situated outside Exmouth and they crossed the wooded land that lay between there and their destination with an almost creaking slowness. Occasionally the wounded man let out a deep-felt groan but other than the flicking of his eyelids gave little sign that he had regained consciousness. He was naked except for the tights he had fought in and a cloak which Nathaniel had flung hastily around him, and was shivering with the cold.

'It is kind of you to take us back to our lodging, Sir,' said Nat, breaking the silence.

'We could hardly have abandoned you,' John answered. He changed the subject. 'I think you should send for a physician in the morning. Jack Beef is in a poor state.'

'Oh, he'll recover,' Nat answered, almost in an offhand manner. 'He's endured worse than this in his time.'

'But I thought he rarely lost a bout.'

'That is true, he doesn't.'

'But you said . . .'

John was interrupted by Joe. 'Draw your pistols, gents. I think we are about to be visited by a gentleman of the road.'

Peering out of the coach's window John saw a shadowy figure moving amongst the trees. 'I'm not carrying a weapon,' he said. 'Are you?'

For answer Joe gave a quiet laugh and drew from the depths of his coat a gun, the butt of which shone silver in the dim light. But his fears were false. The figure disappeared into the woodland and the coach trundled on in peace.

'I wonder who that was?' John murmured.

'Probably one of Lord Lechdale's men,' answered Nat.

'Why should he be following us?'

'Who knows?' came the laconic reply.

Forty minutes later they reached the outskirts of the city and entered through one of the gates.

'Leave us here, gentlemen, if you would,' said Nathaniel.

'Why, is your lodging close at hand?'

'Just across the road. We shall be all right.'

'But you can't manage the Black Pyramid on your own.'

'He'll walk the few final steps.'

'No he won't. Not without help,' John answered firmly.

The coach pulled to a stop and the three men heaved the fighter's inert body out into the street. The Pyramid, meanwhile, was groaning and muttering, quite definitely alive but lacking any will of his own.

'Gentlemen, please leave us,' said Nathaniel with a certain amount of force.

John and Joe did not reply, too out of breath staggering beneath the formidable weight.

As if by magic the door in the house they were approaching opened and a figure stood silhouetted by the candles which burned brightly behind. John stared, hardly able to believe his eyes. It seemed as though the Black Pyramid and Nathaniel Broome had sought lodging with somebody they had met on the coach on their original journey. For it was Paulina Gower who stood there in the darkness waiting to greet them.

Eighteen

'You are sure it was her?' said Joe Jago. stretching himself and still managing to look alert despite the fact that he was yawning.

John put out a hand and touched his arm. 'Positive. Look, Joe, I know this is rather late in the day but will you come and spend the night at Elizabeth's house? I really need to talk to you about this case and we can be private there. Besides it is time you caught up with her again.'

'It will be a pleasure to do so, Mr Rawlings. But I have no clean linen with me. No shaving accoutrements.'

'I can lend you anything you like. Joe, please come. I honestly feel as if I am walking through a maze.'

'Very well, Sir. You have persuaded me. Now, as to Paulina Gower, could it not be mere coincidence that she has rented a room in the same house as the Black Pyramid?'

'But you saw her. She had heard them coming and opened the door to greet them. Surely that is the act of an established friendship. What is going on, Joe?'

'I have no idea, Sir. But as long as she did not get a good look at me I intend to play the role of an ardent admirer and theatregoer who has followed her down from London particularly to see her Lady Macbeth.'

John fingered his chin, a sure sign that he was thinking. 'The light from the door was shining out but you and I stood in the shadows. I would not be surprised if she saw neither of us.'

'Then as soon as I am back in Exeter I shall start hanging round the stage door.'

'A very good plan. Did you notice how insistent Nat Broome was that we should not accompany them to the house?'

Joe nodded. 'Yes, he was pretty firm about that.'

'Then that means that he was afraid we would find out how friendly they are with Miss Gower.'

'No, steady down, Sir. As I said, it could all be a coincidence.'

'There are too many coincidences for my liking, Joe.'

And the Apothecary proceeded to run over the facts of his seeing

Lucinda Silverwood and Jemima Lovell in Lewes, the names of Helen and Richard which had occurred in connection with Vinehurst Place and had then been repeated by Fraulein Schmitt, the fact that William Gorringe had thought he recognized the Black Pyramid.

'They could all be explained away, Sir.'

'I know that. Yet I feel that there is a thread here. Though what it is I have no idea at all.'

'No more have I, Mr Rawlings. But let us hope that something comes up.'

A short while later they turned into the uphill drive that led to Elizabeth's house and Joe, peering out of the coach's window, let out a low whistle as the mansion, lit from outside by lamps, came into view.

'By Jove, Sir, this is something of a palace. I had not expected anything quite like this.'

John laughed. 'You wait till you see inside.'

The coach drew up at the front door which was opened by a liveried footman who bowed to them both.

'This is Mr Jago,' said John. 'I have invited him to spend the night here.'

But he got no further. There was a cry from the staircase and Elizabeth, clad only in sleeping clothes and a night-rail, rushed towards Joe and gave him a smacking kiss on the cheek.

'My very dear friend,' she said, 'I could not greet you properly at the ball t'other night for fear of throwing light on a blind man's holiday. But I cannot tell you how very pleased I am to see you again.'

Joe bowed low. 'And in much happier circumstances, Madam.'

'It seems an age ago now. But you look well, Joe. Come and sit down and tell me all that you have been doing.'

'Precious little, my lady. I lead a dull old life in London.'

'Now that I do not believe.'

As they had been talking she had led Joe into the mighty entrance hall and John smiled to himself to see his old friend's jaw drop open as he took in the details of the painted ceiling with Britannia crowning all.

Elizabeth laughed. 'You remind me of John when he first saw this place. I think he was quite awestruck.'

'I was,' the Apothecary answered. 'With you as well,' he added in an undertone.

She ignored that remark and went sailing ahead, her arm linked through Joe Jago's, chattering and laughing. John stopped in his tracks, filled with a sudden joyfulness that he should have been blessed with such marvellous and giving friends. Friends who knew him well and would forgive him his many trespasses. Friends who would ask no questions but always be at his side when danger threatened. He laughed aloud and Elizabeth turned her head to look at him. She gave him her incredible smile.

'You are happy?'

'Yes,' he said. 'I am truly very happy indeed.'

He and Joe sat up late – Joe smoking his long pipe and drinking port, his wig, which he had slapped back on his head at the sight of Elizabeth's house, at a very rakish angle.

'Well, I reckon we've said all about the case that we can possibly say, Sir.'

'I still think I should go back to Lewes, Joe. There's some link with this affair that none of us can see at the moment.'

'Not before you've visited Fraulein Schmitt again.'

'No, I think that she might hold the key. So shall we go down to Padstow and see if we can find her?'

'I don't see why not. But on the other hand perhaps we should leave the poor old dear in peace until her holiday is over.'

'Very well, I'll be guided by you, Joe. But don't forget that Sir John has given you a fortnight's leave and no more.'

'That thought is uppermost in my mind. So how can we usefully employ ourselves tomorrow?'

'I can call on the Black Pyramid and see how he is progressing.'

'A good idea. You must do that. While I shall go accourting Mrs Gower.'

And so saying Joe downed his port before giving the most enormous yawn.

He was up and out and away at daybreak, leaving John to glimpse his departing figure, riding tall in the saddle, his back straight as a tree. As he watched the departing figure, the Apothecary felt that next to his father he loved Joe Jago more than any other man alive. Then he thought of Sir John Fielding and considered that he was the kind of person that one could not really love as a companion, being too grand and huge an individual, a monumental man in every sense of the word.

For some unknown reason John felt in the mood to hurry and washed and dressed himself rapidly before descending to breakfast. But even sitting before the meal he loved best the restlessness persisted and his eyes kept wandering to the window and the landscape outside. The golden weather continued, despite the fact that it was nearly October. The hills were shot with rose, but where the shadows fell they were purple, dark and mysterious, while the river far below wound like a curling blue ribbon, twisting in the autumn sunshine.

John got to his feet, itching to do something to break the deadlock that this investigation had reached. Indeed he had got as far as leaving the room and going out into the huge entrance hall when he heard feet upon the stairs and, turning, saw that it was Elizabeth, up and dressed and ready for the day. He crossed to the bottom step and watched her descend, loving the way she moved, her body growing larger but still elegant and supple for all that.

'Good morning, my darling. Joe Jago has already gone I fear. He has left you a note − quite formally written − thanking you for your hospitality. I have read it because it was addressed to me as well.'

Elizabeth looked at him seriously. 'John, why are you so uneasy?'

He put his arm round her waist as she arrived at his level. 'Because I think this case is virtually dead. There have been several remarkable coincidences but none of them makes any sense to me. I cannot find the common thread that is running through the whole thing.'

'Is there nothing you can do?'

'I could go to Padstow and ask Fraulein Scmitt to whom she was referring the other night.'

'You mean her mention of Helen and Richard?'

'Yes. But Elizabeth, Joe has advised me not to go. To wait until the poor old dear gets back from her holiday.'

She was silent a moment, her black hair swept up in a pinner, her scar distinctly visible in the morning light, her head slightly bent in concentration. Then she looked at him.

'Do you agree with him?'

'Yes and no. But I feel that if I don't do something I shall go mad.'

Elizabeth smiled. 'Well, we can't have that, can we? Last time you and I paid a visit to Cornwall I came back with this.' She laid a hand on her rounding. 'So let us see what I come back with this time.'

'You mean you would journey with me?'

'Of course. Padstow is not that big a place. Someone is bound to know where they are staying.'

'Very well. When shall we leave?'

'Now. Straightaway. I shall write to Lady Sidmouth and tell her I shall be gone for a few days. And you must write to Joe at his inn. Come along. There is no time to lose. We leave within the hour.'

And she was right. As ten o'clock chimed the last pieces of luggage were being loaded onto the coach and John was helping her into her seat beside him. He turned to her. 'You are quite sure about this?'

'Absolutely positive.' She took his hand and he felt her excitement like a tangible force running into his fingers. 'It will be a mighty adventure. It is time I got out and about and saw something of the world again.'

'And the child?'

She looked at him serenely. 'The child will be well, never fear.'

They travelled up through Crediton, heading over the edge of Dartmoor until by mid afternoon they had reached the town of Bude. Here Elizabeth insisted that they stop for the night as she had no wish to exhaust the horses. They found an inn which was simple but adequate and Elizabeth clapped her hands as she saw the downstairs parlour with its beams, its inglenook in which burned a fire of both coal and logs, and its big oak refectory table on which gleamed various copper pots.

They dined on lentil soup, a capon and a neat's tongue and afterwards they strolled out along the quaintly cobbled streets and smelt the salt of the sea. Then they went to bed and slept like two children, side by side, hardly moving. John, happy to be doing something, anything, to get nearer the solution; Elizabeth content to see him so.

The next morning they set off and arrived at Padstow in the afternoon. But first they drove along the coast track and at John's insistence stopped the coach that he might see the vastness of the ocean. He and the Marchesa stood on the cliff top and said nothing, awestruck by the majesty of the sight before them.

Below, far below, wave upon wave rolled in to shore in a ceaseless flow of tumbling water, each white peak breaking relentlessly upon the yellow sand. The ocean was alive with movement, swelling in great blue humps, rising in cream-topped ripples, glinting aquamarine as it crashed down onto the strand. It was a sight that impinged itself onto the Apothecary's pupils so that in the weeks after he could recall it as if it were before him still.

Slowly he turned to look at Elizabeth but she was gazing out to sea, her eyes clear, her features strong, her shoulders carried proudly, a strand of her hair whipping out on the gusting wind. At that moment he felt immensely grateful that she was carrying his child and he took her hand and held it as if they were the only two humans left alive in all that vast and thundering landscape.

They walked back to the coach in silence, subdued by the mighty splendour they had just witnessed and they exchanged few words until they reached the town of Padstow where they booked themselves in at The White Hart, a coaching inn misted with time.

John turned to Elizabeth. 'The hunt is on for Fraulein Schmitt. Will you come with me or would you rather rest?'

She gave him an amused smile. 'My darling, you go out before it gets dark. I shall wait for you here. I am not as young as I used to be and I find I get tired more quickly.'

He seized the wayward lock of hair. 'You will always be young to me.'

'That is because we are soul mates.'

'Then why don't you marry me? Give the child my name?'

'Because it would not be fair on you,' she replied simply, and after that would say no more, so that John was forced to kiss her and set out alone into the cobbled streets of that ancient Cornish town.

An enquiry at the haberdashers – from where he bought for Elizabeth a beautiful lace cap trimmed with violet ribbons – brought him the information he needed. A Miss Davenport had visitors, both of whom had been brought into the shop and greatly admired the goods, and neither of the ladies was English.

'Did one of them have rather a loud voice?' asked John, fishing in his pocket for some money.

'Oh very much so, Sir. Why, do you know her?'

'Indeed I do. I shall call on them forthwith. Now can you tell me where Miss Davenport's house is situated?'

'Yes, Sir. It is on the incline above the harbour. It stands alone and looks out towards the estuary. You can't miss it. It has a balcony on the first floor.'

It was a pleasant walk down to the estuary, with the smell of salt in his nostrils and the high, mad cry of gulls, wheeling in the sky over his head.

A knock at Miss Davenport's door brought no reply at all, not even from a servant, and John, somewhat disappointed, walked down to the harbour and sat on the wall, where he stared out to the estuary of the mighty river Camel conjoining with the sea. Yet despite the tranquility of the scene, the calmness of the afternoon, John had a feeling he had had many times before. That something, somewhere was wrong. That events were about to take an amazing – and possibly alarming – turn.

Nineteen

How long John sat there, absorbing the sights and smells of the busy harbour, he never afterwards knew. But eventually he noticed that the shadows were lengthening and a chill was coming into the evening, consequently he got up and started to walk back to The White Hart. As he passed the small incline on which Miss Davenport's house had been built, he glanced up towards it, then stopped dead in his tracks. A procession was making its way towards the place: a procession consisting of two weeping women, followed by a couple of burly fishermen carrying a stretcher between them, and a raggle-taggle horde of onlookers, mostly children. Not knowing quite what to make of it, John simply stared.

It was with a shock that he recognized one of the women. It was the little round lady, Matilda Mitchell. Shaking with tears, she had a handkerchief held to her eyes and was being supported by a taller, thinner woman, who had clutched her firmly by the arm. Without hesitation John ran up the path towards them. And then he caught sight of who was being carried on the stretcher and exclaimed aloud. So bruised and battered that it was barely recognizable lay the body of Augusta Schmitt, though whether alive or dead was impossible to tell. Her clothes were shredded to ribbons, her face was pulped, her skull a mass of blood. If John had not known who she was he would not have been able to discern her features.

'God's holy wounds!' he muttered under his breath. Then clearly to Mrs Mitchell, 'My very dear lady, what has happened?'

She lowered the handkerchief and looked at him with eyes puffy as oysters. 'Mr Rawlings, it is you, isn't it?'

He gave the briefest of bows. 'I am on holiday in Padstow, Ma'am. I was sitting on the harbour wall and I noticed your sad procession. What has occurred?'

'My sister, Augusta, she . . . she fell . . . off the cliffs.'

'Off the cliffs?'

'Yes. We took Miss Davenport's trap out some way, then we walked . . .' She could not go on, her voice choking on sobs.

But already into John's mind had come a picture of a lone figure, gazing out at the very vista that he and Elizabeth had looked at earlier in the day, then tumbling off the top of those treacherous cliffs, a dark figure etched black as it fell to its death below.

'Is she . . .?' He could not bring himself to say the word.

Matilda Mitchell shook her head. 'She clings to life but only just. Some fishermen picked her up and made a crude stretcher. They brought her back in the trap. Miss Davenport and I . . .'

But again she could not go on. John put a comforting arm round her shoulders. 'If you would let me examine her, Madam. I am an apothecary.'

She did not answer for they had reached the front door. With trembling fingers Miss Davenport unlocked it and the fishermen carried their burden within.

'Put her on the floor, lads,' said one, and they gingerly laid Augusta down. John crouched beside her, doing his best to relieve her suffering but with nothing further to help him than his smelling salts, which would have been cruelty itself to put to her nose. Instead, with the aid of one of the fisherfolk he gently lifted the suffering woman onto the sofa and arranged cushions beneath her shattered neck.

Matilda came into the room and collapsed in a small spherical heap at the sofa's side. She looked up at John from streaming eyes.

'Is there any hope for her?' she asked quietly.

He slowly shook his head. 'The injuries are too severe. It's a miracle that she is still alive.'

He leaned forward as the dying woman let out a groan of pain and slowly opened her eyes. She had lost one in the fall so all he could see was a huge black bruise with a bleeding hole in it, the other was protruding from its socket in quite the most bizarre fashion. John realized as she turned her head slowly that Augusta Schmitt had totally lost her sight. She began to speak in an un-recognizable voice.

'It voz a game, all of it, Matilda. We vere very good at it, you know.'

'Hush, my dear. Save your strength.'

'Ve deceived zem all, ve did.'

'Yes, I'm sure. Now, try to rest.'

'Is Mr Rawlings zere?'

John spoke. 'Yes, I'm here, Madam.'

'It voz all make believe, Sir.'

'Thank you for telling me,' was all he could think of saying, though he had no idea what she was talking about. Then a different thought came to him. 'Were you standing alone on the cliff tops, Miss Schmitt?'

'The sea called me,' she answered him, and her voice had dropped to a whisper. 'I heard its song.'

'Yes, but were you alone?' he asked, more urgently.

'Vere is Matilda?' the governess said, her voice suddenly changed.

'My darling, I am here,' her sister answered, perching on the sofa beside her, attempting to pick her up in her arms, though John cautioned otherwise.

There was a momentary silence, then Augusta Schmitt said, 'Helen, my dear,' let out a sigh, and became dead weight in Matilda's grasp.

'Oh, God's holy life,' said the little woman, her sobbing hushed in horror. She gazed down at her sister. 'Is she . . .? Is she . . .?'

John knelt down and felt for the pulse but there was nothing, all stilled and quiet. He looked up.

'I'm sorry,' he said. He stood, leant over the corpse and closed that terrible eye. Matilda fell against his legs, her storm of weeping returned.

'My dear Mrs Mitchell, her death has been a mercy. She could not have gone on living in the state she was in. I am sorry but it was inevitable.'

'But she was my sister,' sobbed the little woman. 'I know she may have been loud and terribly overbearing but I have known her all my life and I assure you it will be quite empty without her.'

'I'm sure it will,' said John, gently drawing her to her feet and leading her out of the death room and into the small room next door where stood the figure of the tall Miss Davenport. She looked at him with an enquiring face and the Apothecary nodded. Miss Davenport made the sign of the cross.

'Would it be possible for Mrs Mitchell to have a brandy?' he asked.

'We could all do with one,' she answered, and having finished crossing herself made for a cabinet from which she produced a bottle and glasses.

Having motioned Matilda into a comfortable chair she thrust a brimming receptacle into her hand. 'There you are, my dear, drain that and you'll feel better.' She turned to John. 'I didn't catch your name, Sir.'

He gave a short bow. 'These are hardly the circumstances in which formal introductions can be made alas. But my name is John Rawlings and I am an apothecary of Shug Lane, London. I already know you as Miss Davenport.'

She gave a bob. 'Sibyl Davenport, Sir.' She lowered her voice. 'What tragic circumstances and what a completely shocking thing to happen.'

John motioned to a chair. 'May I?' She nodded and he sat down. 'Tell me, were you near Miss Schmitt when it happened?'

'No, truth to tell, Mrs Mitchell and I are not particularly keen on standing on the edge. We were sitting down on a rug and Miss Schmitt wandered off on her own.'

'But within your sight surely?'

'Barely.'

'What does that mean?'

'We could see her out of the corner of our eye, as it were, but we were busy chatting to one another and were not actually looking at her.'

'I see.' John stared at her very straightly. 'There is no possibility, I suppose, that she was not alone up there?'

Sibyl returned his stare. 'What are you saying?'

He came straight to the point. 'That Miss Schmitt might have been pushed over the edge.'

She went very pale. 'No, absolutely not . . . and yet . . .'

'And yet what?'

'As I said, we were not regarding her all the time. In fact neither of us saw the fall. We only started up when we heard her terrible cry.'

'I see,' said John thoughtfully.

'But what you are saying is ridiculous, Sir. Who would do such a thing? A wandering lunatic? And why should he pick on poor Augusta ? No, it is quite out of the question.'

'Unless, of course, she had an enemy,' John answered into the stillness.

'And what did she say to that?' asked Elizabeth, her face animated in the glow of the candles which were lighting herself and John as they ate a rather late dinner.

'She couldn't reply of course. But at that moment poor Matilda started moaning and wailing and my full attention had to be turned to her. She had been listening to our conversation and the very thought of her sister having been pushed to her death had upset her terribly.'

'I am hardly surprised. But do you think it is possible?'

'Yes,' John answered thoughtfully. 'I do think that is what might have happened.'

He had stayed with Mrs Mitchell until the Constable had come, this one a fisherman who had been loath to do his duty. Eventually the body had been taken off to the mortuary to await the findings of the Coroner and as John had watched the last of Augusta Schmitt being driven away in a small, sad cart – decently covered he was glad to observe – he had felt more than a pang of sorrow for the formidable German woman. He thought of their first meeting when she had regarded her fellow travellers with a fishy eye and uttered a string of complaints. Strangely, he had almost grown to like her.

His mind ran over her last words. What had been a game that they all played? Could she possibly have been referring to something long ago? Had she played some game with Helen and Richard before the girl's sad demise? The Apothecary shook his head, realizing that the questions he had planned to ask Augusta about the origins of the brother and sister would now remain unasked.

'You are sighing,' said Elizabeth.

'Yes, I am indeed. Sweethheart, do you realize that with the death of Augusta Schmitt the trail goes cold once more? I really thought I had a lead with her reference to Helen and Richard but now I shall never find out.'

'Why not ask Matilda?' Elizabeth said practically. 'She is bound to know where her sister worked.'

The Apothecary put his hand over hers where it rested on the table.

'That is an extremely good idea. But I daren't say anything yet. The poor creature is too overwrought.'

'Why don't you call on her tomorrow and take some things from the apothecary's shop with you? After all it would be a kindness if you did.'

'Actually I had planned to do just that.'

'If she would not think it an imposition I would like to come

with you. If the poor wretched woman does not wish to see me
I shall understand perfectly. On the other hand she might enjoy
the company of a stranger.'

'Who knows?' John answered. 'I simply cannot imagine being
in her position. But it is kind of you to offer. You are a good
woman, Elizabeth.'

She smiled. 'I would hardly have applied that description to
myself. I have led too wild a life and you know it.'

'Perhaps motherhood has calmed you down.'

She laid a hand on her body. 'I must say that this little creature
has slowed me up, but as to calming me down I really cannot
agree.'

'Have it your way,' said John, smiling back. 'I have no wish for
an argument.'

The Marchesa suddenly looked very serious. 'John, do I give
you a miserable life?'

He contemplated, thinking about the differing emotions that
she brought about in him. 'Not really,' he said eventually.

She kissed his hand and said, 'Tell me.'

'If you want to know, I am not certain myself. I adored being
married and yet I sometimes felt I was getting staid and a little
dull. But when I became a widower I have never known such
grief. Now I want to marry you but I know that that dream will
remain unfulfilled; yet even if it were not, would we be suited in
the long run? So sometimes I am happy and sometimes I am sad.
And at the moment I am a mixture of both. Sad because of the
terrible events of today, happy because I am here with you. Sad
because I must soon go back to London, happy to see you thriving
and well. And extremely happy when I think of the child that is
to come. For if it is a girl and inherits your beauty, then she will
be an outstanding person.'

'And if it is a boy who takes after his father in both looks and
personality, then we will have a fine son indeed.'

He leant across the table and kissed her, regardless of the other
people in the dining parlour. 'May I propose a toast to the future?'

She raised her glass. 'Please do.'

'To our son or daughter. May they know prosperity and good
fortune.'

'May they do so indeed.'

★   ★   ★

They retired to bed early, having walked a little after dinner. But John's night was fraught with unpleasant dreams. In his imagination he stood once more on the cliff tops and, though he struggled to move found that he was immobilized and thus watched helplessly as an unknown figure fell down and down to the beach below. Then he was once more in the coach journeying to Devon, sitting opposite the Black Pyramid who had grown to the stature of a veritable giant, while a skeleton sat in the corner, a skeleton with a fishy eye that turned its head and grinned at him. The Apothecary woke, drenched in sweat, terrified that he had shouted and woken Elizabeth. But she slumbered beside him, peaceful as a baby.

John got up and crossed to the small window, looking out at the sight of Padstow by moonlight. Nothing stirred except for an occasional marauding cat. Yet he knew that not far away in the mortuary lay the body of a woman who, on a simple visit to the town, had met a cruel and untimely end.

Twenty

The coroner had released the body and pronounced that Augusta Schmitt had died an accidental death. Matilda had immediately arranged for the coffin to be transported back to Sidford on a cart so that her sister might be buried close by in the parish church. Elizabeth had offered the unfortunate woman a ride back to Devon but had been politely refused. Mrs Mitchell and the sensible Miss Davenport were enduring the rigours of travelling with the departed to make sure that the coffin arrived safely. John had most sincerely wished them a safe journey and had stepped into Elizabeth's carriage feeling what it must be like to be a member of the privileged classes and always travel in comfort.

He had arrived back at the Marchesa's house in a positive spasm of impatience to see Joe Jago again.

'He'll only have a few days left before he must return to London,' he said by way of explanation as he immediately went to the stables to find himself a reasonably placid mount.

Elizabeth waved a hand. 'Oh be off with you! Go and find your red-headed alter ego and give him a kiss from me.'

So, despite it being late afternoon, John set forth and found Joe Jago in the taproom of The Blackamore's Head in company with the Exeter Constable, no less.

'Hah,' he said, arriving at their table in a whirl, 'the two men I most wanted to see.'

They both looked up in surprise and Joe sprang to his feet. 'Mr Rawlings, I hope I find you well. How was your visit to Padstow, Sir? Did you get the information you wanted?'

'No, I did not. But thereby hangs a tale.' And sitting down beside them John proceeded to tell them everything that had taken place since he had last been in Exeter. They listened in astounded silence until Joe finally said, 'So you believe Miss Schmitt was pushed?'

'There is no way of knowing. I spoke to the fishermen who picked her up from the beach but they saw no-one.'

The Constable spoke. 'Forgive me if I sound a little slow, Sir. But why should anyone want to shove the lady off the cliff?'

'Because of a possible link with something in the past,' John answered. 'She mentioned a Helen and a Richard to me. Those were the names of the people who lived at one time in Vinehurst Place in Sussex. The place we agreed I should visit.'

Toby Miller sat silently for a moment or two, considering what he had just been told, then he said, 'But there is no firm connection between William Gorringe and the house you visited, Mr Rawlings, as we both hoped?'

'None at all.'

'I see.'

Joe Jago pulled thoughtfully at his ear lobe. 'I have explained to Mr Miller that I am clerk to Sir John Fielding and that I am here to assist you, Mr Rawlings. But as far as I can see the case must now be closed. We have reached an impasse, as it were. The chances that Helen and Richard were connected in any way is extremely remote. Furthermore I must return to London in two days' time. I am sorry that I have been unable to help you further.'

John smiled ruefully. 'You've done your best, Joe. I know you tried hard. By the way, how did you get on with Paulina Gower?'

A dull glow appeared in the clerk's rugged cheeks. 'A very pleasant lady,' he said non-committally.

John, who had found her sharp and unhelpful, looked at him in some surprise. 'Oh,' he said, but decided to leave his most searching questions until later.

Toby stood up. 'I am sorry, gentlemen, but duty calls.' He turned to the Apothecary. 'I am afraid that I agree with Mr Jago, Sir. There is nothing further I can do in the case of the murder of William Gorringe. Should any further evidence come to light I will naturally pursue it. But, alas, I think that is now highly unlikely.'

John was forced to agree. It seemed as if every door had slammed shut in his face. He bowed to the Constable.

'It's been a pleasure to make your acquaintance, Sir. Were you in London I would recommend you as a court runner to Sir John.'

'Hear, hear,' said Joe.

They watched the man go out and Joe, looking at his departing back, said, 'An excellent worker, that one.'

'Yes, indeed.' John's eyes glinted. 'Tell me about Paulina? I take it you got on rather well.'

The colour returned to the clerk's craggy face. 'I found her very charming actually, Sir.'

'Do I detect a hint of romance?'

'No, good heavens, nothing like that,' Joe protested loudly. 'I pretended to be an admirer of her theatrical work and as a result we became quite friendly.'

John collapsed into a fit of wild giggling. 'Oh, Joe, I do wish you could see the expression on your face. You resemble a naughty boy who has been caught at the jam pot.'

The clerk assumed a dignified air which drove John to further excesses. He chortled loudly and clutched his sides, tears pouring down his cheeks.

'I am glad that I give you cause for amusement, Mr Rawlings.'

John calmed down, thinking that he might have wounded his old friend's feelings. But he still had the strongest suspicion that all was not quite above board as far as Mrs Gower was concerned. He wiped his eyes.

'Tell me, did she explain how she came to be sharing lodgings with the Black Pyramid?'

'She said that she struck up an acquaintanceship with him on that original journey and that they have remained cordial ever since.'

'I see. Did you believe her?'

But it was a superfluous question. Joe Jago had clearly done so, more than a little swayed by the power of Paulina Gower's middle-aged charms. John clamped his lips shut and said no more.

'Well, Sir, where do we go tomorrow?' asked the clerk, pointedly changing the subject.

'I would be most obliged if you would attend the funeral of Miss Schmitt with me and Elizabeth. I think it will be a very small affair and I know that Mrs Mitchell would be grateful for all the support she can get.'

'I shall certainly do that, Sir.'

'Good. Then perhaps you would ride out to the big house at eleven o'clock. We can take a coach from there. On second thoughts why don't you come and dine with us tonight and spend the night. I know Elizabeth would be pleased.'

The clerk drained his ale without answering and John guessed with unerring accuracy what he was going to say next.

'I'm sorry, Sir, I have a previous engagement.'

The giggles – not far away – threatened to come back. 'I see. Anywhere interesting?' John asked innocently.

'I am going,' replied Joe Jago with enormous dignity, 'to the theatre.'

Sidford had one parish church and it was to this that Elizabeth's carriage made its way at twelve noon on the day following. John had prearranged that Joe should escort the Marchesa inside while he would follow some ten minutes later and take a seat at the back where he could observe. Much to his surprise when he did eventually enter the church's shadowy interior he saw that the place was full. It seemed that the entire village had turned out in support of Matilda Mitchell and John was hard put to find a pew at the far end. Sitting down, he saw something even more astonishing. Also present – and sitting near the front at that – were the Black Pyramid, Nathaniel Broome and Paulina Gower, all dressed in solemn shades. Remembering how the black fighter had physically put Miss Schmitt out of the coach when they had travelled down with the murdered man – a journey that John felt he could never forget – the Apothecary felt frankly astonished.

The coffin entered, carried by six stout men, followed by Mrs Mitchell, heavily leaning on the gallant Miss Davenport. A couple of elderly people walked with them who John presumed must be friends of the family. Another surprise. The Black Pyramid solemnly rose to his feet and stood with bowed head as the casket passed by him. Nathaniel Broome and Mrs Gower did likewise and the Apothecary felt more puzzled than ever. It was just as if they were paying their final respects to an old friend.

The vicar started the words of the funeral service in a dreary voice most suitable for the occasion. As always John took this as his moment to look round. There was nobody else there from the original coach party but as he had already noted the church was packed with depressed-looking villagers. He concluded that Matilda Mitchell must be a doer of good works and popular with one and all.

He looked again at the extraordinary trio and saw that the Black Pyramid was leaning forward, his clasped hands between his knees. John could have sworn that a tear glistened on the negro's cheek. The other two, however, sat impassively enough, their faces betraying nothing.

Eventually the procession to the grave began and the Apothecary lingered behind as was his usual way. Joe Jago appeared beside him, temporarily leaving Elizabeth to talk to other members of the congregation.

'Well, my friend, what did you observe?'

'I was somewhat surprised to see the Black Pyramid here,' Joe answered.

'I presume that Mrs Gower told you she would be present?'

'Yes, she did. The reason she gave was that she had grown friendly with the German lady during the trip to Devon.'

'I see.' John hesitated about saying anything further, aware that Joe and the actress had struck up some kind of *rapprochement*. But he knew perfectly well that that statement was a lie, that Paulina had had little time for the late Fraulein Schmitt. However he decided to keep this information to himself for the time being. Instead he said, 'I thought I saw the black man weeping.'

'Unfortunately I was sitting in front of him, Sir, so I did not really get a good look behind me.'

'But why should he do that, Joe? That is the question worrying me. Surely it couldn't have been an attack of guilty conscience?'

The clerk's face took on its famous foxy expression. 'I shouldn't have thought he would go that far however badly he felt about his treatment of Miss Schmitt.'

'There's something odd here,' said the Apothecary thoughtfully.

But their conversation ceased abruptly as the black fighter himself strode down the path towards the grave. He paused on seeing them.

'Gentlemen,' he said in tones of great astonishment.

'We came to pay our respects,' John answered hurriedly. 'Tell me, are you fully recovered? The last time I saw you you were in a bad way.'

'I am much restored, thank you. Nat and I will be returning to London in a day or two. I feel I am now ready to undertake the journey.'

Mrs Gower appeared, walking sedately, a pace or two in front of Nathaniel Broome. She dropped a demure curtsy and John thought that her friendship with Joe had improved her manners enormously.

'Why, Mr Rawlings, what are you doing here?'

'I might ask the same of you, Madam.'

'I have come to pay my respects to the departed.'

'Likewise,' said John, and bowed.

Joe Jago stepped forward. 'May I offer you my arm, Mrs Gower?'

'I will accept it gladly,' she responded, dropped the merest hint of a bob, and went trotting off with him down the path towards the grave.

John fell into step with the Black Pyramid, Nat walking a pace behind.

'I didn't realize that you were so friendly with Miss Schmitt,' he said conversationally.

The black man turned on him an uninterpretable look. 'Neither did I realize about you, Mr Rawlings.'

It suddenly seemed to the Apothecary that the conversation could proceed no further. That every remark he made would be met with the same steely resistance. Yet he knew that there was something deeper in all this mystery. That the whole thing was an enormous puzzle. He also knew that he would not stop until he had solved it completely and totally.

Suddenly, on his way home from the funeral, the Apothecary's mind was full of his daughter. Every day he had thought of her and missed her but now he felt a vital urge to take her in his arms and cuddle her. So much so that he felt determined to accompany Joe Jago back to London, provided that this did not upset Elizabeth. Thinking over his situation the Apothecary realized with a kind of helplessness that he was in a very difficult position. When the baby was born next February he would have one child living in Nassau Street, another just outside Exeter. Clearly something would have to be done about it though at the moment he could think of no practical solution.

He and the Marchesa dined together quite informally, having a table set in one of the smaller dining-rooms, and when the meal was done they withdrew to a drawing-room, rather than the grand salon. They sat in front of the fire and Elizabeth picked up a letter she had received.

'John,' she said without preamble, 'I have received a communication from an elderly cousin of mine in Shropshire. He is not very well and I fear he may not be long for this world. I have therefore decided to go and see him.'

'Are you up to the journey?' the Apothecary enquired professionally.

She gave him a slightly cynical look. 'Of course I am. I shall travel in comfort all the way, so you need not worry on that score. But you, my dear, ought you not to return to London soon?'

Guiltily feeling that she must have been reading his mind, John replied nonchalantly, 'Now that you suggest it I feel I should. Rose must be missing me and, truth told, I am longing to see her again. As for Sir Gabriel, he is now a great age and I honestly ought to spend more time with him.'

'Then you must do so,' she replied. She leant towards him. 'Do you not think you spend too much of yourself on solving mysteries?'

'I have been telling myself that since I started working for Sir John Fielding,' he replied wretchedly. 'I felt it took me away from my wife, my father, my child. And yet I am obsessed with the whole idea. If a villain gets away undetected I feel that I have been personally beaten.'

She smiled, just a fraction sadly. 'I can understand that. I once felt similarly about the Society of Angels who brought about the ruin of my son. I could not rest until the last little verminous beast had been put down. But once they were gone all the anger went out of me and I have become a sober citizen.'

John laughed aloud. 'If you are a sober citizen then I am a Greek god.'

'Well?' she answered.

And they laughed together, in total harmony once more.

Later that night John went by coach to Exeter and booked in at The Half Moon. The stagecoach was departing so early in the morning that he preferred to get a good night's sleep to leaving Elizabeth at the crack of dawn. Yet as he said farewell to her and turned to watch her wave him goodbye he had the strangest feeling that it would be some time before he saw her again.

Twenty-One

It was when he reached Brentford that the Apothecary was struck by the feeling that all was not well at home. Into his mind came a picture of Rose, thin and pale and coughing, and he passed the rest of the journey in a fever of impatience to get back. Paying off the hackney which had transported him from the Gloucester Coffee House to Nassau Street, John ran up the steps and was just about to ring the bell when the front door opened to reveal the figure of what could only be a physician.

'Oh,' said the man, clearly astonished to find someone standing in the doorway. 'Forgive me, Sir, I was just making my way out.'

'You've been to call on a member of the household?' John asked, though he knew the answer even before the man spoke.

'Sir Gabriel's granddaughter, I'm afraid.'

The Apothecary gave him a stricken glance, said 'Excuse me,' and fled past the physician into the hall and up the stairs. Without pausing for a second he flung open the door of Rose's bedroom, then stopped as he took in the scene before him.

Sir Gabriel Kent, arrayed in negligent style, sporting an elegant cap upon his head, his shirt unbuttoned, the collar loosely turned down to reveal a ribbon band fastening, a great long gown over the whole ensemble, was sitting quietly on Rose's bed, gently stroking her hand. The child herself lay amongst the white bedclothes, her face an almost identical shade, racked by a most unpleasant cough that had a deep sound within it as if the child were fighting for breath. John's adopted father turned his head at the noise of the intrusion.

'My boy, I was on the point of writing to you to beg your return. Rose is stricken down as you see.'

'How long has she been ill?'

'Three days. Dr Wilde says it is a chin cough.'

'He's probably right. What has he prescribed?'

'I don't know. He's gone round to the apothecary now.'

'Then I'll save him the trouble. Rose must have Sundew. It is the finest form of treatment for such an illness.'

Sir Gabriel sat up straight and looked at John with such a deep expression that his son caught his breath.

'I am pleased you have taken control of the situation.'

'It is not all that common a herb but I have some in my shop. Father, let us send a footman round there posthaste. I'll write a personal note to Mr de Prycke to ask him to compound.'

'Of course. It shall be done at once. And may I say, my very dear child, how good it is to have you at home. Promise me that you will stay with us for a while.'

John put his arm round the old man's shoulders. 'Father, I would never go away again if I had freedom of choice but I cannot desert Elizabeth. Not . . .' he added in a somewhat cynical voice, '. . . that she needs any protection from me.'

'But your duty lies here as well, John. I quite understand about the Marchesa di Lorenzi but meanwhile your other child is in dire need of you.'

'Well, I am returned,' John answered, and throwing off his cloak went to sit beside Rose and take the pale little hand that lay so still upon the counterpane.

'Papa,' she whispered, though her eyes did not open and other than for that whisper she seemed to be utterly lifeless.

'I am home, my darling, and I will not go away again,' he answered.

The fingers tightened round his but she made no further response.

John fought hard to control himself. The guilt which he had felt recently was redoubled in strength and his thoughts ran down a million alleyways as he contemplated the future. But with a tremendous effort he brought his emotions under control. Rising from the bed he crossed to where Sir Gabriel had taken a chair.

'Father, call the nursery maid. She must sit with Rose while I write to Mr de Prycke.'

Sir Gabriel replied with much dignity, 'I prefer to keep the vigil, John. I would not like my granddaughter to feel that she has been totally deserted.'

Wounded to the heart but determined to keep himself in check, John hastened downstairs to the library where he called a footman and simultaneously wrote a prescription for his shop. But at the last minute he hesitated. He did not like Mr de Prycke and Gideon was still too inexperienced to be trusted with such a vital matter. There was nothing for it. He would have to make the distillation himself. He rattled an instruction to the hovering servant.

'Simmons, run into the street and fetch me a chair. I must go to my shop immediately and I need to be quick.'

The man hurried away and John called up the stairs, 'Father, I'm going out. I don't trust anyone else to make up the physic for Rose.' Then he went out of the front door as two stout fellows with a chair between them came up to it. 'The apothecary's shop in Shug Lane,' he said and got inside.

To him the journey was tediously slow, stopping for carts and coaches and large ungainly members of the population. But at last he pulled up outside his familiar – and somehow badly missed – premises and, paying off the chair men, bolted inside. Gideon, looking terribly grown-up and smooth, was standing on the far side of the counter wearing a long, dark robe.

'Good gracious, Gideon,' John exclaimed, 'you dress more formally than I do.'

His apprentice's mouth dropped open. 'Sir! I didn't know you were coming back. What a surprise. How very nice to see you.'

'I'm afraid I have no time for pleasantries,' John said, going straight to the compounding room, simultaneously throwing off his cloak. 'I am worried about Rose's cough and I have come to make her a distillation of Sundew. Where do you keep it?'

He was searching amongst the bunches of dried herbs hanging from hooks in the ceiling. Gideon broke out in a sweat.

'Master de Prycke got rid of that, Sir.'

'What do you mean got rid of it?'

'He sold it to an apothecary in Seething Lane. He was desperate for it – the man I mean. I am sure Master de Prycke meant well.'

'I am sure he did,' John answered through gritted teeth. 'But Rose's life might hang in the balance. Now where can I get some?'

'You could try Master Berry in Piccadilly, and, failing him, Master Wisley in Duke Street.'

'Shut the shop,' John ordered, staring at the stupefied apprentice. 'Now! You go to Duke Street, I'll try Piccadilly. Here's some money. Pay whatever is asked. And Gideon, please run as you've never run before. Do it for Rose.'

And with that the Apothecary was off, sprinting like a hare – the movements of which his own occasionally resembled – towards Piccadilly.

Sundew, otherwise known as *Drosera Anglica*, was a fairly rare plant, grown mostly in Scotland and Ireland. Because of its rarity it was dear to buy but John always kept some in stock having observed over the years its extremely beneficial effects on chin coughs, coughs which made a whooping sound, bronchitis and other illnesses of the chest. But many apothecaries did not stock it, considering it too expensive and believing it only suitable for application to warts.

Master Berry fell into this category and John, feeling frantic, turned in the direction of Duke Street only to meet Gideon at the top, red in the face and gasping but brandishing a parcel which he waved frantically in John's direction.

'Got it, Sir.'

'Thank God! Let's get back to the shop.'

They ran all the way, Gideon being far the faster was ahead of John sufficiently to allow him to open up and let in a grumbling Mr de Prycke.

'Why did you lock up in the middle of the day, boy? I can't take my eye off you . . .'

'He did it at my behest, Mr de Prycke. You apparently sold the last of my Sundew to another apothecary. And now I need some urgently for my daughter.'

De Prycke's face took on a slightly cynical expression. 'Is the poor child suffering with warts?'

John did not answer but made immediately for the compounding room, Gideon hot upon his heels. Mr de Prycke hovered in the doorway.

'May I assist?'

'Thank you, but no,' John answered, trying to hide the irritation in his voice. 'If you wouldn't mind taking over behind the counter.'

'But Gideon . . .'

'Gideon knows my ways,' the Apothecary answered abruptly and turned away to the pan of water which he had placed on an oil-lamp and which had already started to bubble.

An hour later and it was done. The plant had been boiled in just the right amount of water and now stood cooling on the side. John turned to Gideon.

'You can hurry on home, my boy. I'll bottle this up as soon as it has cooled down. You are to explain to Sir Gabriel the cause of the delay. Now, look sharp.'

The apprentice struggled out of his long black garb and into his cloak, then bolted out past a staring Mr de Prycke.

'Really . . .' he started to exclaim but John forestalled him.

'I've sent him home early, Mr de Prycke. And I shall shortly be returning myself. Would you mind very much locking up before you return to your lodgings?'

'On that point, Mr Rawlings, may I enquire whether you have returned to us for good? Or is your intention to take your leave again? I merely ask because I want to know where I stand.'

John answered without hesitation, somewhat irritated by the man's attitude but determined to remain civil. 'I am back to stay, Sir.'

'Does that mean you will no longer be requiring my services?'

'Mr de Prycke you are more than welcome to work out the rest of the time that we contracted. In fact it would help me very much if you did. I intend to remain at my daughter's bedside until she is fully recovered so I will not be able to devote my time to the shop.'

'In that case, Sir, I shall work next week and then I will take my leave of you. Quite frankly I find your apprentice a wretched little beast and I shall be glad to see the back of him.'

'I am sure the feeling is mutual,' John answered pleasantly and turned his attention to the pan of cooling liquid.

He arrived at Nassau Street to find Sir Gabriel reeling with fatigue, so much so that he had to be helped by a footman down the stairs. John, meanwhile, carefully measured out ten drops of the Sundew fluid into a small amount of water and raised the cup to Rose's mouth.

'Here, drink this, sweetheart. It will make you better I promise you.'

The poor child did not open her eyes but gulped down the medicine and immediately had a violent fit of coughing. John listened intently and recognized the familiar sound of the whoop. His heart sank, knowing that many a child had died of this illness, exhausted and fighting for breath.

He began to talk to Rose in a soothing voice. 'Papa is home now, darling. And he will stay at home until you are well and able to play games with him again. And then we'll all go off to Devon for Christmas and you can ride your pony. Would you like that?'

After a while he noticed that Rose's breathing had become a little deeper and realized that she had dropped off to sleep. He took a seat in the chair in which Sir Gabriel had sat and stared at her beautiful little face. She meant everything to him and he wondered how he could have left her for so long without the father she loved.

Suddenly he found himself questioning his relationship with Elizabeth. Was he a fool to have offered his love to her? Was he heartless for abandoning his family in order to pursue her? Yet she was soon to be the mother of his child as a result. Feeling ill at ease with himself the Apothecary rose and slowly began to pace the room.

The nursery maid arrived and said, 'I'll watch Rose now, Mr Rawlings. Sir Gabriel is waiting for you in the library.'

'Very well. Just for half an hour. But if she should wake you are to send for me immediately, is that clear?'

'Very good, Sir.' And the girl bobbed a curtsy.

Downstairs the library offered its usual warmth and comfort. A fire of coal and wood gleamed in the grate and the curtains were drawn against the night. In one of the two wing chairs set close to the blaze sat Sir Gabriel, his eyes closed, his breathing deep. John looked at him with enormous tenderness and tiptoed past him to pour himself a sherry.

'John?' said a sleepy voice.

The Apothecary turned. 'I'm sorry. Did I disturb you?'

'I was only dozing, my son. How is Rose?'

'She has fallen into a natural sleep. I have given her ten drops of the compound and will administer another ten in three hours' time.'

'And what is your prognosis?'

John sat down in the chair opposite and, putting his glass on a small table, leaned across the space and took Sir Gabriel's long and fine fingers between his own. 'Father, believe me, I am as worried as you but I have given her the finest medicine there is. I can only pray that her natural strength will pull her through.'

'I see. Pour me a sherry if you would.'

John did so and handed a schooner to the great old man who sat before him.

'I give you a toast,' said Sir Gabriel Kent. 'To my granddaughter's total recovery – and to her father's permanent return to London.'

It was on the tip of John's tongue to ask about his duties to his unborn child but something told him to remain silent. He looked at his adopted father with enormous love.

'I'll drink to that,' he said.

Twenty-Two

Throughout that night John administered the drops of Sundew to his daughter. He had not admitted to Sir Gabriel how terrified he was for the last thing he wanted was to add to his father's fears. But secretly he was in torment, his spirits never lower, as he contemplated a future without the shining presence of Rose. John had never felt closer to her than he did now, longing for that terrible cough to stop, longing for her to have enough strength to fight the illness away.

At about five o'clock in the morning he heard her speak and opened his eyes from where he sat dozing in a chair by the bed.

'Papa?'

It was said as a question and John immediately came to full consciousness and knelt down beside her, taking her hand.

'I'm here sweetheart.'

'I have seen Mother. She was here in the room with me.'

Despite himself John peered into the shadowy depths of the chamber, but nothing moved.

'What did she say?'

'Nothing. She just stood by the bed and smiled.'

'I'm glad she came to see you, darling. Now go back to sleep.'

'Will you stay with me, Papa?'

'I shall not leave your side until you are better.'

She turned to look at him, her eyes the colour of gentians. 'You promise it?'

'I promise.'

She slept a little after that but an hour later was woken by a violent fit of coughing. John, trying desperately to act as an apothecary rather than as a father, listened intently and thought that the whooping noise was diminishing. As soon as Rose had settled down once more he gave her some further drops of Sundew and at last saw the cold finger of dawn lay itself across the room.

The physician had sent round an infusion of Willowherb which, though effective in the cases of coughs, was nothing like as powerful as that which John had prescribed. The Apothecary decided that to mix them would not be advisable and therefore when the doctor called the next morning he saw his bottle of physic untouched.

'What's this, Sir. Have you not treated the child?'

'I most certainly have, Dr Wilde. I have given her Sundew and I compounded it myself.'

'I take it you are an apothecary?'

'Yes, Sir. I own a shop in Shug Lane, Piccadilly.'

'Then I see that the girl is in good hands. I'll examine her now, if you please.'

John stood aside while the physician bent over his daughter and thought how strange the world was. He had come back to London because Elizabeth had dismissed him and now he knew that he would never, could never, leave Rose again. Any future visits to Devon – or anywhere else for that matter – would be in the company of his daughter or not at all.

The doctor straightened up. 'There is a definite improvement, Mr Rawlings. If the child lives through today then she will survive. I shall call again this evening. Good day to you.'

He had spoken bluntly, as one professional to another, but John felt cold at the very words. Tired beyond belief he nonetheless sat beside Rose until she slept once more before sending for the nursery maid.

'I must go and change my clothes and get a bite to eat. You promise to call me if the child wakes.'

'Immediately, Mr Rawlings. You can rest assured.'

Sir Gabriel, looking rested but still drawn with worry, was sitting at the breakfast table, delicately peeling a grape. He looked up as John entered.

'How is Rose, my boy? Is there any change?'

'Father, there is. The doctor said there was a marked recovery.'

'And that is all?'

'All,' lied John, and gave Sir Gabriel a confident smile.

All that long, long day the Apothecary spent sitting beside his daughter, every four hours giving her ten drops of the substance, realizing that soon he would have to make up some more and wondering where he would be able to buy the herb Sundew. The physician called at five o'clock and pronounced that the child would live. But John already knew this; knew by the increase in his daughter's colour, by the way in which that racking cough was starting to subside. Though not a religious man by any means he found himself thanking God for Rose's return to life and at last, at long last, left the child in the care of her grandfather and staggered downstairs and into the library. He almost fell into one of the chairs and looked up as a footman entered the room.

'Is Master Purle at home?' he asked.

'Yes, Sir. He's in the kitchens.'

'Send him up to me, would you.'

The servant hesitated in the doorway. 'Miss Rose, Sir. How is she?'

'She will live, thank God. And thank you for asking. You may tell the rest of the servants.'

A few minutes later the figure of Gideon appeared at the entrance, looking slightly embarrassed at being invited into the inner sanctum.

'You sent for me, Sir?'

'Yes, sit down and have a drink with me. Rose is going to be all right, my friend. Thanks to your efforts to get Sundew.'

Gideon perched uncomfortably on the chair opposite John's. 'It must be running short by now, Mr Rawlings.'

'That's what I want you to do tomorrow, my boy. I want you to scour the apothecaries in London and buy some more of the herb.'

'I'll go and gladly. Poor little girl. I hope I'm not too bold in saying that she misses you, Sir.'

'No, Gideon, you are right to remark it. I have been away too long. In future I shall not allow my business in Devon to keep me there more than two weeks at the utmost.'

His apprentice gave him the kind of look that had doubt at its heart but merely nodded his head in silence. John poured him a glass of sherry, a decanter of which always stood in the library.

'There you are, my friend, drink a draught of that.'

Gideon did so – and choked, coughing and sneezing. John glanced at him with a smile.

'You're a good lad even if you have no head for alcohol.'

'Thank you, Sir. Though I am afraid that Master de Prycke would not agree with you.'

'I think,' the Apothecary answered with a smile, 'that Mr de Prycke likes no-one but himself.'

Three days later and John was walking down Greek Street when he suddenly stopped dead in his tracks. He was on his way back to Nassau Street from Shug Lane but had taken the long way round in order to buy some olives. In his pocket he had another bottle of physic for Rose, who by this time was sitting up in bed and reading, quite restored to her former self, her hair having regained its bounce and curling splendour, her skin its lovely creamy shade. The Apothecary, erring on the side of caution, had just prepared another tincture of Sundew for her – Gideon having located the dry herb somewhere in the city – and was making his way home having made his purchase, when his attention was drawn by a shop. It was a hat shop and in the window, just removing a creation of bows and ribbons from a stand, was someone he knew.

John stared and as he did so had the most curious sensation. It was as if he had seen the face he was looking at – a face that he knew reasonably well – before somewhere. But not exactly that. It was more as if the face reminded him of someone else. Just for a second the Apothecary nearly grasped who it was and then the whole thing slipped away and was gone.

The owner of the face was as surprised as he was and acknowledged his presence with a small bow of her head before she retrieved the hat and disappeared back into the shop. Unable to help himself, John went inside. A tall woman with a face that had once been pretty but was now beginning to show the signs of ageing, bore down on him.

'Can I help you, Sir?'

She made a coy mouth as she spoke and smiled at him by pulling both her lips upwards without any accompanying warmth.

'Yes, I want to buy a hat,' John answered.

In the corner he could see Jemima Lovell serving a short plump woman, who had removed her wig the better to try on headgear, and made her a bow.

'You know Miss Lovell?' asked the proprietoress.

'We have met,' John answered, and concentrated on the matter in hand.

'Is the hat for your wife, Sir?'

'No, actually it's for my daughter. She is only five. Do you have anything in a small size?'

The owner rearranged her lips to look motherly. 'Yes, we do. Miss Lovell perhaps you would like to serve the gentleman. I shall take over your client.'

Children's headgear clearly did not interest her and Jemima, having given the plump lady a polite curtsy, made her way to John.

'Mr Rawlings, what brings you here?' she asked in an undertone.

'Seeing you in the window,' he muttered back. Loudly he said, 'Please can you show me a selection of hats for little girls.'

'We do not have many. They are usually made by individual milliners.'

'Well if you would be so kind as to bring out what you have got.'

'Certainly, Sir.' And giving him a little bob she made her way into the back.

John prevaricated and procrastinated over his choice and during that time managed to have a *sotto voce* conversation with the girl.

'So your stay in Devon is over?'

'You knew that, Sir. Madam Sophie released me to Lady Sidmouth but then I came straight back.'

John, recalling the moment he had seen her in Lewes with Lucinda Silverwood, walking and talking so closely together, almost felt like contradicting her but held his tongue.

'Tell me, Miss Lovell, where do you live?'

She smiled. 'Very close by. In Thrift Street.'

'Then I wonder if you would do me the honour of coming to dine with me at my family home tonight. My father will be present. We eat at five, by the way.'

'That is when the shop closes. I could be there by half past.'

'Then I shall give orders for the meal to be served thirty minutes later.'

Eventually John bought two hats for Rose and made his way outwards carrying a couple of boxes. He had surreptitiously given Miss Lovell his card before leaving and she had whispered to him that it would be a pleasure to come. Feeling quite pleased with himself, John made his way home.

His father was sitting in the library dressed déshabille, a habit he was beginning to adopt more and more, John noticed.

'Father, I have invited a young woman to come and dine with us. I do hope you don't mind.'

Sir Gabriel sat up straight. 'Not at all, my boy. Tell me of her.'

'Her name is Jemima Lovell and she is the one person I believe is innocent of the crime that was committed in Devon recently. That is I am fairly positive it had nothing to do with her. Yet I believe that somehow she is connected . . .'

The Apothecary broke off and stared into space.

'What exactly *do* you mean, my dear?'

'I'm not sure,' John answered, coming back to earth with a thoughtful look on his face.

'Well, I must go and dress,' said his father, heaving himself out of his chair. 'I look forward to meeting this young woman greatly.'

'I shall change too, but first I must go and see Rose.'

'You will find her improved since this morning.'

John gave him a broad smile and rushed up the stairs with the two hat boxes. Not wanting to leave her as she turned her sweetest grin on him and put the hats, one after the other, on her head, the Apothecary found himself with precious little time to change. Despite this he put on evening clothes of dove grey with a pink waistcoat, and a fine shirt into which he pinned a brooch set with amethysts which glittered brilliantly when he moved. Coming downstairs he saw that his father was – as was ever his habit – dressed in sombre black with a white adornment here and there, the starkness of the ensemble relieved by a brilliant zircon, which shimmered a sparkling blue whenever Sir Gabriel made the slightest gesture. No sooner were the men assembled when there was a ring at the front door and John went into the hall to greet the new arrival.

'My dear Miss Lovell, how very nice to see you. I am afraid that the only other female present is my daughter and she is a little young to entertain you. So you will be the only woman sitting down to dine. I hope that is acceptable to you.'

Jemima gave a small curtsy. 'Perfectly, Mr Rawlings.'

'Excellent. Do come and meet my father.'

Sir Gabriel may have reached a great age but he had not lost one whit of his charm. John watched, very slightly amused, as Miss Lovell melted beneath the shower of care and attention that his father poured on her. And when they went in to dine Sir Gabriel stood tall and straight and courteously offered the dark-haired beauty his arm in order to support her. John was left to walk behind and notice how fine the pair looked as they made their way into the dining-room.

The meal was a great success, the cook having surpassed himself, and Miss Lovell declaring that each course was delicious. John, looking at her in the light of the many candles which lit the room, once again had the fleeting impression that she reminded him of someone but yet again was unable to recall who that person was.

'You do know of course that poor Fraulein Schmitt died very suddenly in an accident,' he said quietly, watching her reaction as he poured her a port.

She looked horrified. 'No, I had no idea. How awful. What sort of accident was it, pray?'

'She fell off a cliff.'

'Oh no! Where was this?'

'In Cornwall. She and her sister had gone to Padstow for a holiday but went for a trip to visit the cliffs near Polzeath. Miss Schmitt went off on a walk by herself and plummeted to her death.'

There could be no doubt that Jemima was genuinely upset, in fact she seemed more distressed than John would have expected in view of the couple's somewhat strained relationship.

'Please don't upset yourself,' he added. 'It was a terrible death indeed but I am sure she felt no pain.' He did not add that Miss Schmitt might not have died instantly but could well have crawled round in agony after her fall.

Sir Gabriel spoke up. 'I consider this a highly unsuitable conversation for the dining-table, my son. Let us talk of happier things I beg you.' And he led the chat to the amusements of London and whether Miss Lovell went to the theatre and, on hearing that she did, her thoughts on various plays.

John sat back and let them babble on but in a way he was slightly annoyed. He had intended to lead the talk to questions about whether Miss Lovell had seen anyone from that fateful coach party subsequent to her leaving Devon. Yet he knew that Sir Gabriel was right. He should not have broached the subject of Miss Schmitt's frightful demise when he had.

After dinner they repaired to the parlour, a room much used by Emilia but somewhat neglected of late. Jemima, it seemed, was reasonably good on the harpsichord and played them an air or two before rising to her feet and saying, 'Gentlemen, it is getting late. I am afraid that I must leave you.'

'Allow me to escort you home in my coach. I assure you it will be no trouble,' John offered, forestalling any objection she might make.

Travelling along in the darkness Jemima said, 'I had not realized you were quite so well-to-do, Sir. Your father is obviously a man of distinction.'

The Apothecary smiled. 'Has it put you off? I'm sure your father was someone of good quality.'

There was a fraction of a second's pause before she answered, 'I think he is one of the best men in the world.'

'So he is still alive?'

'Very much so,' said Miss Lovell, and with those words fell silent.

Twenty-Three

The next two weeks passed with the Apothecary feeling exactly as if he were living an orderly life. He rose early each morning, ate his breakfast, played with Rose for about twenty minutes, then walked to Shug Lane – the shop already opened by Gideon – and looked through calls booked for that day. Then, if there were none too urgent, he would go into the compounding room and prepare his herbs amongst the joyful smell of well-remembered things. That done he would set out at about noon to visit his patients and take with him the medicinal properties either prescribed by himself or by a physician. He would return home in time to dine and would then spend the evening chatting to Sir Gabriel or – now that Rose was getting so much better – venture forth to the theatre. He had also taken to visiting his friends again, seeing something of the now decidedly wealthy Samuel Swann, the de Vignolles, flitting between London and their Surrey home, and the great man himself, Sir John Fielding.

But none of these people quite compensated for the sight John had one day of King George, riding along and looking extremely cheerful in an open carriage, waving his gloved hand in a most amicable manner. The Apothecary waved back and bowed and by the time he had straightened up again the royal party had passed by.

The King had clearly been on his way to St James's Palace and had been heading down Piccadilly towards St James's Street. John had been standing on the corner of Swallow Street, bound to see a shopkeeper suffering horribly with trapped wind, when he had encountered the monarch. Having returned the royal salute, the Apothecary continued to make his way up the street when his eye was caught by a vividly painted and decidedly garish sign. It depicted a crudely painted representation of a woman's foot with pointing toe and a legend reading 'At Number twenty-four, Little Vine Street, Dancing Lessons are give daily at the hour of ten onwards for the sons and daughters of Gentlefolk. 1/6d per hour paid in advance. Persons of More Mature Years by Special Arrangement.'

What led John to walk past the place he could not have said but as he drew nearer he became more and more convinced that it had something to do with Cuthbert Simms. And sure enough as he drew within earshot he heard the sounds of a tune being scraped out on a fiddle and a familiar voice calling out, 'No, not like that. Like *this*,' followed by the sounds of scampering feet. Drawn as if by a magnet, John entered the premises and walked into the large room in which the dancing lessons were taking place.

It being during school hours, Cuthbert's class consisted of a half dozen or so middle-aged women – shopkeepers' wives John presumed – who were bored and had nothing else to do but gossip with their friends. Also present was a very elderly man.

They turned in a body at the sound of the Apothecary's entrance and he was fixed by a dozen pairs of eyes, ogling for all they were worth.

'Have you come to join us, Sir?' asked one, bolder than the rest.

'Well, I might try a step or two,' John answered, putting down his parcel of physic.

'Join in as best you can,' said Cuthbert snappily, not looking up from a sheaf of music which he had lying on the floor in front of him.

'Certainly, Mr Simms,' John answered, and had the pleasure of seeing the little man look up in some surprise.

'Well, if it isn't Mr Rawlings. Why, bless me! So you have returned from Devon, Sir.'

'As have you, Mr Simms. Alas, all good things must come to an end.'

'Indeed yes. But I must not neglect my work. Have you come for a lesson, Sir?'

'I'm afraid I don't have time. But I'll dance a quick measure now that I am here.'

'That will please the ladies greatly. Now form up. Several of you will have to take the man's part. Mr Ponsonby . . .'

There was no reply from the old fellow who stood, stumpy legs spread out, dusting snuff off his well-worn damson breeches, clearly not hearing a word.

'Mr Ponsonby,' Cuthbert yelled, 'we're just about to dance *Haste to the Wedding*.'

The old chap cupped his ear, gave a grin which revealed one or two rotting teeth and shuffled onto the end of the line. John, finding himself standing next to the old dodderer, gave him a broad smile. Mr Ponsonby replied by displaying his teeth and pushing up his wig which looked decidedly in need of care and attention. With a great show of bravado, Cuthbert Simms struck up.

The Apothecary, who reckoned himself a reasonable dancer, knew the steps and whirled through the set piece with great elan. Several of the ladies, however, grew out of breath and Mr Ponsonby surprised one and all by jigging about at great speed though not one whit in time to the music. In fact he seemed to be doing a dance that he had invented himself and gave an appreciative cackle if any lady should be so fortunate as to meet with him during its course. John decided that Cuthbert Simms truly earned his money and was pleased to produce a shilling and a sixpence which he pressed into the dancing master's hand as he made his way out.

'A break if you will, ladies and gentleman,' said the little man, perspiring copiously and somewhat red in the face. 'I really do not require this money, Mr Rawlings. Thank you all the same.'

'Nonsense. I enjoyed the dance and would have stayed longer but am on my way to see a patient. But I would appreciate it if we could have a chat some time. Do you live nearby?'

'My humble abode is in Great Wild Street, not far from the Seven Dials. It is very small and somewhat dingy.'

'But why did you choose this place to teach? Surely you could have found somewhere nearer?'

'Cost, Mr Rawlings. Cost.' And Cuthbert tapped the side of his nose. 'Besides the better class of person would prefer a dancing master to have rooms in a more prestigious part of London.'

'I suppose you're right. So could we not meet in a tavern?'

'Very well. The Royal Saracen, if that would be convenient to you. When did you have in mind, Sir?'

'Tonight. When you finish teaching. What time would suit you?'

'I shall close my classes early. Shall we say seven o'clock?'

'That would be most convenient. I shall just have time to see my daughter into bed.'

'Then seven it is, Sir.'

Having left the dancing class in full swing John hurried up Swallow Street to where a barber waited in a back room, groaning loudly, while his assistant was rushed off his feet with a queue of customers growing impatient.

'Heavens, Sir,' said John, opening his bottle of physic and pouring out a spoonful, 'I had not thought to find you in extremis.'

'I had a bite midday,' grunted the barber, whose name was Fields, 'and the pain has come on again. You are sure it is wind?'

'Positive. The physician has been to see you has he not and confirmed the diagnosis?'

'Indeed. But the pain is so intense.'

'Swallow this,' said John, and proffered the spoon.

The barber did so but still sat doubled up, his face pinched and pointed with pain. John decided on an old-fashioned solution. Taking his cane he laid it across Fields's stomach at the same time telling him to lean forward. Then he pressed as hard as he could and was rewarded by the barber letting loose a rouser, followed by another and finally a third.

'That's better,' Fields announced, standing up straight.

'Take the physic as prescribed,' John said, taking his handkerchief from his pocket and raising it to his nostrils. 'That will be two shillings, Sir.'

'Worth every penny,' answered Fields, and going to a small cupboard unlocked it and counted out the money.

'Back to work for both of us,' John said cheerfully, and giving the man a brief bow made his way out to Swallow Street and from there to Shug Lane where he and Gideon spent a pleasant afternoon compounding simples.

The Royal Saracen was in Newport Street, close to St Martin's Lane, and from the outside looked a reasonably well-run establishment. Stepping inside John was pleased to see that it was moderately clean and that booths had been set up in which people were sitting round tables. Spotting Cuthbert, who was looking somewhat exhausted to say the least of it, John made his way to join the dancing master.

'You seem weary, my friend.'

'Alas, I am. I feel I am getting somewhat ancient for this work. Believe me I was ready to lie down and die by three o'clock.'

'Oh, surely not. You don't look old,' John lied gallantly.

'I have been teaching the Terpsichorean art for forty years, my friend. I began as a bright young spark of twenty-odd and now you find me at sixty plus still nobly doing my best.'

John had a sudden rush of tremendous pity as he did for all old and benighted people who struggled to make ends meet and toiled themselves into the grave as a result. He turned to Cuthbert Simms with a look of great affection.

'It is working that is keeping you young at heart, Mr Simms. 'Zounds but if you were some retired old ninny with naught to do all day but sip chocolate and read the newspapers you would soon feel the pinch of the years. Why I shall continue to work in my shop until the day they carry me off, I swear it.'

'Well said, my boy. The only trouble is that my body is beginning to let me down, don't you know. I cannot caper as once I used.'

'You will have to get a young assistant.'

'But where to find the fellow at the price I can afford to pay him? That is the question.'

John looked sad and sipped his wine. 'Never mind. The right person may turn up. You never know.'

Cuthbert was growing somewhat red in the face and was imbibing quite freely and John, watching him, wondered whether it was going to loosen the man's tongue. He asked a discreet question.

'I'll warrant you were one of the finest dancers of your day, Mr Simms.'

'Oh, I was, my friend. Why I once led out the Princess Augusta.'

'The King's mother?'

'The royal lady herself.'

'And where was this?'

Cuthbert emptied his glass and held it out for a refill. John obliged.

'It was at a private party at which we were honoured with her presence. I did tell you, did I not, that I was once attached to a great household as dancing master to the young people?'

'Yes, you did. Did you live in or have lodgings nearby?'

'I lived in. The master of the house was very keen on his children having daily lessons, d'you see. Which suited me perfectly as an unmarried man.'

John hid a smile. The thought of a woman in his bed would undoubtedly have given poor old Cuthbert a fit of violent trembling. Small wonder he had remained a bachelor all his life. With a bit of an effort the Apothecary dragged his attention back to the conversation, praying that Mr Simms was going to fulfill his hopes and reveal more about his past.

'It sounds like a wonderful house. Where did you say it was situated?'

'I didn't – and I don't believe I will. You see a great tragedy took place there. Something which I feel I ought not to discuss.

All I can say was that my life was completely shattered. I had to give up my place and was lucky to get another at Lady Sidmouth's. But alas, as you know, her children grew up and I was out on the road again.'

'Poor Mr Simms,' said John softly, 'I wonder if it is true what they say about Vinehurst Place?'

'What do they say about it?' asked Cuthbert in a hoarse whisper.

'That the place is accursed,' John answered, lying through his teeth. 'That ill fortune attends all who live there.'

The dancing master rallied. 'I've never heard such nonsense. Where did you learn a story like that?'

John paused a moment before he spoke, realizing that Cuthbert had not contradicted him regarding the name of the house. Then he grinned. 'My dear Mr Simms, you are looking at an ape. I heard that legend an age ago about a place in Surrey and got totally muddled. Of course it wasn't Vinehurst Place. It was Vinecroft Manor. How utterly stupid of me.'

Mr Simms looked faintly relieved. 'Oh, that's as well.' He changed the subject. 'You told me you had a daughter who had been poorly. How is she now?'

'Much better, thank you.' And John rattled on until he had run out of things to talk about and poor old Cuthbert Simms's eyes were starting to close. At this the Apothecary rose, paid the bill, and escorting the old man into the street, called him a chair and a linkman and sent him happily on his way home.

An hour later John got into bed himself and lay awake for a long time. He had put his head round the door of Rose's bedroom and seen her sleeping peacefully, and had listened outside Sir Gabriel's door to hear his steady breathing. Up in the attic Gideon slept alongside the servants. The house was locked and shuttered and safe for the night. But sleep would not come to the Apothecary as his mind turned over the mystery of Vinehurst Place.

Had Cuthbert Simms been so overwhelmed that he had simply forgotten to say that the house in which he had once dwelled had not been called by that name? Or was his silence a kind of complicity? Had he lived in that beautiful place that John had seen standing so proud and so empty outside Lewes that day? Whatever the answer, the Apothecary knew that he must visit it again – and soon at that.

Twenty-Four

Rose was up early next morning and insisted on extending her playing time with her father, tickling him and making him laugh. She was in her sixth year and had all the beauty that childhood can bring with it. Her skin was finely textured, with a snowy quality relieved from being too stark by the poppies that glistened in her cheeks. Her eyes, a rich hyacinth blue, were wise yet had a distant quality about them. She was small for her age though neatly made, with delicate hands and feet and well-placed limbs. But her most attractive feature was her hair, a spiralling mass of red, rich and true in colour as a fox's coat. Where this colour had come from was a mystery to John though he presumed it must be connected with his unknown father, a member of the great Rawlings family of Twickenham. All he knew of the man was that he had been of good stock, had fallen in love with and made *enceinte* one of the serving girls, and had arranged to meet her when she had run away to London. His non-appearance had meant that both John and his mother had been forced to beg on the streets until they had been rescued by Sir Gabriel Kent.

The Apothecary always considered that his life had really started there. From dire poverty he had moved into comfort and cleanliness, a happy home indeed. Eventually Sir Gabriel had married Phyllida, John's mother, after he had taught her about the finer aspects of living. But she had died in childbirth – the baby daughter as well – and so the young boy had become the only child, the object of all the grieving widower's affection.

John often thought of how different everything would have been had Phyllida and the baby lived. He would have had a sister, maybe more than one; a brother too perhaps. He would have been able to watch his mother and his stepfather grow into old age together. There would have been peace and harmony and a great deal of love in the house. Yet he could not complain of lack of that. He had been frankly adored by Sir Gabriel but now John realized that that situation was drawing to its inevitable conclusion. His adopted father was over eighty and his time was running out. Soon John's only living relatives would be his daughter and the child yet to be born.

He hugged Rose tightly and she said, 'Why are you squeezing me?'

'Because I love you, my wild rosebud.'

'And I love you too, Papa. Do you still love Mama?'

'Of course I do. I shall never stop doing so. But love is a strange thing. It flows along like a mighty river which, in turn, flows into tributaries.'

'What are they?'

'They are the little rivers that come off the big one.'

Rose tossed her foxy mane. 'I don't think I quite understand.'

John stood up and took her hand in his. 'I think perhaps you will one day.'

'I hope so.' She looked out of the nursery window. 'Are you going to the shop today?'

'Yes, in a minute. When you give me permission to go.'

She smiled up at him. 'I don't mind it when you are in Shug Lane but Devon is a great way away, isn't it?'

'But you like it there. You like Mrs Elizabeth and your pony.'

Rose looked at him and said simply, 'I like anywhere that you are, Pa.'

'Are you trying to tell me you miss me when I am not here?'

'Very much,' she said, and pulled him down so that she could kiss his cheek.

He went to work shortly afterwards, his thought that he could never leave Rose again uppermost in his mind. One day he knew she would marry and live a great and successful life and part from him to go to her husband with much joy. But now she was young and soft and motherless, and needed a father to take care of her. She loved Sir Gabriel and he adored her but that was not enough. In future, the Apothecary decided, Rose would remain at his side until such time as she went to school. Indeed, when he returned to Devon – as the birth of the forthcoming child insisted he must – he would take his daughter with him and stay in an hostelry if Elizabeth refused to have her. But that situation was hard to imagine. The Marchesa was a wayward woman of strange and capricious temperament but she would never turn Rose away, indeed was fond of the child and spoiled her to a certain extent.

'Ah, good morning, Sir,' said Gideon, looking up from dusting the jars and alembics.

'Good morning to you. Gideon . . .'

'Yes, Sir?'

'I have decided to make a brief visit to Sussex and I wanted to discuss the details of running the shop with you.'

'Oh Zounds, Sir. You are surely not going to ask Mr de Prycke to take over again!'

'I don't think I could bear to make you suffer it. But I must find someone.'

'But why, Sir? You left Nicholas in charge once he had been with you a certain number of years. Why can't you leave me to manage the shop? I can deal with many of the patients and those that I think are beyond me I can ask another apothecary to attend to. I can serve potions and physics as well as you can. I promise you, Sir, that I will be industrious and mindful of your affairs.'

John gave a crooked smile. 'You certainly present a good case.'

'Sir, I will even sleep in the shop if you should wish. Anything but Mr de Prycke, I beg you.'

'I shall only be away for a few days, of course.'

Gideon did not answer but turned his large eyes on John and looked at him pleadingly. The Apothecary laughed.

'Very well, you may run the place in my absence. But anything that is beyond you – and I mean anything, Gideon – you are to send down the road to Piccadilly. Do you understand?'

'Yes, perfectly. Thank you, Sir, for putting your trust in me.'

'Well now, let us get on with the business of the day.'

John put on his long apron and walked into the compounding room as the door of the shop rang and the first customer entered the premises.

John let Gideon serve the sick that day, partly to give him good practice and partly because the Apothecary wanted to be silent with his thoughts. He had no firm evidence to go on but the thought that Vinehurst Place was somehow connected with the murder of William Gorringe was growing into something like an obsession. John knew that he would not be happy until he stood once more on the grass, looking across the space to where that beautifully proportioned and elegant piece of architecture, which now, to him, had become the House of Secrets, towered before him.

His mind then turned to Rose. He most certainly would not leave her behind and yet there would be times when the presence of a five-year-old girl might make life difficult. John pondered this and then the answer came to him. He would take Sir Gabriel as well, treat him to a little sojourn in the country, indeed get his views on anything he might discover in Lewes. Feeling suddenly cheerful he whistled as he made some suppositories in a special little rolling machine and Gideon, alone in the shop at that moment, joined in in a melodious light baritone voice.

Eventually it grew dark and the two of them locked up for the night, blowing out the candles and throwing covers over the various displays. Gideon turned the key in the compounding room door, while John locked the main door in the front. Tapers had just been lit in the rooms above the shop and the Apothecary felt reassured that two law students lived up there. He had heard tell that women visited them from time to time but other than for that – or perhaps because of – they were excellent tenants who paid their rent on the day it was due.

He and his apprentice walked home through the gloaming, John falling in love all over again with the city in which he had been brought up. He relished this hour of day when there was enough darkness to hide the filth in the streets, the dead dogs, the human detritus, the strewn litter. But the attraction of every window as it came to life, as chandeliers were hauled up, as servants drew curtains across the space, entranced him. There was a softness about it that appealed to him, a beauty that raised his soul. Beside him Gideon trundled along, whistling and cheerful, pleased that he had been granted jurisdiction over the shop in his master's absence. But John ignored him, in a kind of spell, adoring everything about this time of day including the delicious smells of dinner that wafted from the various residences he walked past.

Some twenty minutes later they arrived in Nassau Street where they parted company – Gideon going off to eat with the servants, John having a quick wash before he went to join Sir Gabriel in the library. Tonight Rose was still with him, wearing her night-gown, her feet bare and held out to the fire for warmth.

'Goodness, child,' said John, 'you're only half dressed.'

She turned to look at him, her hair glinting in the firelight. 'But I'm quite comfortable, Papa. Grandfather and I were just having a chat.'

'What about?' asked her father, pouring himself and Sir Gabriel a small sherry and handing the older man a glass before sitting down.

'About life,' she answered so seriously that John could not help but smile.

'What particular aspect were you discussing?'

'History, actually,' she answered, and gave him a look in which John saw Emilia.

He exchanged a glance with his father.

'I was telling Rose about the Great Plague of 1665 and the Great Fire that followed a year later.'

'The Plague, eh?' said John thoughtfully. 'That was a terrible time. Hundreds died every week. And no apothecary and no physician could do anything about it.'

'Is it true that the people were buried in plague pits?' Rose asked.

'Yes, there are several dotted round and about.'

'Where?' she enquired eagerly.

The Apothecary became deliberately vague. 'Various places in London. Their actual location is secret.'

'Why is that?'

'So that curious people won't go digging them up and start the epidemic all over again.'

Rose pulled a face. 'What a horrid thought. I do not care for the sound of it.'

John grinned. 'Then the best thing is to think about something else. How would the two of you like to come away with me next week?'

Rose jumped in the air. 'Oh, yes please. Where to Papa?'

'To Sussex. To a small country town called Lewes. I've got some looking around to do and it would be so nice to have your company. Father?'

'I don't know, my son. I don't move about much anymore as you well know.'

'Nonsense, Sir. You are known for your walks round Kensington.'

'They are on the level. I pant going up slopes and what I can remember of Lewes is that it is very hilly.'

'Indeed it is. But if we travel in my coach Irish Tom can take you wherever you please so that you need only perambulate on the flat.'

Sir Gabriel considered, putting his superbly turbaned head on one side so that the zircon adorning it glinted in the light of the flames. John, as he had so many times in his life before, silently drew breath in wonderment at the magnificence of the great man.

'Please come, Sir,' he said quietly.

Sir Gabriel raised his head. 'Put like that, my boy, it would be impossible to resist.'

Rose leapt to her feet and gave her grandfather a thorough hugging. 'T'will be a great adventure, Grandpa. We might discover something.'

'What sort of thing?' he asked, holding her at arm's length and looking at her quizically.

'I don't know exactly, but something exciting and mysterious,' Rose answered, and throwing her head back laughed the laugh of a happy child.

Twenty-Five

They set off in fine fig two days later. The coach which Sir Gabriel had given John for his wedding present had been newly washed and polished by Irish Tom, who was seated on the box wearing a long caped driving coat, boots and a three-cornered hat. A footman sat beside him acting as guard, while within a nursery maid – a quiet, shy girl, quite flustered by the thought of going to Sussex – excitedly adjusted her best scarf. She had dressed Rose very neatly in a dove grey travelling cloak and a straw hat trimmed with flowers, while Mr Rawlings himself was sporting the very latest fashion – a double-breasted coat. Sir Gabriel was resplendent in an old-fashioned but stunning ensemble of black with silver buttons.

John, not wishing to tire his daughter too greatly, decided that they would spend the night at East Grinstead which they made comfortably by early evening. They put up at The George and after Rose had gone to bed, John and Sir Gabriel enjoyed a meal together served with two bottles of particularly fine wine. Next morning they set off once more and arrived at Lewes some four hours later, heading straight for The White Hart. That done there were several hours before the time to dine and John filled these by taking his daughter and Emily, the nursery maid, on a tour of the town and a climb up the hill to what remained of the ancient castle. Rose gazed at the ruinous buildings wide-eyed.

'Does anybody live there, Papa?'

'No, I don't think so. It used to belong to the Earls of Surrey but the family died out and I don't think it's inhabited any more.'

'But I can see a lady sitting outside in a garden chair. There.' She pointed.

John stared and sure enough a woman in a pink gown wearing a shady hat was taking her ease outside the keep.

'You are right, Rosebud. Somebody is obviously in residence.'

And enquiries over dinner at the inn revealed that the castle, ruinous though it was, now belonged to the Earls of Arundel who had decided to convert the keep into a summerhouse and were currently in situ.

'I must say,' Sir Gabriel stated, having taken a gentle stroll round the town while his younger relatives braved the heights, 'that Lewes is quite fashionable. I passed several well-dressed men and women, to say nothing of coffee houses. And I also saw a poster advertising a prize fight.'

John was all attention. 'Really? How interesting. Who were the fighters?'

'That I can't tell you. My memory is not what it was, you know.'

The Apothecary gave his adopted father a fond smile. 'Yet you still manage to win at cards, Sir. I think you protest too much.'

Rose piped up. 'When are we going on an adventure, Father?'

'Tomorrow, my darling. We shall go and visit Vinehurst Place tomorrow morning. Will you come, Sir?'

Sir Gabriel waved a long thin hand. 'I shall sleep late and then stroll to a coffee house and read the newspaper.'

'Will you be requiring the services of Irish Tom?'

'I may do so later in the day.' Sir Gabriel patted Rose on top of her foxy head. 'Are you looking forward to venturing forth with your father, my child?'

'Very much, Sir,' she answered in such an adult way that John saw the older man supress a smile.

'Then I shall get him to drop us off and ask him to return to Lewes,' the Apothecary said, also concealing a grin.

'That will be most satisfactory,' answered Sir Gabriel and, very subtly indeed winked a sparkling eye.

Later that evening after Rose had retired to bed, ably assisted by a still-excited Emily, John permabulated through the town with his father, noticing that Lewes was indeed turning itself into a place of interest. Small wonder, he thought, that the Earls of Arundel had decided to convert a part of the castle into a summer residence. John briefly let his mind wander to Coralie Clive, the widow of the late Lord Arundel, and he wondered how she was faring. At one time he had loved her so deeply, would have laid down his life for her, but now his thoughts and commitment lay elsewhere, with the mother of his unborn child. He presumed that the Earl of Arundel must be related to Coralie by marriage and wondered if she would ever be invited to the summerhouse in the castle.

Sir Gabriel interrupted his train of thought. 'There is the poster for the prize fight I told you of.'

John stared, hardly able to believe his eyes, feeling at that moment that he and the Black Pyramid must have some strange spiritual link. For the bare-knuckle fighter was coming to Lewes in two days' time, almost as if he had known that the Apothecary would be there.

'Damme,' he exclaimed. 'He's coming here. The black fighter who is involved in the case I am trying so hard to solve.'

'A strange coincidence,' Sir Gabriel answered.

'It is indeed. Well, if we are still here I shall take you to see him.'

'Now that would indeed give me pleasure. There is nothing I like better than seeing a good and well-fought mill.'

'Then go we shall,' answered John, but his thoughts were a million miles away.

The next morning he got up early and knocked at Rose's door. Emily answered, very pink in the cheeks and full of excitement. She dropped him a curtsy.

'Good morning, Sir. Miss Rose is just getting dressed. I will bring her down to breakfast in ten minutes.'

'Very good. I'll go ahead and have a quick look at the papers.'

But in the few moments before his daughter joined him John had a strange feeling of disquiet. She was still a little girl for all her adult manner and he felt that to expose her to any kind of danger would be wrong. Yet what danger was there in going to look at that most beautiful of houses, that scene of rural tranquility? Though he had to admit that he himself had felt a touch of ice when that solitary, unmoving figure had come out and so silently stared at him. Thinking about it brought the scene back quite clearly and the Apothecary had just decided that he would go to Vinehurst Place alone when Rose rushed to join him in a flurry of sweet-smelling soap and over-strong tooth cleanser. She looked at him knowingly.

'We are going to visit that house you told me of today, are we not Papa?'

'Well, I . . .' he began.

Rose cut across him. 'Please, Papa. You promised me an adventure and I shall be so disappointed if I can't have one.'

'But sweetheart, isn't coming to Lewes and seeing the town enough excitement for you?'

'Oh it is, Papa. But I truly want to walk with you today. Just the two of us together.'

She was playing the scene for all she was worth, John realized that, but as with her mother, Emilia, he felt hopelessly out-manoeuvred by such a barrage of charm.

'Very well,' he said, somewhat reluctantly. 'We shall go for a little while. But if you feel tired you must tell me at once and we will return to the inn.'

Rose nodded her head, said, 'Of course, Papa,' very sweetly, and addressed herself to her breakfast.

An hour later, both father and daughter having eaten heartily, they were clambering into the coach which Irish Tom had brought round from the stables.

'Now where are we going, Sorrh?' asked the Irishman, whose rubicund features had changed not a whit with the passing of the years.

'Outside Lewes, on the road to Brighthelmstone. We turn left at the first crossroads. If you drop us there we shall walk the rest of the way.'

'And what do you wish me to do, Mr Rawlings?'

'Come back to Lewes and see if Sir Gabriel needs you. But even if he does be sure to come back for us in an hour.'

Rose looked at him. 'Can't we stay longer, Papa? An hour is very little time for an adventure.'

John gave her a firm glance. 'An hour, Miss, and that is all. And I'll hear no argument.'

'An hour it is, Sorrh,' answered Irish Tom, and with a crack of his whip the team of horses started off.

What had seemed like a long walk was now traversed in a short space of time and it seemed to John that no sooner had they got into the coach than they were getting out again. Before him lay the narrow lane which led to the gates of Vinehurst Place. With a slight tightening in his stomach, John took Rose's hand and started to walk down it.

'Is this the way to the house, Papa?'

'Yes, my girl. But remember that we will be trespassing once we are through the gates. In other words we will be there without an invitation from the owner.'

'But does he live there?'

'No, he resides in London apparently.'

'Then he can't be cross with us for having a look,' Rose answered happily.

'I'm not so sure about that,' John answered.

They walked on until the land opened out and there before them were the gates with that long green driveway bearing the faint marks of carriages that had passed that way years ago. Nature had now reclaimed it but John could picture the house in its heyday, with horses clip-clopping on their way to a great assembly within its graceful walls. But now the place stood empty and somehow forlorn, as if it were remembering the fatal shooting that had occurred there one terrible night.

As they drew nearer that elegant and beautiful building John felt Rose quicken her pace.

'Be careful,' he warned. 'Somebody might see us.'

'Somebody already has,' she answered. And breaking free from his hand started to run towards a distant figure that had just plodded into view, coming round the building.

'Hello,' she was shouting, and John, terrified of the consequences, began to hurry after her.

The figure stood stock still, very similar to the one that had greeted John on his first visit, except that this one belonged to a child. A somewhat startled child judging by the way he gazed at the newcomer.

John sped on but Rose was too fast for him and hurried up to the figure, which, on closer inspection, revealed itself as a boy. Her voice echoed back to her father.

'Hello, Sir. I'm Rose Rawlings. Who are you?'

The boy continued to gawp but after a moment or two gave an awkward bow.

'I be Michael, Miss.'

'Do you live here?' Rose continued in her brightest manner.

'I lives in the gamekeeper's cottage. My father be keeper, see.'

His accent was deepest Sussex and John started to relax. At least this was no sprig of nobility who might order them off the premises with some authority. He caught them up.

'Hello, Michael. I am Rose's father. Do you mind if we have a look at the house?'

'No, Sir,' said Michael, giving another stubby bow. 'Are you a relation or something?'

John put on his honest face – though feeling rather badly about lying to the child – and said, 'We're remote cousins of the Bassetts.'

Rose turned to him, genuinely surprised, and said, 'Are we?'

'Yes,' John replied firmly. 'We are.'

The boy looked at his boots, then said, 'I think perhaps I ought to ask my da' about you seeing round the house.'

'Oh that will be perfectly all right,' Rose answered promptly, giving John the vaguest notions of smacking her. 'Shall we wait here, Papa, while Michael goes to find him?'

He heaved a sigh. 'Whatever you say, my dearest.'

She looked at him then and saw that he was upset. 'I'm sorry,' she whispered, and put her hand in his. Instantly his irritation flew away and he smiled at her.

'Yes, that's fine, Michael. You go and ask your father. Rose and I will sit on that bench over there,' he said.

But as soon as the boy was out of sight he turned to his daughter. 'I am afraid we are going to make this a proper adventure, sweetheart. We are going in to the house without permission.'

'But suppose Michael comes back with his father. Will he shoot us?'

John laughed. 'Heavens no, we will have looked round and be gone before he finds him.'

'You are sure?'

'I am positive. His father is gamekeeper and could be wandering around anywhere on the estate. It will probably take him half an hour to locate him.'

Rose gave him a glance and he read mischief in her eyes, a deep sparkling glee.

'Let us proceed then,' she said.

They walked slowly round the house looking for some means of entry. Eventually, John saw a small window leading into what he imagined would be a pantry, standing open sufficiently to allow Rose to squeeze through. He looked at her.

'Sweetheart, are you game to go in there, then make your way to the kitchen door and let me inside?'

She gave him a gallant smile. 'Of course I am,' she said, but he saw that her chin was shaking slightly.

'Rose, you don't have to go.'

'But I want to have an adventure.'

He lifted her into the air and she tried to push the window –

which was a four-paned sash – up a little. But something was jamming it at the top and she gave her father a hopeless look.

'It's stuck, Papa.'

'Can you get through the space?'

'Yes, if I breathe in.'

He felt terrible about asking her to do it but what harm could possibly come to her in an empty house? Nonetheless his heart plummeted as she squeezed herself through the small gap and vanished from his sight. Straining his ears he could hear her feet scampering away – then came silence. John stood anguished as the moments went past. He drew his watch from his pocket and realized that he had been standing outside the kitchen door for almost twenty minutes. Then, distantly, he heard the sound of approaching voices. Glancing over his shoulder he saw that the keeper's boy was coming back with a tall, burly individual wearing a surly expression. So far they had not seen him but it would only be a matter of minutes before they did. John did the only thing possible and dived down behind a bush, and it was at that precise moment that the kitchen door opened and Rose stood there, red in the face with excitement. The Apothecary took a flying leap across the space, praying as he did so that Michael and his father would be looking in the opposite direction.

His daughter was staring at him. 'What's the matter, Pa?'

He put an urgent finger to his lips. 'Not so loud. Michael and the gamekeeper are coming.'

Rose looked troubled. 'Did they see you?'

'No, I don't think so. What took you so long to open the door? Couldn't you find it?'

She gave him her wonderful smile. 'Oh yes, that part was easy. But I've been talking.'

A thrill of unease chilled John to the bone. 'Talking? To whom?'

'A black man.'

'What black man? The house is empty.'

'No, it isn't. There is a black man here. I came through the window and went into the hall by mistake and there he was, sitting in the grand saloon.'

'Is he there now?'

'Yes, as far as I know. I'll take you to him.'

She thrust her small hand into John's and led him through the glorious interior of that fine and delicate house. But he was not in the mood for admiring its lovely lines, full of a strange fore-boding. They reached the hall and turned into a large and beautiful room that led off it. It was completely empty.

'Oh!' exclaimed Rose, stopping dead in her tracks. 'He's gone. What a shame.'

John squatted down so that their eyes were on a level. 'Did you really see someone here, sweetheart?'

'Yes, I did.' Her face screwed up as if she were about to weep. 'Don't you believe me?'

John straightened his back. 'Yes, I believe you. But the question is, where has the man gone?'

A tear trickled down Rose's cheek. 'I don't know, Papa. It seems that he must have vanished.'

'Yes,' answered the Apothecary thoughtfully, 'it seems as if he must.'

Twenty-Six

They left by the kitchen door, John's plan of examining the house totally thwarted by the arrival of the grim-faced gamekeeper. As they crept outside he could hear the man's voice.

'Well, where they gone then? Michael, I'll tan your arse if you be telling me one of your stories.'

'I'm not, Da'. They was here. The man and a little girl called Rose.'

'Well they ain't here now, are they.'

It wasn't a question, it was a statement.

The boy began to snivel. 'But I spoke to them, Da'. They must have got into the house somehow.'

'Then we'd best go and look for them.'

John turned to Rose. 'Come along, darling. Let me give you a piggyback.'

And scooping her up in the air and onto his shoulders, he started to run. Behind him he heard shouting and then shots were fired, more in warning than attempting to injure, he thought. Nonetheless he increased his speed as best he could carrying the extra burden of the child. The gates came into view and he hastened through them and had never been more relieved in his life than to see his coach drawn up, Irish Tom on the box and Sir Gabriel's face peering anxiously through the window. Gasping, John covered the last few paces, bundled Rose within, then stepped inside himself.

'My dearest child, did I hear shots?' asked Sir Gabriel, pretending nonchalance but clearly worried.

'You did indeed, Sir. It was the gamekeeper who mistook me for a hare, I don't doubt.'

'Foolish fellow,' answered Sir Gabriel, and took a pinch of snuff. John noticed with tremendous tenderness that the old man's hands were shaking.

'I suggest that we repair to The White Hart and have a small libation,' he said.

'What an excellent plan,' answered his father. He patted Rose's cheek. 'And how did you enjoy your adventure, my love?'

'It was splendid, thank you Sir.'

'Which part did you like best?'

'I enjoyed chatting to the black man. He was so interesting.'

John leant forward. 'Tell us about him. What was he like?'

'He was very tall and massive, and he had a nice voice.'

The Apothecary had a sudden mental picture of the Black Pyramid. 'Did he tell you his name?' he said.

'He said it was Jack,' she answered guilessly.

Over her head John and Sir Gabriel looked at one another and exchanged a silent message.

Later that night, after the child was in bed, the two men strolled out briefly. It was a cold evening and they did not stay outside long. A wind had got up and was whipping through that small and ancient town clinging to the side of a hill. But though Sir Gabriel strode out bravely John could not help but notice that he was now taking far longer to walk. He felt glad when they got inside The White Hart and he was able to settle his father down with a cognac.

'Father I must talk to you in earnest. I saw nothing of that house today, my entire attention having been seized by Rose thinking she saw a black man within, yet, as you know, the house is totally uninhabited except for a handful of servants.'

'Perhaps he was one of them.'

'I suppose it is possible. But two things bother me. Rose described the physique of the negro perfectly and it matched that of the Black Pyramid. Furthermore she told me that the man said his name was Jack. Which is the Pyramid's real name. Sir, I have the strangest feeling that he was there, present in that empty house.'

'Well, there's only one thing for it,' answered Sir Gabriel.

'And that is?'

'To ask him.'

'When?'

'Tomorrow when we go to see him fight. That will be your time, John.'

'Yes, I suppose it will. Father, I am getting the strangest idea about the murder of William Gorringe.'

'Which is?'

John Rawlings lowered his voice and whispered something so odd that Sir Gabriel just sat there, shaking his head in disbelief.

*   *   *

The next day they set out to see the Black Pyramid fight. As usual the crowd had gathered in a field nearby and John took Rose, not to see the scrap but to sample the delights of the fair that always seemed to accompany such events. But he had another reason for taking her. He wanted her to identify the man she had seen in the house, to say whether it was the Black Pyramid or not.

Irish Tom strode ahead of the group, looking a little like a bare-knuckle fighter himself. Behind him walked Sir Gabriel and John, with Emily and Rose following on. They made quite an interesting set of people as they cut a swathe through the crowd and several persons turned their head to get another look at them.

The fight had been arranged in a meadow beside a river that wound its way placidly through the countryside. In the distance, high up, towered the ruined castle and in a hastily erected box, which consisted of a faded awning over a few planks put down so that the chairs would not sink into the grass, sat two important people, that John thought must be the Earl and Countess of Arundel.

In the middle of the field some strong sticks had been thrust into the ground round which ropes had been tied in very much the same kind of arrangement as John had seen in Devon. It was here that the fight would take place at the hour of three o'clock. At present there was no sign of the Black Pyramid or Nathaniel Broome, or any representative of his opponent. But the festivities were very much under way. Rose and Emily broke into a run as a puppeteer set up his stall.

John smiled at Sir Gabriel, who was looking like a grandee as he strolled through the mob.

'Would you care for a little refreshment, Sir?'

'A small glass of canary would not go amiss.'

'There's a tent over there where I imagine we could obtain one. I'll put Irish Tom in charge of Rose and Emily.'

'Splendid,' answered his father and made his way to the liquor tent where a chair was immediately found for him.

On the dot of three o'clock the Black Pyramid, completely recovered from his fight in Devon, his dark skin gleaming with the sheen of ebony, stepped through the ropes and raised his arms aloft. John and his father, the older man sitting on a camp stool right at the front, gave a small cheer. His adversary – a dark young man with a mass of curling hair who called himself Gypsy Joe

Summerfield – then came into the ring and made menacing gestures in the direction of his opponent. The Black Pyramid turned disdainfully away.

The fight was by no means a walkover for the black man as Gypsy Joe pounced on him with a welter of flying, brutal fists. But inevitably the range of the Black Pyramid's powerful arms and the use of his muscular legs, encased as they were in black tights, won him the day. The gypsy was knocked to the ground and had to be helped out of the ring by his clique of supporters. It was then, with the black man jubilantly receiving the accolade of the crowd, that John ran back into the fairground, where Rose was sitting with the maid and the coachman, having a light meal which Emily had packed before they left The White Hart.

'My darling, come with me a minute, if you will,' and before she could say a word he had taken her hand and was leading her towards the ring.

The Black Pyramid was just climbing out and would have turned away but Rose broke free and ran towards him calling out, 'Hello Mr Jack.'

He spun round, looking to see who was hailing him. Then he saw the child – at least it seemed as if he did – and abruptly turned his back and hastened towards a group of cheering admirers.

Rose did something unusual and burst into tears and John sped towards her and scooped her up into his arms.

'Don't cry, sweetheart.'

'But Papa, he turned away from me. And yesterday he was so nice, even thought I startled him.'

'Then it was the same man?'

'Definitely. I am certain of it.'

'I see.'

'I think perhaps he was trying to hide from me. But why, Papa? Why?'

That, my dear child, John thought, is precisely what I would like to know.

That night John and his father sat in a snug after dinner had been served. There was a comfortable silence between them, the Apothecary's thoughts being miles away as he ran the details of the case over and over in his mind. There were so many questions left unanswered but one in particular came back to John with vivid clarity. Why had the Black Pyramid put Fraulein Schmitt out of the carriage – had it really been because she grumbled so greatly? And what had she meant by her last remark to him that it had all been make believe? Could it have been possible that the two of them were acting out some piece of theatre? But for whose benefit – and why?

John's thoughts turned to the other people in the drama. There was Mrs Lucinda Silverwood, so calm and so capable who lived somewhere in Lewes and obviously knew that dark-haired beauty Jemima Lovell better than she had admitted. There was the actress Paulina Gower who the Apothecary had not liked all that much but who had clearly taken the fancy of the redoubtable Joe Jago. As to the men who had travelled on the coach that night, there was mincing little Cuthbert Simms – who John could not help but feel sorry for – and the enigmatic Black Pyramid, together with Nathaniel Broome. A disparate group of people if ever there was one. Yet they had all shared in that extraordinary journey which had culminated in the violent doing-to-death of William Gorringe.

The door to the snug opened and in came the waiter who had served John breakfast on the occasion of his first visit to Lewes.

'Can I get you anything to drink, Sir?'

John looked across at Sir Gabriel. 'Father?'

'A cognac for me, if you please.'

'And I will have the same.'

'Very good, Sir.'

'By the way, before you go, do you remember me talking to you about Vinehurst Place and its occupants on the occasion of my last visit?'

'I do indeed, Sir.'

'If I were to draw a man could you tell me from the likeness whether or not it was the vanished Fulke Bassett?'

The waiter looked somewhat startled. 'I think I could. Yes, sir.'

While he was out of the room John summoned up his vivid pictorial memory. Then he started to sketch as best he could the features of the man known to him as William Gorringe.

'Do you think that that is the key to the mystery?' asked Sir Gabriel.

'I think it has to be. If it isn't then I'm afraid I must drop the whole thing.'

'That is not like you, John.'

The Apothecary sighed. 'Alas, it is a fact. This has been the most baffling set of circumstances I have ever encountered.'

At that moment the waiter returned bearing a tray with a decanter and two fresh glasses upon it. He put it down, then solemnly and in silence John handed him the sketch. The man merely glanced at it.

'Yes, Sir,' he said, 'that's Mr Bassett. Cruel and evil man that he is.'

'Thank you,' John answered. 'I think everything has just become clear.'

Twenty-Seven

The search for the Black Pyramid was renewed with great urgency. Early the next morning the Apothecary went down to the remnants of the fair, busy packing up and removing what had been left of the stalls, and asked the man's whereabouts. He was informed that the victorious fighter had moved on to Brighthelmstone – indeed had gone that very night – and was shortly due to fight in that small town. Nobody seemed quite sure when. John had thanked them and returned to The White Hart in something of a quandary.

'What is the matter, my child?' asked his father, seeing the anxious look on his son's face.

John sat down and ordered himself some tea and food. He had left the inn before breakfast, a meal which Sir Gabriel was now picking at.

'It's that wretched fighter. He has already departed Lewes.'

'Do you know where he was bound?'

'To Brighthelmstone.'

'Well if you need to question him, follow him and do so.'

'But, Sir, I vowed to myself that I would never leave Rose again. Yet I realize that I would be much quicker on my own.'

'How long do you think you will be gone?'

'A day or two. Three at the most.'

'Then why are you making such an alarm? The child will be perfectly safe with me. Have I not looked after her properly in the past?'

'You have guarded her as well as any grandfather possibly could.'

'Well then?'

John squirmed, sensing that this was a battle he was about to lose.

'But I swore . . .'

'Oh fiddle-faddle,' said Sir Gabriel, and snapped his long white fingers.

Rose, too, seemed very relaxed about the situation. 'Oh are you going away, Pa? But not far I believe. Only to Brighthelmstone Grandpa said.'

'Yes, that's right, darling. But if you really object I won't go.'

She stared at him in blank surprise. 'Oh no, that would be foolish. I think you should go and try to find Jack. And when you do could you ask him why he was so horrid to me at the fight. All I wanted was to greet him.'

John laughed, he could not help himself. It was like being in the presence of a very small adult.

'You're sure?'

'I am positive. Emily and I have some walks planned. We're probably going to have an adventure.'

'Well don't make it like ours, whatever you do. I don't want you going near Vinehurst Place, do you hear?'

Rose gave a demure curtsy but refused to meet John's eyes.

'I repeat, you are to leave that house alone.'

'Yes, Papa,' she answered, but behind her back she was crossing her fingers.

John took the public stage to Brighthelmstone, a relatively short drive, and arrived there in the late afternoon. Booking himself a room in The Ship he immediately set out to explore the place, which was small and somehow rather sad-looking. However, walking by the sea he spied several bathing machines with brave souls venturing into the waves. Immediately he was seized by the desire to swim, having been sitting long enough in the cramped conditions of a coach. Acting purely on impulse he went down to one of the machines, tramping over the pebble on his booted feet, and booked himself a place behind a portly young man, obviously in agony through gout-ridden toes.

The attendant hired him a pair of flannel drawers and an oilskin cap for his hair, which John refused. Stepping out of the machine and down the steps the Apothecary strode manfully into the waves and in a few minutes was swimming strongly out to sea. He had always loved the sport, probably because he was good at it, and now he felt happy and more relaxed that he had in an age.

In front of him, even further out than he was, he could see a single swimmer, his arms rising and falling as he executed a perfect crawl. At the rate he was going, John thought, the man would soon end up in France. An urge to catch him up possessed John and he increased his speed. Ahead of him he saw the swimmer turn his head as if conscious of his pursuer and though he could not be certain because of the distance, the Apothecary had the fleeting impression that the man was black.

A strange feeling overcame him at that moment as he became convinced that the man he had come to Brighthelmstone to find was swimming but a few yards away from him. Striking out for everything he was worth, he determined to catch him up. And then, at that very moment, the man's head vanished. John stared round as best he could through the waves but there was no sign of him anywhere. And then he felt a pair of strong arms encircle him and he was dragged down beneath the water.

Holding his breath John shot to the surface again and saw that it was indeed the Black Pyramid who held him in a potentially lethal grip.

'Right, you little bastard,' said the black man, his face streaming, 'exactly what game are you playing with me?'

'I might ask the same of you,' the Apothecary gasped back.

'You have no right to spy on me. Who are you, you miserable little worm, wriggling all over the place?' And without waiting for a reply the black man dragged him under the sea again.

John truly thought that he was drowning and felt more terrified than he had ever done before. He started to fight, beating at the brawny black chest with his fists and kicking as powerfully as was possible in that vast and unfriendly ocean.

They came up for air once more. 'Frightened, huh?' said the Black Pyramid in such an aggressive tone that John once more feared for his life.

'Yes, I'm frightened,' he spluttered. 'In fact I'm scared witless.'

'Good,' answered the Black Pyramid, and baring his teeth he pushed John under and held him down.

What saved him he never afterwards could tell. Whether another intrepid swimmer drew near or whether the black man decided that John was simply not worth running the risk of being caught for was forever moot. But the fact was that he was suddenly released and floated up to the surface in a kind of stupor. His future hung in the balance but he somehow managed to pull himself together and struck out for the shore. In the distance as he turned towards the Brighthelmstone coast he could see the Black Pyramid swimming out further than ever – and faster too.

Somehow the Apothecary made the shingle at the foot of the

bathing machines and there he collapsed, lying flat on his face and gasping. A bathing attendant came down the steps.

'Are you all right, Sir?'

He literally could not speak, having saved the last of his breath to swim to the beach. Instead John gave a weak nod of the head.

'Well, you don't look all right, Sir, if you'll pardon my saying. I'll give you a hand into the machine.'

He assisted the trembling Apothecary to his feet and half carried him up the few steps into the bathing machine from which he had started his perilous swim.

'I'll just sit down for a minute,' gasped John.

But it was half an hour before he could make the effort to get dressed and then he walked very slowly back to The Ship where he went into the residents' parlour and ordered himself a large brandy. He was just sipping it when his would-be murderer walked into the room.

'You survived then,' the black man said laconically.

'Yes,' John answered, equally briefly, then added, 'Why did you do it?'

'Because,' said the Black Pyramid, looming over the Apothecary's chair, 'I was sick of the sight of you. Wherever I went, there you were.'

John took another mouthful of brandy, then said, 'Did you know William Gorringe – or should I say Fulke Bassett – before that coach ride?'

The black man hesitated, sucking the air in through his teeth, before saying, 'Yes, I knew him.'

'Did you kill him?'

'What makes you ask that?'

'You've just demonstrated that you are capable of it.'

'Oh yes, I am quite able to take a life.'

'Then did you?'

'I refuse to answer that.' The Black Pyramid suddenly gave a slow smile and John thought how handsome he was and how transformed he was by smiling. 'Listen, my friend, let me buy you a drink and you can answer some of my questions for a change.'

'Very well. I accept.'

The fighter lowered his enormous length into the chair opposite John's. 'Tell me,' he said, 'what is your interest in this killing?'

'Did I not inform you that in the past I have worked with Sir John Fielding of Bow Street?'

'I do not recall it.'

'Well, I have done so, many times. And though this is not one of his cases I can honestly say that I am deeply interested in this particular affair. Probably because I was travelling in the same coach as the victim.'

'I see.'

At that moment the girl arrived with their drinks and the conversation ceased until she had gone. Then the Pyramid said, 'And so you think that one of the passengers is guilty, do you?'

'Obviously so.'

'But surely it could have been an outsider who attacked him.'

'It could have been but I don't think it was.'

There was a long silence during which both men drank a draught, then the black man said, 'Well, you need look no further.'

'What do you mean?' asked John.

'Because I killed him,' said the Black Pyramid, and once again smiled his slow dark smile.

It was too easy, thought John. He had never before received an admission of guilt and now that he had he was frankly flabbergasted. Every instinct he possessed told him that the fighter was telling him the truth, yet still he had the small niggle of doubt.

'You are certain?' he said feebly.

The Black Pyramid boomed a laugh. 'Good God, man, I've just confessed to you. What more do you want?'

'Proof,' answered John, rallying.

'Of what kind?'

'Tell me how you did it?'

'Well, I had met him before, as I've already told you. He recognized me despite the passing of the years. But that was not why I killed him. The reason was that I loathed him, hated him, every bit of me despised the evil bastard.'

'Why?'

'I have no intention of answering that.'

'You might have to when you come before your judges.'

'I shall deal with that if and when the time arrives,' the Black Pyramid answered calmly.

John stared at him and found himself liking the man, liking the way he handled himself under pressure. Yet determined as he was to get to the heart of the mystery, the Apothecary had come up against a brick wall. The bare-knuckle fighter steadfastly refused to elucidate further.

'So how did you do it?' John asked.

'I crept up in the night and beat the bugger's brains out.'

The Apothecary shot into his pictorial memory the image of that stealthy figure walking along the landing. He could see it quite clearly, cloaked and mysterious and completely sexless. And even though he was observing it from above he knew then that the Black Pyramid was lying – or at least telling him only part of the story.

'I don't think so,' he said slowly.

'What do you mean?'

'What I say. You are only telling me a small portion of what really happened.'

The Black Pyramid got to his feet. 'That is all, Mr Rawlings, that I am prepared to say.' He made a deep bow. 'Good night to you, Sir. I leave you to take whatever action you deem necessary.'

And with another brief salutation he left the room.

Twenty-Eight

All the way back to Lewes John berated himself with thoughts of
the million and one questions he should have asked the Black
Pyramid, the most important of which should surely have been
what he was doing in the great house known as Vinehurst Place.
Because the more the Apothecary thought of it the stranger it
seemed. And yet . . .? His mind once again raced down that frightening track which led to the most extraordinary idea he had ever
had. An idea so outrageous that he could hardly comprehend it.
An idea which he had whispered to Sir Gabriel who had looked
at him askance. And now he was heading back to that little town
that clung beneath the castle to wind the whole affair up – or at
least to try and do so.

But how to start – that was the thought that bothered him. For
whichever way round he looked at the problem it always began
and ended with the black fighter. And John could not help but
feel that if he had questioned the man properly this current situation could have been completely avoided. Or could it?

He was in such a whirlwind of thought that the Apothecary
felt extremely nervous as he stepped off the public stage and into
the confines of The White Hart. His incredible idea was, after all,
pure supposition and to tie it in with the murder of Fulke Bassett,
passing under the name of William Gorringe as he had been, was
going to be practically impossible.

John's mind went to Joe Jago – safely returned to London
long since – and at that moment he wished for the steadiness
of the clerk's company and felt that he would know how next
to proceed. Mentally bracing himself for what he believed was
going to be a rocky ride ahead, the apothecary looked for his
family.

There was no sign of any of them and he imagined that they
had all gone out in the coach, probably into the surrounding
countryside. Feeling somewhat at a loose end the Apothecary
dumped his bag in his room – which he had kept on – and
wandered out into the street. He found his feet turning towards

the castle and he climbed up to where he could see the keep. It was a very warm October day and there were several figures sitting outside. Then his heart lurched violently as a female stood up and he recognized her as Coralie. A younger girl stood beside her whom he took to be Georgiana. John felt as if he were watching some enormous play with the ruins of the once-mighty castle as the backdrop and the woman he had once loved taking the leading part. At that moment he longed to call out, to attract her attention, but knew that he never would, never could. He just stood silently as Coralie put her arm round her daughter's shoulders and walked slowly into the keep without so much as glancing round.

As if this were an omen the Apothecary felt a chill wind come up from nowhere which made him suddenly go cold to the bone. He hurried into The White Hart and into the guests' parlour, and who should be sitting there but Sir Gabriel.

'Father!' John exclaimed. 'I've been looking for you.'

'Well, here I am. And glad to see you back, my son. Did you run down your quarry?'

'Yes, I did.'

'And?'

'And he confessed to the murder.'

'He confessed?'

'Yes, but Father there's something not right about it. I know he's hiding someone.'

'Ah yes, your extraordinary idea.'

'I know it sounds incredible but I am truly beginning to believe it is the truth.'

Sir Gabriel said nothing, compressing his lips and shaking his head slowly, and the two men sat in silence, thinking about what John had just suggested. And it was into this strange quiet that Irish Tom walked some quarter of an hour later. He looked somewhat perturbed.

'Oh, I'm sorry to bother you, Sorrh. I wondered if you had seen Miss Rose and Emily.'

John snapped to attention. 'No, I've only just got back. Where are they?' He looked at Sir Gabriel.

'They went off in the coach for a jaunt. Surely you didn't leave them?' The older man directed this at the coachman.

'It was at Miss Rose's insistence, Sorrh Gabriel. She asked if she might have a little walk with Emily and could I pick them up in half an hour.'

'And they weren't there?' asked John, a terrible fear making his voice catch.

'No, Sorrh, they weren't. I waited for thirty minutes and then I came back here because I thought they might have walked back.'

'By God!' John was on his feet. 'Not again! That little imp went missing in Cornwall and I nearly lost her for good. Where the devil did you take them, Tom? Don't tell me Vinehurst Place?'

The coachman had gone red as a soldier's coat. 'Not exactly, Sorrh. But it was close to the walk that led up to it.'

'Then let's get there – and fast.'

'I shall attend also,' said Sir Gabriel.

Poor Tom, looking fit to weep, rushed from the room in the direction of the stables while Sir Gabriel hastily pulled on a cloak.

John Rawlings turned to his father, his face the colour of chalk. 'Why did she have to wander off? What possessed the child?'

'You will have to deal with that in the future. What we must concentrate on now is finding her.'

John nodded, hardly able to speak, and a second or two later they heard the sound of hooves on the cobbles and saw Irish Tom ready and waiting for them outside. Without saying anything further they got into the coach and sped off up the road in the direction of Vinehurst Place.

John sat tight-lipped, thinking of the time in Cornwall when his daughter had hidden from a black coven and had taken refuge down that deep and terrible well in which lay another body. At that moment all he could think of was how much he loved Rose, despite the fact he could cheerfully wring her neck for running off in the way she had. Yet he was forced to admit that she had probably inherited her spirit of adventure from him and he supposed that there would be little he could do about it. With a feeling of dread the Apothecary sat back against the coach's cushioned seat.

It was only a few minutes' drive to the lane that led to the entrance to Vinehurst Place yet it felt like an eternity to John. As soon as the carriage came to a halt he leapt out but then he remembered himself and turned to Sir Gabriel.

'Father, you'll be safer staying here. I would rather do this on my own.'

'My child, what makes you think that Rose is within?'

'I don't know. But she was fascinated by the house. Besides I have a feeling about it. I can't explain.'

'You'll take Irish Tom with you?'

'Yes. That is if you don't mind being left alone.'

'Don't worry I am armed. But I shall only shoot to kill if it is strictly necessary.'

Despite everything, despite his worry for his beloved child's safety, John could not help but give a crooked grin. His father – age being no hindrance to him – was speaking in total earnest.

'That's excellent news, Sir,' he said, straight-faced. He called up to the box, 'Tom, come down. I want you to go with me.'

'Should I bring my shillelagh, Sorrh?'

'Bring anything that can inflict damage.'

And at that John fingered the pistol in his own pocket and felt a little more secure.

It was dusk as he and Tom set out, the dying autumn sun casting strange shadows and making the Apothecary's heart beat faster. Indeed he had rarely felt more nervous as he worried about Rose and where she could possibly be. He cleared his mind and tried sending her a message, just as he had done in Cornwall when she had vanished before. But unfortunately this time it did not work. Concentrate as he would no answer came.

He and the coachman reached the end of the lane and then stopped short. The gates, never used and seemingly permanently closed, stood wide open, and even while they stood gaping at them there was the sound of wheels behind and a dark carriage thundered past them. It hurtled up the overgrown drive and round the sweep to draw up at the front door and simultaneously every candle in the house was lit. It must have taken an army of servants to achieve this effect but Vinehurst Place blazed with light.

'God's teeth, Sorrh, what the deuce is happening?'

'I have no idea, Tom, but I'm going to find out.'

'Well, I'm right beside you, Mr R.'

They proceeded up the drive, this time keeping to the shadow of the trees for the lights of the house blazed out over the lawns. And as they drew nearer they could hear sounds – a harpsichord played a welcoming air, together with muted laughter and somebody whistling a merry tune.

Tom looked at John. 'How do we go about this, Sorrh? Do we just knock at the front door?'

John silently shook his head. 'No,' he whispered, 'let's creep round the back and see if we can get in that way.'

'Do you think Miss Rose is in there?'

Once again the Apothecary shook his head. 'I have no idea but I am prepared to try anything to find her.'

As they drew nearer the house the noise grew louder and they were able to identify it as coming from the grand saloon at the rear of the hall. Moving in complete silence they circumnavigated the side of the building and at last reached the large French doors of the room, hung with floor-length curtains as it was and opening on to the gardens behind. And then John stood aghast, motioning Tom to be still. For the curtains were not drawn and the interior was as brilliantly lit as a stage set.

They were all there, every last one of them, with the exception, of course, of Augusta Schmitt. There was a stranger in their midst, however, a man that John had not seen before, a man of about fifty, tall and well made. He had a glass in his hand and as the Apothecary looked round, wide eyed, he saw that so did the others. The man raised his glass.

'To just deserts,' he said.

Nobody answered but they all downed the contents of their glass with extreme solemnity. John stared in ever-growing amazement as he let his eyes wander over the assembled company. For though this had been the very thing that he had whispered to Sir Gabriel it still took his breath away to learn that he was right. Lucinda Silverwood stood with Jemima Lovell and Paulina Gower, her arm casually draped round Jemima's shoulders. Nathaniel Broome was in earnest conversation with Cuthbert Simms, the dancing master's little face quite flushed with drink and excitement. Everyone who had ridden in the coach that fateful evening was present, other than for the Black Pyramid and the German woman. John thought grimly that the only two people not connected with them had been himself and Martin Meadows.

He took a step forward, anxious to hear what was being said and the movement must have caught Cuthbert's eye. He gave a little scream and said, 'Oh my goodness, there's somebody out there.'

John and Irish Tom turned to run but at that moment a vast shadow loomed up in front of them and grabbed John by the collar of his coat.

'So we meet again, my friend,' it said.

John was just able to gasp out, 'Run, Tom, run. Find Rose for God's sake,' before he was lifted in the air and carried unceremoniously into Vinehurst Place.

Twenty-Nine

John had never made an entrance like it. Thrown onto the Black Pyramid's shoulder like a doll, he was carried into the grand saloon and dumped unceremoniously onto the floor.

'Look what I have found,' said the black man. 'The nosy creature who has been snooping round us all has just committed his final act of spying and followed us here.'

There was a snicker of laughter but generally the faces that regarded him were tight with suspicion.

'Mr Rawlings,' said Lucinda Silverwood, 'I would have thought better of you. What on earth brings you to Vinehurst Place?'

John swallowed and made a gallant attempt at regaining his equilibrium. 'I have come in search of my daughter,' he said, his voice sounding somewhat hoarse to his ears. 'She has gone missing and I had a feeling she might have come here.'

'And why should she do that, pray?' asked Cuthbert Simms.

'Because she is fascinated by the house as apparently are all of you.'

'Aye, as well we might be,' answered Nathaniel Broome in a tone so bitter that the Apothecary scarcely recognized it.

The man standing in the midst of them all, the only person that John did not know, gave him a peremptory bow. 'Allow me to introduce myself, Sir. I am Richard Bassett.'

'The brother of Helen, the one who was . . .'

'Shot? Yes, I am he. Pray take a seat.'

And suddenly the whole situation became as strange and weird as anything the Apothecary had ever seen upon the stage or read in a novel. Here were almost the whole contingent of that coach ride from London to Devon, the ride that had ended in a man being bludgeoned to death, all knowing one another as John had suspected and now gathered together as guests of Helen Bassett's brother.

'Would you like something to drink?' Richard asked.

'Yes, I would. Anything. This has come as something of a shock.'

Yet it hadn't really. It was just that the whole situation was utterly

bizarre. Beyond anything that the Apothecary had ever had to deal
with or had experienced. Far from knowing how to handle himself,
he decided that the best policy was to keep quiet and let them
question him. Yet they seemed strangely silent, almost nonplussed
by his presence. It was the Black Pyramid who was the most vocal.

'Well, I must say, Mr Rawlings, that you did a clever job in
tracking us here. What put you onto it?'

John sighed. 'Actually it was a chance remark of the coachman
who drove us to Devon. He recognized Gorringe and said he had
taken him to a stop near Lewes where a carriage had picked him
up. He also remembered that the man had used another name
though he could not recall it.'

'So you came to Lewes on the off chance?'

'Yes, I did. And then I heard about Vinehurst Place, that a terrible
tragedy had been enacted within its walls. But at that time I had
not made the connection.'

Richard Bassett interrupted them.

'He's got this far, Jack. We may as well tell him the whole story.'

'But Richard, that would make him the most dangerous person
to all of us.'

'He doesn't look dangerous to me. He looks like a man of
honour. Are you, Sir?'

John gulped the cognac which had been passed to him and
found he had drained the glass.

'I believe that I am,' he answered. 'I tell lies sometimes, I adopt
guises in order to aid Sir John Fielding's enquiries, but I think I
can answer that I am generally an honourable person.'

Richard leant his face close to the Apothecary's. 'Then I want
you to take a solemn oath that what you hear tonight will remain
your secret and yours alone.'

John was silent, considering his options and feeling the seriousness of the occasion. He either had to make a swift escape – which
was an impossibility – or go along with their instructions. He
looked round the room. Paulina Gower was shooting him a very
black look. Mrs Silverwood, though serious, was giving him a half-
smile, while Jemima actually seemed sympathetic. Nathaniel Broome
was expressionless, Cuthbert Simms was looking perturbed, but the
Black Pyramid seemed utterly fearful. He spoke.

'What is the alternative, Richard?'

Richard – a tall man of medium physique with fair hair that

had started to recede – answered very simply, 'We should have to kill him.'

John sat rigid, then said, 'In that case you leave me little choice but to swear an oath.'

There was an indrawing of breath from the onlookers and Nat Broome called out, 'Let's kill the bastard. He's been a regular pain in the arse since we first met him.'

Richard was clearly in charge of the meeting because he said, 'Do we need another death on our conscience?'

Lucinda Silverwood spoke up firmly. 'No, we don't. Let Mr Rawlings take an oath to remain silent and that will satisfy me.'

There were general murmurs of approbation and John gulped, almost certain that his life had been saved. But added to this feeling of relief was an enormous sense of curiosity. He longed to know the secret of Vinehurst Place. He longed to know which of them had actually murdered Fulke Bassett.

'Get me a bible,' he said, 'and I will swear.'

Richard went out of the room and in his absence the Black Pyramid murmured, 'If you let us down, Rawlings, I vow I'll come after you, hunt you down, and this time I will kill you.'

But John hardly listened, feelings of worry for Rose consuming him once more. Had Irish Tom found her? Or was she not at Vinehurst Place at all? Had she, in fact, gone for a walk somewhere entirely different?

Richard Bassett came back into the room bearing a large and heavy family bible. He placed it on the table and told the Apothecary to raise it in his right hand. With a struggle John managed to do so. Then he said in as solemn a voice as he could manage, 'I swear by Almighty God that everything I hear tonight shall be kept secret by me until the day I die.' He turned to the Black Pyramid, alias Jack Beef, 'There. Is that good enough for you?' he said.

The black man merely shrugged his shoulders in a gesture that needed no words. Richard spoke again.

'Please, all sit down. I intend to tell Mr Rawlings the story of how my father murdered my beloved sister – and the aftermath of his actions.'

There was a general shuffling of chairs and John, too, sat down on a small sofa. Richard began, his voice pitched so that everyone could hear him.

'I think the tale really begins when my mother acquired a little blackboy to accompany her as was the fashion in those days amongst ladies of rank and fortune. She bought him when he was six and a frightened little fellow. We were living in town at the time but subsequently my father made a considerable amount of money in the City of London and built this house and moved Helen and myself out of London to live here. She was ten and I was twelve. Indeed I was the same age as the blackboy whom we had christened Jack.'

Even before Richard had said any more the Apothecary had made the connection.

'Anyway the boy reached puberty a year or so later and my father was all for sending him to the plantations but my mother insisted on keeping him. She did not have any more living children. She lost two, born after we were, and then died giving birth to a stillborn child. By this time Jack had reached the age of sixteen and had become a useful servant with whom we often unofficially used to play. It was inevitable that he and Helen should fall in love. Inevitable but heartbreaking.'

Richard paused and looked straight at Jack Beef who had plunged his face into his hands.

'They kept their secret with difficulty, even when Helen became pregnant. She was eighteen and in a state of despair lest my father should find out. Eventually she made the excuse of going away to stay with an aunt but in fact she rented a house in the company of our housekeeper and it was there that she gave birth.'

John was utterly silent, waiting to hear that the child had died, but much to his surprise Richard added, 'To my beautiful niece,' in such a pleasant manner that the Apothecary immediately assumed that she was alive after all. And then something totally astonishing happened. The dark-haired Jemima Lovell got to her feet and crossed the room to where the Black Pyramid was clearly weeping. Putting her arms round him, she said, 'Don't be upset, Papa. You know I love you.'

John was too astonished to do anything more than stare openmouthed. Jemima smiled at him.

'My adopted mother – or the woman I regard as such – is Mrs Silverwood. She nursed me from birth and brought me up in her little cottage on the estate. I owe her so much.'

The Black Pyramid wiped his eyes. 'When Mr Bassett instructed Helen that she was to wed that filthy and ancient swine the Marquis of Dover, she refused, saying she loved another. But Bassett insisted and she blurted out that she had a daughter. Then he took a gun to her and shot her in the heart.'

'He was always a violent man,' said Richard. 'Many's the time that both Jack and I had a thrashing or were locked in the cellar. I don't know what punishment he exacted from Helen.'

'I do,' said Jemima quietly, but would say no more.

John asked a question. 'But how do the rest of you fit in? And what about Fraulein Schmitt? Were you really angry with her, Jack? Or was it all play-acting?'

'It was a masquerade,' the Black Pyramid answered sorrowfully. 'She decided to moan all the way down – thought I must admit that that performance was not stepping very far out of character . . .'

He was interrupted by Paulina Gower who had remained silent up to this point. 'She was a kind old creature, once you got to know her.'

'But that was difficult,' answered Nathaniel Broome.

'And where did you fit in?' asked John.

'I was a footman here and when Jack decided to become a professional fighter I offered to go as his manager.'

'And when was that?'

'Just after Helen was shot. When Mr Richard Bassett closed the house and went to London.'

'I picked up my child and took her on the road with me. That was until she was seven years of age when I placed her in a school. I tried to be a good father, Mr Rawlings,' put in the Black Pyramid sorrowfully.

'So Fraulein Schmitt's death was a total accident?'

'It was indeed. The poor old thing must have wandered too near the edge and fallen off the cliff.'

What a sad ending, thought John, and remembered the woman's dying words and how at last they were fitting into the jigsaw. Unconsciously he turned his head towards Paulina Gower and she, seeing him look at her, raised a supercilious eyebrow.

'No doubt you are wondering where I fitted into the household.'

'The thought did occur.'

'I was a lady's maid, first to Mrs Bassett, secondly to Helen. I knew all her secrets – and she knew mine. How I longed to go on the stage because my mother had done so. How all I needed was a chance. It was she who advised me to leave my position and try to make my way in London. And thank God I took it and went. But not before I knew my little lady was pregnant by a black slave and had Lucinda's solemn word that she would care for her and keep the child in secret.'

John cleared his throat. 'So I presume you all decided to murder the man?'

Richard spoke. 'We decided to be avenged for Helen's death and put down a being who wasn't fit to live. But we had great difficulty in hunting my father down. It took years but my son, Charles – the boy who staggered off the coach the night you got on it, Mr Rawlings – finally found him and followed him and told us his movements.'

'Bassett's own grandson!'

'Yes. Never seen by him because he had run away and hidden before I was even married, let alone had a child.'

John shook his head, his mind almost cracking under the weight of the facts which had just been given to him.

'But how is it that he didn't recognize you all and get off the coach?'

'I think you can put that down to the passing of the years,' said Cuthbert Simms, speaking for the second time. 'Alas we are all a little fatter – or thinner as the case may be. We have lines and wrinkles. We do not look the same.'

'And you forget one thing,' said Paulina Gower. 'They were all altered facially by the use of theatrical make-up.'

'Except for me,' replied the Black Pyramid. 'The bastard recognized me. Did he not complain to Martin Meadows that he had seen me before somewhere, that he believed that there was a plot abroad to kill him?'

'Yes, he did. And Mr Meadows asked me about it.'

Richard spoke again. 'The truth is that I think he recognized all of you and knew that his life was in danger.'

'Then why did he not get off? Why not change coaches?'

'Who knows? Perhaps he thought he could outwit the lot of you. It was part of his character so to do. And it was an evil, black character, Mr Rawlings. He had done much harm in his life and so, finally, the man got his just deserts.'

'So which of you committed the crime?' John asked.

There was a moment's silence and then the Black Pyramid answered slowly, 'We all did.'

John held out his glass and Richard filled it without saying a word. The Apothecary was quite literally speechless. He had never in his life heard such a story, almost to the point where his brain rejected it. Yet he knew it was true. That everyone of those present had gone into that room and beaten their tormentor about the head. It was a terrible, ghastly thought but yet there had been a dark justice in it.

Though the Apothecary was staring into his drink he knew that every eye in the room had turned upon him expecting some reaction. Eventually he said, 'It's a terrible story,' but could think of nothing further to say.

'My father was a terrible man,' Richard answered solemnly.

'Indeed he was,' Jemima added quietly.

There was a weighty silence into which spoke a familiar voice.

'If any of you daredevils so much as approach my son I'll blow your blasted brains out, so I will.'

John shook his head and almost laughed aloud. Sir Gabriel had crept up on them intent on saving the day. John rose and went towards him, where he stood outside the French doors one of which he had opened quietly.

'It's all right, Father. Put that pistol away. I shall leave here quite safely, I can assure you.'

Sir Gabriel glanced round the room. 'A dastardly clutch of criminals,' he murmured under his breath. Then he paused, ''Zounds, isn't that Miss Lovell? What is a decent girl like her doing with this motley crew?'

'She's the Black Pyramid's daughter,' John said with a smile, and watched his father go pale and sink into a chair.

Richard spoke. 'It would seem, Sir, that your father has come to collect you. I take it that you will not be visiting Vinehurst Place again.'

John nodded. 'No, we shall go back to London first thing tomorrow morning. Provided, that is, that I can find my daughter.'

'The little imp was brought back to the coach by Irish Tom and I must inform you John that I gave her six smacks on her *derrière*.'

'Which she richly deserved.'

John bowed to the assembled company who were still staring at the amazing sight of Sir Gabriel decked out in stunning black and white, his three-storey wig adding to his already considerable height. Then Jemima Lovell found her delightful voice.

'Goodnight, Sir Gabriel, goodnight, Mr Rawlings. I trust that you will keep the promise you swore to honour.'

'I assure you, Madam, and the rest of you,' answered John, giving another, more formal, bow, 'that the secret shall go with me to the grave.'

Thirty

Despite the fact that he wrote several times to ask how she was faring John had no reply from Elizabeth until early in the month of December when a letter arrived telling him that she had returned to Devon. He was overjoyed to get it, naturally enough, but for all that he could not deny that he had thoroughly relished his time in London – living in Nassau Street, seeing Rose every day, working contentedly in his shop in Shug Lane. But when the letter came it contained a charming invitation for the entire family, including Sir Gabriel Kent, to join her at her house for Christmas. John had been hoping all along that this would happen and immediately wrote back accepting.

This time they travelled in John's coach with Irish Tom driving, a footman with him carrying a shotgun, and Emily inside to look after Rose's requirements. It was difficult to say who was the more excited but John thought it was probably the maidservant rather than his daughter.

'Rather different from your last trip, John,' said Sir Gabriel drily.

'You mean the one that ended in murder?' He had checked that Rose was asleep before mentioning the word.

'I do indeed. What an extraordinary night that was in Vinehurst Place. To see them all gathered together and hear them admit jointly to the crime. What a terrible person Fulke Bassett must have been to raise such emotions in the breasts of everyday people.'

'I think the last straw for them all was the shooting of Helen. They were all devoted to her in their different ways.'

'Quite so. I take it you are not going to do anything about it with regard to our friend the Blind Beak?'

'What can I do? I am sworn to secrecy. As for you, it would be only one man's word against all the others. I think the best thing we can do is forget the whole incident.'

'I think, my son, that you are right.'

Stopping every night for the sake of Rose and Sir Gabriel – though he would rather have died than admit that he could no longer travel at speed through the countryside – it took them several days to reach Devon. Thus they arrived at Elizabeth's home just as the evening was drawing in. Sir Gabriel looked up at the house, etched dark against the twilight sky.

'Damme, but she has a fine place here, your Lady Elizabeth.'

'Yes, and I think it has become the hub of her universe. She won't come to London despite everything I say.'

John's father lowered his voice. 'And she won't marry you, you know that.'

'Yes, I know.'

The coach drew to a halt and the footman from the house raced forward to pull down the step. Rose jumped out and rushed up the flight of stairs and into the doorway where Elizabeth awaited. Sir Gabriel raised his quizzing glass.

'She's a fine-looking woman, my boy.'

'I know that too.'

'Well, let's hope she produces you a clever child.'

'Of that, my dear Father, I feel quite certain.'

And linking his arm through Sir Gabriel's, John slowly walked up the great flight of steps and back into Elizabeth's life.